LOST ANGEL

A Wasteland Chronicles Prequel

KYLE WEST

Ragnarok Press

Prologue

The world ended on December 3, 2030, with the impact of the meteor, Ragnarok, in the American heartland. When the world ended, a new one began – one which most of humanity didn't live to see.

Most did not die in the impact, but in the months following it. The meteor dust clouded the skies, filtering sunlight. As infrastructure collapsed, billions died from lack of food, medication, and shelter. Violence and gangs rose from the ashes of civilization, skirmishing for control of limited supplies.

Within a decade, only a tiny fraction of the world's population remained. The dust lingered, sending global temperatures plummeting, heralding the beginning of a new Ice Age few would live to see.

The U.S. and Canadian governments, pooling their resources before the impact of Ragnarok, constructed 144 underground installations within their borders to survive the apocalypse.

Only the brightest, wealthiest, and highest-ranking individuals were allowed inside, which collectively contained room for thousands of people, complete with anything needed to sustain large populations for an extended period. When the dust settled, bunker residents would reemerge to rebuild society.

But life underground was fraught with unforeseen difficulties. Disease, rebellion, and internal breakdowns took the bunkers offline, one by one. Surface dwellers and roving bands of raiders overran the bunkers out of desperation for shelter and supplies.

And on the surface, unknown except among the scientists and administrators of Bunker One, a new threat was evolving. For Ragnarok was not merely rock and dust. A long dormant form of alien life was buried within the meteor. Vast fungal blooms sprouted within the vicinity of the impact site. For thirty years, it spread at an alarming pace, completely unchallenged.

By 2048, the denizens of Bunker One would learn the true threat Ragnarok posed . . .

Chapter 1

Samuel Neth ran alone through the corridors of U.S. Bunker One, his footfalls rattling off the metal surfaces. He panted, breathless, thinking a prayer for deliverance over and over.

Let them be home. Let them be safe . . .

From behind came a hideous, inhuman screech, distant but terrifying. The sound was like nothing Samuel had ever heard. That screech was shortly followed by another scream, this one human.

After that, silence reigned, the only sound being Samuel running home as fast as his feet would carry him, to the wife and children who still didn't know about the threat above.

People were opening their doors to look at the source of the disturbance. All of them watched Samuel as he ran by, as if *he* could have made a noise like that. Some of them cast him dirty looks.

"Hide!" he shouted, cutting off their questions. "They're inside!"

There were shouts and questions as he ran by, but Samuel had done his part. He had warned them. Those . . . *things* . . . had overrun the surface agripods, cutting their way through the sheer plastic with serrated pincers. The cold air of the surface had rushed in, and the openings had revealed the monsters' three glowing white eyes, each of them set in angular, insectoid faces. Just remembering them made his skin crawl, the way those tongues flickered out, or how their sharpened mandibles clicked as they opened and closed, the scuttle of their spindly scorpion legs. He still heard his friends' dying screams resonating in his mind. He could hardly believe what he'd seen. It was beyond reality, but he couldn't deny it: monsters were invading Bunker One.

Samuel was one of the few lucky ones to get to the elevator before the doors closed, shutting out the screams of his falling comrades. Once inside Bunker One itself, Samuel saw no signs of alarm. The corridors were empty, save for a few patrolling security officers, which themselves didn't seem to know what was happening. Some of the escaped workers went to warn them, but Samuel only had one thing on his mind: his family, sleeping and unaware. Several of those officers had tried to accost him for breaking curfew, but Samuel was too fast. They would soon be drawn off for more pressing things, anyway.

Samuel's apartment was clear across the Bunker, on L20, near the bottom. Maybe there would be time to get to his wife and kids. He kept expecting to see one of those monsters at every turn, but there was nothing but silence.

Samuel turned into the final corridor, which was a dead end, and ran to the last door on the left. He and his family had been a last-minute entry into Bunker One, and as such, their apartment was small and out of the way. He had hoped they could move to a larger home as his family grew, but his appeals were always declined by Bunker Admin. As an agriculture worker, what he had now was probably the best he and his family could ever hope for.

Now, his home's isolation was a blessing. If those monsters were as fast as they seemed on the surface, then they would be devastating the upper east wing by now. That was where Security was. While only a few of those creatures had invaded his agripod, he got the sense there were many more out there in the Wasteland, waiting to pour in.

If there were, Bunker One might not last the night.

The lights of the corridor flickered a moment, and then steadied. Samuel scanned his card on the reader, and the door slid open. He turned on the lights to reveal his children, Makara and Samuel, blinking drearily from the bed they shared, while his wife, Violet, lay in their shared bed across the room. She stirred at her husband's entrance, looking at him first with confusion, and then second, with alarm.

"Samuel," she said. "What are you doing home so soon?" Then, she noticed his face. "Has something happened?"

He had left not two hours ago for the night shift. Never once had he come home early.

Several screams sounded from the corridor outside, to which the door was still open. Samuel hastily scanned it shut.

As he watched Violet's frightened brown eyes, her kind face, he almost immediately broke down. But both children were staring at him, wide-eyed. He looked at little Makara, who was seven, and Samuel Jr., who was eleven. Samuel couldn't bear to tell them the truth, especially Makara, who clung to her threadbare panda plush with sad, droopy eyes. She had named the bear, appropriately, Panda.

He walked to his wife and embraced her tightly, trying to hold back the tears that wanted to come. He was afraid; for himself, yes, but mostly for his family. He needed to be strong for them.

"What's wrong, Daddy?" Makara asked.

"What's happening, Dad?" Samuel Jr. asked, his voice cracking a bit.

Samuel closed his eyes. "We need to stay in here, kids. There's been an emergency at the agripods. We need to stay in here and be very quiet."

Violet pulled back from his embrace and looked at him fearfully. "Sam? What's going on?"

"Why?" Samuel Jr. asked.

Samuel ignored his son and looked into his wife's eyes. "You would never believe me."

"After everything we've been through?" Her eyes became stern. "Tell me. Tell me right now."

Samuel sat on the bed, trying to ignore his two kids staring at him. They would know soon enough, and that fact alone was almost enough to make him break down right there. All the same, Samuel couldn't bring himself to say it out loud. He had hoped his kids might remain blissfully ignorant.

But Violet had to know. She wouldn't accept anything less than the truth.

"Monsters," he whispered in her ear. She stiffened in his arms, but Samuel continued. "They're fast. We'll never outrun them, so we have to stay in here. Let Security take care of it."

It was a long time before Violet responded. She must have been full of questions and doubts. There had long been rumors that there were things more dangerous than gangs out there in the Wasteland, things Samuel and Violet had never put much stock in.

It appeared now that there was something to those rumors.

Violet whispered back. "Okay."

"What are you talking about?" Samuel Jr. asked, with rising frustration. "What's going on?"

"We're staying here for a while," Violet said, in a firm voice brooking no argument. "All right?"

"What was that screaming outside?" Samuel Jr. asked, looking at his father. "Dad?"

"I'll tell you later, son," he said. "For now, be quiet."

Either from the way Samuel said that, or the expression on his face, neither of his children argued against it.

The Neth family waited.

Chapter 2

Samuel played cards with the kids, feigning interest, while Violet brewed a pot of tea on the apartment's tiny stove, taking care that the water didn't boil and cause the kettle to whistle. There were no more sounds from outside, but Samuel's eyes nervously darted to the door in between hands. He anxiously watched the speaker mounted to the wall for an announcement.

But there was nothing. Absolutely nothing. It was almost as if he had imagined the whole thing.

His wife kept looking at him nervously, while forcing a smile for the children's sake. Makara was getting into the game, even giggling and forgetting the tense atmosphere, but Samuel Jr. still knew something was wrong, and seemed angry at not knowing what that was.

Violet poured a cup of tea for her husband, then herself, and took a seat on the children's bed.

As Samuel got ready to deal another hand, a bead of sweat made its way down his forehead. A sudden crackle from the room's speaker caused his hairs to stand on end.

"Announcement," Samuel Jr. said, his dark brown eyes hungry for news.

Samuel closed his eyes, bracing for impact.

There was only silence for a moment, even though the line to the other side was open. Voices then argued, indiscernible, somewhere close to the mic.

"Err . . . sorry about that. Everyone's under orders by President Garland to stay in their homes until further notice. Bunker One is on full lockdown. Remember your drills. We will advise you when it's safe to come out. Once again, we are on full red alert and lockdown. If you are out of your homes, proceed to the nearest auditorium, café, or gym, whichever is closest. There is no need for alarm or panic, this is simply a drill . . ."

Someone cursed in the background, and then, there was a horrendous screech, followed by the automatic fire of an M5 or M16. Violet raised her hand to her mouth, her face a mask of horror, while Samuel Jr. stared at the speaker intensely. Little Makara dropped her cards, her smile completely gone, while she reached for Panda.

Thankfully, the P.A. clicked off, leaving the Neth family in uneasy silence.

Everyone looked at Samuel. He swallowed, then wiped the sweat from his brow.

"We're to stay here," he said, so quiet that it was almost a whisper. "Await further orders."

Both children nodded while Violet took hold of Makara, who was shaking.

The following silence stretched for at least two more minutes. Samuel wasn't sure what comfort to offer his family. He had *seen* those monsters. Whatever comfort he had was a lie. He had taught his children to never lie, and he had never lied to them. It was a point of pride, but he might have to break that commitment tonight.

"Maybe Security will take care of it," Samuel Jr. said. His small voice was hopeful, but to Samuel, that hope sounded forced. The kid was smart enough to know this wasn't a drill. Those screams and gunshots were too real to be faked.

"Maybe so, son," Samuel said.

"What was that scream, Daddy?" Makara asked. "I don't like it."

Samuel didn't like it, either. Violet watched him, her eyes afraid. They seemed to say, *Don't tell her. Don't be honest this time.*

"I don't know, Mak," he said. "We'll have to see."

He thought about dealing another hand, but neither child seemed interested. Samuel Jr. was staring at the door in fascination. To his mind, something exciting was finally happening.

Samuel Jr. was still so young.

"Come here, son," Samuel said, nodding toward the corner farthest from the rest of the family. Though it was farthest, the Neth home was so tiny that it was only about twenty feet away.

Samuel Jr. followed him there, and his father held his head close.

"You're going to need to be strong, son," he whispered. "For your sister. You're going to have to protect her."

"What do you mean, Dad?" he asked, loud enough for the rest to hear.

Samuel's stern look warned his son to be quieter. "I don't know what's going to happen. The situation is dangerous. This isn't a drill, like they said."

"What's going on?" Samuel asked. "Is it . . . is it a rebellion?"

It had happened once before, when Samuel Jr. had been all of four years old. It was probably one of his son's first memories. That had been terrifying, but it was nowhere close to this.

"Might be worse than that, son," he said.

Samuel Jr's eyes widened. "How can I be strong, Dad? I don't even know what's going on. You won't tell me."

KYLE WEST

His son's voice had risen, and once again, Samuel struggled about whether to tell him the truth. It always tore him to say something that would threaten Samuel Jr's innocence.

He had thought his family would be safe in Bunker One. When they had won the lottery to be assigned here, he couldn't believe it. He'd thought they'd live down here a few years at most before reemerging on the surface above to start a new life.

But here the family had lived for eighteen years. Both of his children had been born in Bunker One. And if tonight went the way he was afraid it was going, both would die here, too.

"I always wondered why they never let us out of here," Samuel whispered to his son. "Soon enough, you'll know the reason, too."

"Are the rumors true?" the boy whispered back.

So, he had heard them, too. The government always insisted the surface was still too dangerous — too cold, too desolate, too many roving looters and gangs. Only authorized military personnel were allowed on recons.

The rumors had seemingly originated from Bunker One's lower Lab Levels. The meteor Ragnarok, having crashed just eighteen years ago, had not only brought widespread devastation to the planet, but something else. Demons now prowled the world above, and it was for this reason alone that the U.S. government had never given the order to vacate the Bunker, as had been the original plan.

"The rumors are true," Samuel finally said. "They're true, son."

Samuel watched his son's face remain neutral, if a bit paler than usual, and was relieved to see him nod. Samuel Jr. accepted the news in stride and seemed to be the calmer for it. His son knew what the threat was, to an extent, and was ready to do his part.

"Be strong, son," Samuel said. "I'm going to need you. Be ready to take charge. Makara can't know."

At the mention of her name, his daughter looked up. She had been playing with Panda, twisting its arms around and making it do flips.

"Be strong," was all Samuel could manage to say.

Both father and son returned to the center of the room.

"We're going to eat," Samuel said. "And pack. But before that, we're going to push all our furniture against the door." He looked at everyone firmly, to make sure his instructions were understood.

"Okay," Violet said.

Chapter 3

The family set to work, even little Makara helping in her own way by moving the family's smaller possessions to the far corner of the room, freeing up the furniture — the two beds and the one wardrobe everyone shared — to be pushed in front of the door.

Once done, Violet cooked a meal and the family ate. No one was hungry, but Samuel insisted they eat anyway. They might need the energy for later.

After eating, they packed. All they had for this purpose was the luggage they had brought with them into Bunker One eighteen years ago, two large wheeled bags covered with dust. Most of the things they had brought in had been confiscated by Bunker personnel or traded away. But the bags had remained. The family filled them with clothing and food, as well as the cards they had played with earlier.

Samuel also took the heavy, cast-iron skillet his wife had just cooked in. It was still warm from the stove and soapy water she'd used to clean it. He felt foolish, picking it up and feeling its heavy weight. Would its heft be enough to smash in one of those monster's heads?

It was better than nothing, he decided. No one said

anything as he set the skillet in his lap and sat against the wall with the rest of his family.

There, they waited in silence.

~

SAMUEL FADED in and out of sleep. He couldn't help it. Working the agripods was backbreaking labor, and the adrenaline of running had taken its toll. Violet kept watch, drinking more tea to stay alert.

He felt her hand pinch his shoulder, and his eyelids fluttered open.

She raised a finger to her mouth. Samuel nodded to show he understood. Both children were asleep. Violet then nodded toward the door.

At first, Samuel didn't hear anything. His hearing wasn't as good as Violet's. Years of working around the pods' hydroponic recyclers had somewhat deafened him. But soon, the sound was loud enough to where even he couldn't deny it.

Click. Click. Click.

It sounded as if it were coming from the hallway outside.

Click. Click.

Makara stirred, and her eyes drowsily opened. As soon as she heard the noise, she looked confused, and then frightened.

Samuel hastily covered her mouth, while Violet raised a finger to her lips to keep her daughter silent.

It was quiet for a long time. Samuel Jr. let out a snore, and Violet woke him to cover his mouth, too.

Click, click, click, click . . .

The sound faded down the corridor. Samuel let out a breath.

A few minutes later, the hiss of a door sliding open made his skin crawl. At first, he thought it was *their* door, but it must have been someone else's.

I thought there was a lockdown, Samuel thought.

He heard footsteps venturing into the hall. Low voices talking.

No, no, no, Samuel thought, wincing. *Get back inside!*

Then, muffled through his door: "Did you hear something?"

Jeff Tonioli, his nosy neighbor. Samuel had often dreamed his prying ways would get their comeuppance, but never like this.

His wife, Clara, spoke next. "I think it's around the corner. Maybe we should check on the neighbors." Her nasally voice carried all too well, despite the fact she probably thought she was being quiet.

"Don't come here," Violet prayed. "Please, God, don't come here."

"Let's start knocking on doors, then," Jeff decided. He had always styled himself some sort of self-appointed sheriff. Samuel had half a mind to go to the door and point the foolish man and his wife back into their apartment, but he wasn't going to risk anything.

He closed his eyes and tried to will them away. They were a few doors down, so it wasn't likely they'd come to his door first.

Knock-knock-knock.

It was his neighbor's door, a quiet family who kept to themselves.

Don't answer, Samuel said. *Don't answer.*

They answered. The door hissed open. More voices filled the hallway outside.

Samuel closed his eyes, as if bracing for a punch. Over the next few minutes, half the hall was outside, talking, conjecturing, sharing information. Some even laughing, albeit nervously. If it kept going like this, there'd be a full-on block party in ten minutes.

None of them know what's happening, Samuel realized. The announcement had given no information. As for the bullets and the screams, maybe that was what they were trying to rationalize away.

"Maybe it's safe?" Violet asked. Her eyes scanned the furniture piled against the door. There was doubt there, as if it had all been just a giant overreaction.

Samuel felt a sliver of doubt himself, much to his surprise. It seemed *he* was the only one who knew the truth. If his neighbors got wind of an overreaction, he would become the hallway laughingstock.

"No," he said. "If they saw what I saw, they would not be out there."

She nodded. "I trust you."

There was a knock at their door. No one moved to answer it.

"Quiet, kids," Samuel said. But the admonition proved needless. He had well-behaved children, and Samuel Jr. was making sure Makara stayed silent.

Samuel heard the footsteps wandering off.

"Are the Neths home?" Clara's voice resonated from outside, above the buzz of conversation. Her voice could probably pierce ten feet of pure wall.

"Should be," Jeff said. "Samuel works till 7 on the weekends, but Violet and the kids should be home. Give it another knock."

Samuel's face heated with irritation. The damn guy probably knew his schedule better than he did.

"I'm just worried about them," she said. "That man works a lot. I hope his kids are okay."

Violet squeezed Samuel's hand to calm him. It didn't do much good.

There was a sudden silence as all the voices went quiet at once. Something was happening.

"Disperse to your rooms!" came a commanding voice through a megaphone. Security. "You are *not* to leave your housing units. We are on full lockdown."

There was a general murmuring, but Samuel heard the footsteps returning to their homes.

"Sarge," another voice resonated. "Up ahead."

There was a moment's pause, and then a screech.

"Shit. Open fire!"

The corridor became a din of bullets, inhuman screeches, and human screams. Makara wailed and hid her face against her mother, while Samuel Jr.'s eyes looked as if they would pop out of his face. Samuel grabbed his son with his left hand, while his right wielded the skillet.

The horrible shrieks drowned out all else. Only a few of Security's M5's fired, and the men wielding them were screaming. It was impossible to tell just how many of those monsters there were, but soon, there were no more screams, and just the clicking of the monsters' legs and mandibles, accompanied by disgusting slurping and sucking sounds.

For some reason, Samuel could still hear the screaming and crying of his neighbors.

Why were their doors still open?

The answer came soon enough. "I can't close it, Mom! The reader's red!"

From down the hall: "Close the damn door, Clara!"

There were similar shouts from up and down the hall. It seemed as if whoever had gone out could not close their doors. The lockdown was bugged, allowing people to open their doors but not close them. It should have been the opposite.

The slurping sounds ceased as a series of clicks — far more than there had been earlier — scuttled down the hall. There were anticipatory chortles and screeches as the monsters found their way into open homes. More dying screams filtered through the Neths' apartment door. Samuel even heard some people run into the corridor. But the hallway was a dead end, and there was nowhere to flee.

Violet covered her daughter's ears and commanded her to

close her eyes, while Samuel held onto his son, covering his ears as well. They endured that hell for the next two minutes, before there were no more screams and only slurping, crunching, and revolting sucking sounds. And always, those horrible clicks and gurgling coos.

The monsters slammed against their door a few times, rattling the furniture piled against it. Makara's scream was cut off by her mother's hand. The monster clicked and slammed the door again before wandering off in search of easier prey.

It was another five minutes before the clicks had receded into the distance, leaving an eerie silence behind.

Chapter 4

The Neths waited. Makara clung to Panda, squeezing it into her chest. Samuel Jr. stared emptily at the door, looking like a statue. Violet had her eyes closed, while her breaths were controlled to force calm.

Samuel was just trying to think of what to do.

Either the monsters would win, or Security would win. Samuel's next decision had to be predicated on each of those outcomes.

If Security won, the best move was to stay in place. Their food would last long enough for Security to regain control, unless the fighting lasted weeks. Samuel didn't think that would happen, though. The outcome of this battle would be decided within hours, or at the most, a couple of days.

If the monsters won, the best move was escape. To grab whatever supplies they could, especially food and warm clothing, and head for Bunker One's entrance to try and force them to open it. Every passing minute meant more dead security officers, and more of those things filling the bunker.

It was a long shot, but perhaps it was the only shot.

Outside the Neths' door, Samuel knew there would be dozens of dead people, at least two of them being officers. As grisly as the task would be, the officers would both have standard issue M5's, or perhaps even the heavier M16. Samuel had received training on the M5, although it had been years. They had stopped doing gun training for civilians after the Rebellion.

There was another concern about getting out, too. If the Neths' apartment was like the others, their door could not be shut once opened. And it wouldn't take long for one of those creatures to bully its way through the Neths' shabby barricade.

The question was, who would win the battle? Samuel tried to puzzle it out. The monsters had utterly overwhelmed not only the agriculture workers, but Security in the hallway. They had also pierced this far into the Bunker within an hour's time. The Neths' apartment was about as far from the elevators as you could get.

Worse, there had been no further announcements from Bunker Command. If the battle was going well, wouldn't the higher-ups have offered some updates, some measure of hope? The only conclusion was that none of the updates were encouraging. Or worse, there was no one left to even *make* updates. Samuel had heard the monsters and gunshots during the last announcement. How long ago had that been? An hour?

There was only one conclusion that made sense. Bunker One was being taken over, and they had to escape while there was still a chance.

"Get the bags ready," Samuel said, his voice quiet.

Violet's eyes widened. "*What?* Samuel, we can't go out there!"

Samuel almost gave into his wife. For all he knew, she was right.

But Samuel had to go with his gut. "This Bunker won't last the night, Violet. It's over."

Makara squeezed Panda tighter, while Samuel looked at his father. "What do we need to do, Dad?"

"I'll go first," he said. "Get whatever weapons I can." He looked down at his skillet. It just wasn't going to cut it. "After that, we'll head for the westside utility stairwell. It goes all the way to Level 0."

"That's locked to civilians," Violet said.

Yes, that was true. "One of the guards should have a card on them. And it's hard to imagine one of those . . . things . . . being able to fit into a stairwell. We should be safe there."

Violet nodded. The stairwell was close. Go out into the hallway, hang a left, and keep going until the end of the corridor. For now, the Bunker seemed to be powered, which meant keycards would work. That might not be the case soon, another argument for leaving. Escape might become impossible later. If Samuel could find a card, they could get into that stairwell. He was confident of that.

"After that?" Violet asked.

"We go to the entrance," Samuel said. "We force them to open the doors."

Samuel didn't say *how* he was going to force them to open it, and he didn't know what he would do if there were any more of those monsters out there.

"What about the hangar?" Samuel Jr. asked. "If you really think this place is going down, won't one of the ships be the way to get out?"

Samuel Jr. was right. The hangar was on the northside of the Bunker, on Level 2, right below the tarmac of the runway built into the side of Cheyenne Mountain, where Bunker One was located. If there was any safe way out, that was it.

There was only one problem: only the highest security clearances had access to the hangar. Samuel highly doubted a security officer's card could get in unless their rank was high enough.

But the hangar was closer to the Neths' position in the Bunker. Getting to Level 2 would be the easy part. After that, they still had to make their way across the Bunker itself. But the entrance was farther, and located on Level 0.

"I think you're right, son," Samuel said, after thinking it over.

Violet looked at Samuel fearfully, while Makara continued to play with Panda.

"Let's do it," Violet said. "I'm trusting you, Samuel."

He looked her in the eyes and held both of her hands. "Stay close to me, Violet. I'll protect you."

She nodded. "Okay."

"We'll leave the bags, actually," he said. "They'll just slow us down. And cause noise."

Samuel did plan to take a backpack, though, which he filled with some food, water, and another layer clothing for his kids and wife. It would be dreadfully cold outside at this high elevation. Once the pack was on his shoulders, he stood before the doorway, removing a chair and pushing the wardrobe slightly to the side, giving just enough room for him to squeeze out. Violet handed him the skillet.

"Samuel?"

He looked at her. She kissed him on the cheek.

"Please be careful."

Samuel nodded. "I'll be back in a few. Stand in the corner, away from the door."

Violet ushered the children to the far corner of the room, where they would be out of sight.

Samuel hesitated only a moment before pressing the button. The metal door hissed all too loudly as it slid open, revealing the scene of a massacre.

Chapter 5

Blood covered everything. The walls, the ceiling, the floor. Entrails and viscera were caked onto every solid surface. Mangled corpses, half of which weren't even recognizable, littered the hallway. The smell alone made Samuel want to heave. It was like an open sewer, combined with the metallic tinge of blood. And beneath that, there was something worse. Rotten.

It's them, he realized.

His eyes trailed up the hallway, toward the two dead security officers sprawled across the floor, their gray military fatigues blood-soaked and covered with a strange, violet liquid. One of those scorpion-like creatures was splayed on the floor next to them, the purple fluid still leaking from it and pooling underneath the officers' corpses. The two bloods, human and monster, intermixed to produce an even darker shade of purple.

Samuel promptly threw up as his vision went hazy. He was forced to put his hand on the wall for support. He felt chunks of flesh beneath his palm, and violently pulled his hand away with a sob.

Focus, a voice seemed to say from outside himself. *Don't look.*

Don't smell. Get the card, get the gun, and get back to the room. Your family's depending on you.

In obedience to the voice, which seemed to be a better, calmer version of himself, Samuel quietly made his way forward. He heard a horrible screech, but the sound seemed distant. There would be enough time to get to the officers and find what he needed.

He made it to the intersection of his hallway and the larger corridor, one of three that made up this level of Bunker One's western wing. He knelt, pushing down the need to heave again. His hands were already dirty, covered with blood, small chunks of flesh, and the purple fluid that belonged to the monster. The thing was beside him, unmoving. Samuel watched it a moment, to be sure it was dead. In the ten seconds he stared at it, it hadn't so much as twitched.

Samuel didn't think it was an insect, though it did share some of an insect's features, only on a much larger scale. Its chitin shell was grayish pink and dappled with light purple spots, like open sores. He counted the legs, six on each side, thin and spindly. Those legs could poke through anything living like a needle. Its tail was like a scorpion's, with a long, cruel spike pointing from its end. For all that horribleness, it was the monster's three, all-white eyes that unsettled Samuel the most. They were set in the center of its triangular head, which sported two serrated mandibles. The eyes no longer glowed, as they had in the agripods above.

Samuel knew, without being told, that this thing — whatever it was called — did not come from Earth. It was the result of Ragnarok, though he didn't understand how such a large creature could survive the meteor impact, or why it was inside Bunker One eighteen years after the fact.

Samuel rifled through the nearer guard's pockets. It didn't take long to find his keycard, assigned to Sergeant Lucien Mendez. He also took Mendez's M5, doing his best to clean it on the officer's uniform. It felt disrespectful, but Samuel didn't want him or his family touching monster guts any more than they had to. It could carry diseases, for all he knew.

Samuel hurried back to his apartment, his boots sticking to the floor as he walked. He poked his head through the open door.

"Coast is clear."

Violet and the children came forward. She handed him the pack, which he put on, while the children stared wide-eyed at his carbine.

"Come on, kids," he said. "Close your eyes, Makara. And hand me Panda."

She shook her head violently, squeezing the plush tighter to her chest.

"Hold on to him tight, then," he said.

She nodded, then dutifully closed her eyes.

Samuel Jr. was the first to step through. A choked sob escaped his mouth as he looked at the surrounding carnage.

"Keep your eyes up, son," Samuel said, his eyes watery. He hated for his children to experience such butchery. "We'll be out of this soon."

Violet squeezed out of the room last, carrying Makara. The little girl's legs were wrapped around her mother's torso, while her eyes were shut tightly, with her nose buried in her mother's chest. Samuel Jr. wrapped an old shirt around the lower half of his face.

"Let's move," Samuel said. He looked at his wife. "Is she too heavy?"

Violet shook her head. She was a strong woman, used to heavy lifting at her job in the warehouse. Samuel could not both carry his daughter and wield the M5. They would have to make it work for now.

The family started moving, turning left at the intersection. Samuel lifted a finger to his mouth.

They passed two intersections, with one more to go until the stairwell.

The corridor was mixed-use, with some larger residential apartments, classrooms, and offices. Most of the doors were closed, and those that were open seemed to be empty within, and dark. There may or may not have been casualties inside. Samuel didn't care to find out.

When they approached the last intersection before the stairwell, Samuel heard tell-tale clicking to his right. A creature was moving slowly, roving for victims. As soon as they entered the intersection, it would be alerted to their presence. But if they made it to the stairwell door first, which couldn't have been more than fifty feet away, and if the officer's keycard worked, the family would be safe inside the stairwell, at least temporarily.

"Take the kids ahead," Samuel whispered, giving Violet the keycard.

Despite the quietness of Samuel's words, there was a gurgling chortle from around the bend. The clicking approached the intersection.

"Go, Violet," he said. "Now!"

As Violet ran with the children, Samuel stepped sideways into the intersection, unclicking the safety and opening fire on the beast not thirty feet away. The carbine shot fully automatic, the first few bullets spraying the floor. After half a second, Samuel found his target when the monster charged forward into the stream of bullets. The monster began gyrating, letting out a long, hideous shriek. Samuel didn't stop firing, not until it collapsed fully and slid toward him, its mandibles clicking weakly. The beast came to a rest not five feet away from Samuel's boots.

Samuel cursed at not thinking to get more ammunition. How much of the magazine had been emptied in that brief three seconds he'd been shooting? There was no time to go back. At best, he might have a few bullets left.

More screeches sounded from down the corridor, and within moments, more of those monsters showed up — two from the end of the corridor he was facing, and one from the direction the family had come from.

Samuel sprinted for the stairwell door, where his wife was already scanning the keycard while Makara wailed.

"Daddy!"

To Samuel's relief, the door clicked open. Violet ushered Samuel Jr. inside, and then stepped in herself, holding the door open for her husband. Samuel dove through while Violet slammed it shut.

It only took a few seconds for the first of the monsters to crash against it, denting the two or so inches of reinforced steel.

Samuel heard other voices in the stairwell coming from above. He had not been the only one to think of coming here.

"Upstairs," he said, in between breaths.

Violet let Makara down, who was sobbing uncontrollably.

"Come on, Makara," Violet said firmly. "Go up! Give Mommy's arms a break."

Samuel Jr. pulled his little sister along, until both children were hurrying upstairs ahead of their parents. Samuel kept the M5 pointed at the door and backed away slowly, not leaving anything to chance. Only after two flights of stairs did he lower the weapon.

He heard voices whispering above and a girl crying. He let his family catch its breath, all while listening to the harrowing sound of the monsters slamming into the lower door. He nodded at them to proceed upward.

On the next landing, they passed a pair of teenagers sitting against the wall, a boy and a girl, who looked similar enough to be siblings, each with blonde hair, blue eyes, and pale skin. The girl was covered with blood and crying, while the older brother was trying to comfort her, to no avail. She didn't seem to be in pain, though. That blood wasn't her own.

"We have to take our chances out there, Terra. If we stay here . . ."

"They can't get in here," she said, her voice quavering. "They can never get in here."

The boy looked at her hopelessly, and only now seemed to notice the Neths. Samuel didn't recognize either of them, but then again, Bunker One was a big place, with several thousand occupants.

"Sir," the boy said respectfully, his attention going to Samuel's gun. "My name is Clint. Clint Richards. This is my sister, Terra. Can you get us to the entrance?"

Terra looked up, tearfully, and seemed to calm down when she realized they were no longer alone.

"We're not going to the entrance," Samuel said. From below, the door slammed again, causing Terra to sob. "I work near there. At the agripods. That's where they broke in. We're going to the hangar." He eyed both the boy and the girl. "You're welcome to join us."

"Sir!" the boy said. "Thank you, sir. We won't get in the way, I promise."

He pulled his sister up, but she threw away his hand. "Leave me here, then. I'm staying."

"Terra, we *can't* stay here. You saw what they did to . . ." His eyes filled with tears. "Terra. Our parents might have . . . we can still get out of this alive."

"I don't want to," she said, her face a mask of pain. "I don't want to be alive anymore."

"Do you want to die in here of starvation? That's what's going to happen, Terra. I won't let that happen."

At this, Terra started crying again, burying her head in her arms, while her long hair screened her face.

Violet knelt. "Terra?"

Her voice came out gently. Slowly, Terra lifted her face.

"I know it's scary," she said, "but you don't want to stay here. You want to get out of this place. You want to live a long, long time."

Terra shook, tears falling, and then nodded.

"You're coming with us," Violet said, her tone gentle. "We're going to the hangar. We're going to find a ship out of here. You and your brother are going to be fine." She took Terra's hand. "Okay?"

She nodded, sniffling. "Okay."

Terra allowed herself to be pulled up, and even let Clint lead her by the hand.

The four became six as they continued the long climb up to Level 2.

Chapter 6

They reached Level 2 all too soon, despite the twenty or so flights of stairs they had to climb. Samuel shouldered his M5, carrying Makara most of the way. They had passed no one else on the way up. Either no one had thought to enter the stairwell, or they didn't have the required clearance for it. The teenagers' parents must have been higher-ups.

Each floor they passed brought new horrors. There were screams, screeches, gunfire, along with the sickening crunching and slurping of people getting mauled. When they reached Level 2, the mayhem was just as bad, if not worse, than other levels. But this was where the hangar was, and the Neths and the two teens had little choice except to step out into that chaos of gunfire, screams, and death.

"There's no way we can make it," Clint said. "The hangar is, what, a thousand feet from here?"

"Not quite that," Samuel said. He heard a stream of people run by in the direction of the hangar. Just a moment later, the clicks of a scuttling monster chased after them. "Not sure how much ammo I have left. We should wait a minute longer."

There were screams as the monster caught up with the

fleeing people. Violet covered her daughter's ears. She was now twisting Panda's arms in anxiety.

They waited a few more minutes, until the sounds had completely dispersed.

Samuel ventured to open the door and poked his head both ways. There were several mutilated corpses, a scene he was fast becoming numb to. From somewhere up ahead came the sound of gunfire. The lights flickered a moment before going steady.

It was as clear as it was ever going to get.

"Follow me," he said. "And run when I tell you."

They walked quickly down the corridor. They heard a clamor of voices and gunshots from up ahead. Samuel didn't want to lead his family toward people — people were targets — but it was also the direction of the hangar.

Anytime there was an intersection, Samuel waited and poked his head around the corner. The next two times he did so, it was safe to cross. They approached the end of the corridor, which Samuel knew to be the extreme northeast of Bunker One's layout. He looked around the corner to the right, to see a pair of monsters scuttling in the other direction. He waited until they disappeared around the corner of the intersection ahead.

He nodded toward an open doorway. "In there."

All six of them piled into what appeared to be a classroom, with its desks and chalkboard. The door was stuck open, while a couple of bodies littered one of the corners farthest from the door. Obviously, it wasn't safe to stay here long, but Samuel needed a place to hide temporarily.

Samuel wondered just how long they should wait when clicking came from around the corner. He raised his M5 and pointed it toward the open doorway. He raised a finger to his mouth to indicate silence. Violet covered Makara's mouth, to make sure she didn't let out a peep.

The creature scuttled by the room with not even a glance

inside. Samuel had been afraid they would have a strong sense of smell, but it didn't seem so. If anything, they seemed to see and hear remarkably well. It was important to remain quiet and still when they were close.

Once the clicking had receded, he explained his theory to the rest.

"Remain completely still and quiet when they're near, and they might miss us, like that one just did." He nodded toward the doorway. "Let's head out."

"Close your eyes, honey," Violet whispered to Makara.

Makara promptly obeyed.

The family and the two teenagers followed Samuel out of the classroom, after he had checked in both directions. Once they were in the hallway, he looked around the corner. There was nothing.

"Now's our chance," he said.

They walked quickly down the corridor, Samuel leading the way. They passed two intersections, the teenagers lagging. Samuel gestured for them to keep up, but Terra was moving slowly, almost stumbling, and Clint didn't want to leave her behind.

Poor girl, he thought.

Samuel caught Clint's attention, and gestured for him to get his sister to pick up the pace. Clint complied, pulling her along.

When they got to the next juncture, Samuel checked it quickly, then urged the others along.

They had made it a few steps when Samuel heard the scuttle of legs.

"Run!"

Even as the Neths started to flee, Samuel looked back, recognizing that it would be too late for the teens, still lagging. A pair of monsters rounded the corner, and he watched in horror as Terra gave a bloodcurdling scream. Her hands reached out, as if to grasp her brother. The second monster leaped onto Clint, those bladelike points puncturing him as easily as they would a sack of flour. The boy didn't even scream.

While the monsters were momentarily distracted, Samuel urged his family to run ahead while he backed away, his M5 raised to his shoulder. Both monsters were slurping noisily at the teens, but Samuel didn't shoot yet, knowing that every bullet could save his family's life down the line. He rounded the corner and ran after his family.

They joined a stream of fleeing people, all with the same idea.

This won't end well, Samuel thought, but there was nothing else to be done. The screeches emanated from behind, and the monsters rounded the corner. Samuel and his family were at the tail end of a dozen or so people running for Bunker One's northside.

The monsters were lightning fast and would easily catch up to them. But when all seemed lost, a Security detachment rounded the bend ahead, comprised of eight or so men, the front two with riot masks and shields, while the ones behind hefted heavy M16s.

"Move, now!" called out the leader. "Get behind the shields, or you *will* be shot!"

Samuel was bringing up the rear, sprinting forward past the first two shield bearers, young men whose eyes were wide with fear.

"Fire!"

The hallway became a raucous din of bullets, and the screeches of the monsters pierced even above the storm. Samuel didn't pause to look; he and his family kept running, unlike some of the other civilians who thought themselves safe behind the line of officers.

The Neth family rounded the corner ahead, the final one before the hangar. The solid double doors lay straight ahead, perhaps a hundred feet away down the wide corridor, but those doors were closed. About five or so dead bodies lay around it. Samuel looked down at his keycard doubtfully. Would it be enough for him and his family to get inside?

Before he had time to consider it, screeches sounded from ahead, shortly followed by human screams. They needed a place to hide before they were surrounded.

Samuel ran to the nearest door, scanning it open to reveal a supply closet. He rushed his family inside, but there was no room for him.

"Sam . . ." Violet said.

"Stay here," he said.

Before she could argue, he scanned the door shut.

His attention was drawn to the hangar doors, where a man screamed as he tried to beat it down. Two monsters tackled him from behind. Samuel tiptoed across the corridor while the creatures tore into their hapless victim. He scanned open a door directly across from the closet. He stepped inside what appeared to be an office. Once inside, he scanned it shut.

He turned to face a desk, behind which were crowded bookshelves. A globe stood on the desk's corner, along with a few knickknacks and a couple of pictures of a gray-bearded, middle-aged man and his wife, a pretty brown-haired woman.

That same man lifted his head from behind the desk, where he had been cowering on the floor, his state shell-shocked and eyes reddened.

"Leave me," he said, with a slight, southern drawl. "It's over."

Samuel scanned the nameplate on the desk. Dr. Cornelius Ashton. He recognized the name, had even seen him a few times, though their paths rarely crossed. He worked down in the L-Levels, but Samuel supposed he was important enough to have an office up here too, next to Admin.

"Dr. Ashton," Samuel said, calmly. "I'm not going to hurt you."

The man rolled his sharp blue eyes. "Of *course* you're not. Those crawlers have done that enough already."

"Crawlers?"

Ashton nodded his head toward the hallway. "Those things. I knew it would come to this. *Always* knew it would come to this. I kept my damn mouth shut when I should have raised hell." He stood, and then sat in his chair, fingers raking his gray hair that had half-turned snowy white. "Now, she's paid the price. Now . . . she's dead."

He took a picture off his desk and looked at it. Tears formed in his eyes.

"I'm sorry," Samuel said, awkwardly. He thought about his family, and when it might be safe to get back to them.

"Don't bother trying to get to the hangar," Dr. Ashton said, looking at Samuel again. "I know why you're here. You want in." He looked at the gun. "You probably mean to force me to open those doors." He shook his head. "It's all pointless. Those crawlers . . . the thing controlling them. They're going to kill us all. They'll finish what Ragnarok started."

"Listen," Samuel said, stepping forward. "I don't know what you're blabbing about. I'm sorry about your wife. My name's Samuel. Samuel Neth. I need your help. My family is locked in the closet across the hall. My wife, Violet, is locked in there with our two kids, Samuel and Makara." Ashton's sharp blue eyes focused on Samuel, and for the first time, the doctor seemed to be coming out of his head. "They're all scared, and so am I, for that matter. I need your help, Dr. Ashton. You said you can open the hangar doors. I can't bring your wife back, but if you intend on dying here, maybe you can give me your keycard. Give me and my family a shot at getting out."

Ashton barked a bitter laugh. "There *is* no shot of getting out. You realize President Garland is dead, son? The president was one of the first to fall. That was planned. These crawlers are more intelligent than even I realized." His blue eyes looked at him, haunted. "We knew about this, Samuel. We fucking *knew*. It's in the Black Files."

"Listen," Samuel said. "I don't know about any of that. I'm not giving up. I'll have that keycard from you, if you please."

Ashton sniffed. "Fine," he said. "But you ain't getting anywhere without a pilot. Last they updated me, none of the ships had taken off yet. Can only mean all the available pilots died in the initial wave."

"There's got to be somebody who can fly," Samuel said.

"There is," Ashton conceded. "Me." He looked from Samuel's gun, then right back in his eyes. His cold, blue gaze was harrowing. "Are you willing to die to protect your family, Samuel Neth?"

Samuel didn't need to think about it. "Of course. Are you going to help me or not?"

Ashton thought for a moment. After a time, he sighed. "I'll try." He opened a drawer, pulling out a six-shooter that looked quite old, but well-maintained and polished. "Planned on using this on myself. Better than letting them get me."

"You're a pilot, Dr. Ashton," Samuel said. "You can still save a lot of people. Including my family. Don't kill yourself because you failed at something."

Ashton took a moment to think about it. "I don't think there's a snowball's chance in hell of getting out of this alive. I deserve a bullet. I could have stopped this. I could have told people what was out there, publicized those files." He shook his head. "I was too chicken shit, though. I let them get to me." He hung his head.

To Samuel, seeing a man give up all will to live, or to even save others, was the saddest of sights. Would he do the same, if he lost Violet and the kids?

"Get it together, Doctor. *Find* your redemption or die trying to get it. If you just save my family, then you can make up for it. At least a bit."

Then you can die after, if that's what you really want. Samuel kept the thought to himself, though.

Ashton gave a bitter smile. "Don't imagine I'm much good shooting this thing." He looked at Samuel's M5. "I hope your aim is better than mine, son. Let's go."

Chapter 7

They waited for the right opportunity and exited into the corridor. Samuel keyed open the closet, and his family piled out, blinking drearily. Violet threw herself on him.

"Daddy," Makara said, reaching for him tearfully.

"This is Dr. Ashton," he said. "He'll take us to the hangar."

Ashton was already jogging up ahead. Samuel urged his family to follow.

Already, clicking filled the air. The sound was coming from *everywhere*. They passed an intersection, and down either hallway were dead bodies and roving crawlers. They scuttled after the fleeing family to the hangar. They were halfway there.

Samuel fired a few shots before the magazine ran out, scoring a hit on the lead crawler. But two more were coming up from behind, and more still from the hallway by Ashton's office.

"Go, go!" Ashton called, who was already by the doors.

The Neths ran harder and were nearly there. Samuel noticed his wife lagging; Makara must have been getting too heavy for her to carry. He cast aside the gun, useless without ammo, and took his daughter from his wife's hands.

He let her go on ahead, running through the now open doors, through which they could see the massive hangar with its large, metallic ceiling doors. Inside the massive space, a small crowd was milling about, some of them shouting for the doors to be shut. Samuel himself hurried through just as the doors were closing.

The crawlers slammed into the doors' other side while the family and Ashton rushed forward.

"Bay doors are closed, still," Ashton said, looking up. "Should be able to open them from aboard *Odin*." He scowled. "Given that there's enough juice to move them."

Samuel now noticed the orbital spaceship in the center of the hangar. During the Dark Decade, which had lasted from 2020-2030, the United States had publicized almost all its secret research, collaborating with private business. This ship, along with several others housed at Bunker Six, were the product of the country's desperate innovation.

The ship's design was roughshod, not sleek like the old movies Samuel liked to watch. It was powered by a miniature fusion core developed toward the end of the Dark Decade, powerful enough to fuel the thrusters underside and aft of each vessel. Retractable wings made the ship viable for atmospheric operations, though each ship had the capability of going into space for orbital maneuvers.

The ships were rarely used, but always well-maintained.

People were running up to Ashton now, many crying tears of gratitude. Ashton was blind to it all.

"Let's get this show on the road," he said.

The Neths followed Ashton to *Odin's* boarding ramp, several security officers parting to let the doctor through.

"I need a minute to get things ready," he said.

Ashton entered alone, and after half a minute, the sound of *Odin's* engines powering on filled the hangar. Samuel felt its reverberation to his very bones. Both of his kids looked at the ship with awe. Only the highest security clearances had access to the hangar, so this was the first time any of them had laid eyes on the ship.

The security officers were now allowing people to board, but before doing so, they checked their passes. Surely, after all they had gone through, Samuel and his family wouldn't be turned away. They had come in with Ashton, after all. All the same, Samuel watched the others nervously, noticing that most of them wore the nicer clothing of the Bunker's upper reaches. All of them had the look of Admin on them, or scientists. He recognized a couple of councilors and their families.

The Neths approached last of all, the sound of crawler shrieks piercing through the metal hangar doors.

"Passes?" the officer asked.

"We don't have them," Samuel lied. He had a feeling showing the officer his worker level pass might not get him on board.

"No problem. It's been crazy. Name?"

Samuel couldn't lie about that. "Samuel Neth."

The officer pressed a few buttons on his tablet, frowning after a moment. "Samuel Neth, from Agriculture? And your wife, Violet, from Inventory?"

There was no use denying it. "That's right."

The officer exchanged a glance with his comrade, before turning back to Samuel. "I'm sorry, Mr. Neth. I can't let you on board. It's Priority A individuals and their families only."

Samuel's face reddened. "Priority A? What's that supposed to mean?"

"I'm sorry, sir. These are orders from Command. They can't be counteracted."

"I want to speak to Dr. Ashton," Samuel said. "He brought us here. Who's your commanding officer?"

The guard, a youth not even ten years older than Samuel Jr., looked at him nervously. "Captain Dulaney, Mr. Neth."

"Call him up," Samuel said. "Ask his permission."

"Sir, this goes up to General Meyer. I can't disobey a direct order, sir."

This was beyond belief. Samuel took a deep breath to remain calm. "All order, in case you haven't noticed, has broken down. Your commanding officer and General Meyer are probably dead. My family and I have been through hell to get here, and if a little twerp like you says I can't get on board, then I'll *make* a way on board."

Samuel knew he shouldn't berate the kid, but he was so keyed up from the past two hours that he couldn't help it. If the reason he and his family couldn't board was *bureaucracy*, he was going to murder someone.

Violet touched his arm, to calm him down. "Is there anything to be done, Officer? What can we do to get permission to go on board? Is talking to Dr. Ashton enough?"

"I'm afraid not," the other officer said.

"Officer," a new man said, approaching from behind. Apparently, more people had filtered in, from the entrance opposite of where the Neths had come in. "We are Priority A evacuees."

"What is this bullshit?" Samuel asked. "What does Priority A mean?"

The new arrival blinked from behind his glasses, greatly alarmed. "You haven't heard the announcement?"

"What announcement?" Violet asked.

"They're bottom-dwellers," the second officer explained. He seemed to forget the Neths were even there.

"Ah," the man said, as if that made sense. "Guess they didn't make the announcement down there."

Why could that be? As Samuel thought about it, everything clicked in an instant. The government hadn't announced an evacuation for the bottom levels. They had planned to let them *die*, to be bait while the higher levels got away.

Samuel felt a fury such as he had never known. He clenched his fist, and with a roar, punched the second officer, the one who'd called them bottom-dwellers, right in the face before he even knew what was happening.

"Samuel, no!" Violet screamed.

He was on top of him. It was all too much. He landed one more punch before the other officer pulled him off.

"Sir, stand down, now. That's an order!"

Samuel was overpowered. Another couple of officers, seeing the commotion, helped to pull him off.

The second officer got up and wiped his nose, which was bleeding. Whatever hope Samuel had of getting his family on board *Odin* was completely gone, now.

The bespectacled man looked at Samuel derisively. "You bottom-dwellers are all the same. All passion, no intellect. That's why you're down there, and we're up here."

"Sir, don't antagonize him," the first officer said. The second one had retreated, another officer helping him to clean his nose. "I'm afraid you and your family have to move along, now."

"Move along *where*? You would send us out there to die?"

The man with glasses was waved on board, and he went hurriedly.

"Join the evacuation for the general population, Mr. Neth," the officer said. "The ship is for Priority A individuals and their families only."

"Get on, kids," Samuel said.

But the officers stood, barring their way. All of them had M5s.

There was absolutely nothing to be done. Samuel glanced over at the cockpit, waving toward it, but it didn't seem to be doing any good. Ashton would be busy prepping the ship for takeoff. He had probably completely forgotten about the Neths by now. Makara was crying, while Samuel Jr. looked as angry as his father.

"You know Dr. Ashton wouldn't even *be* here if not for us," Samuel said.

"Where is the general evacuation?" Violet asked, finally.

"The runway," the officer said. "Last I heard there were a few copters left."

Samuel stared hard at the young man, who looked at him without pity.

"Your general is a bastard, and you're even worse," Samuel said. "You go to hell. I hope this haunts you for the rest of your miserable life."

The Neths turned to leave, leaving the officers in silence to guard an empty hangar and a half-empty spaceship.

Chapter 8

There was nothing else to do. They ran.

The Neths exited the hangar on the north side and were back into the chaos they had just left. Here, things were more controlled. Security officers had formed something of a perimeter. It became clear there weren't many "bottom dwellers", but mostly middle-tier families that had been worth giving an announcement for. Here, however, it didn't seem as if they would be asking for identification.

The Neths joined the stream onto the tarmac, one among several hundred scared, panicked people. Snow fell in droves, and the night was horribly cold. Despite the situation, Samuel marveled at the vast amount of space, while his children gazed at the snow in wonder.

It was the first time either of them had been outside.

Samuel could hear the collective roar of rotors in the distance. Streetlights flooded the runway, illumining a crowd all pressing as a single organism toward the two remaining copters that had just landed.

There was no way the Neths would get there in time.

"We should go back," Samuel Jr. suggested.

That would be impossible. Ashton had the keycard to the

hangar, and if those officers were guarding the ship, they wouldn't be let on board. Security was known for being fanatically loyal to authority, no matter how senseless or cruel the order.

The somewhat orderly press of people became panicked as several screeches filled the air. Dozens of crawlers materialized from the darkness at the side of the runway, pushing forward in an unrelenting wave. The people screamed and pressed in closer like sheep before wolves. Half ran back to the Bunker, while the other half, closer to the copters, pressed toward their only lifeline.

The Neths ran toward the copters, despite their relative proximity to the Bunker. Samuel knew there was no hope back there. He held his wife's hand and carried Makara with his other arm. Samuel Jr. ran on ahead, his smaller size allowing him to weave through the crowd with ease. Samuel let him go, wanting to give him the greatest chance of escape.

Already, the crawlers were cutting the Bunker off from the runway, and people were falling. Screams filled the air as the crawlers' mandibles tore at their prey. Security was no help. Half of them were running rather than shooting at the teeming mass of monsters.

"Go, Violet, go!"

"Samuel!"

He was running too fast, and his poor wife, fatigued as she was, could hardly keep up. He slowed down for her sake.

But then, Makara screamed.

"Panda!"

Her bear had fallen several feet behind them. Its long, sad face was lost to the violence of the crowd's stomping feet.

"Violet, no!"

His wife had disappeared. She had knelt to pick up the plush, and Samuel waited anxiously for her to reemerge. She never did. People ran her right over, and she couldn't get up. Samuel tried to get to her, but the press of the crowd was too great. He heard his wife's screams, even above the din of the crowd and shrieking crawlers.

"Violet!" he cried. "Violet!"

The crowd had pushed him past the point of no return, with a gravity he couldn't escape.

Makara wailed. "Mommy! Mommy, get up. Mommy, please. Why won't she get up, Daddy? You're leaving her, why are you leaving Mommy behind?"

Makara's tears soaked Samuel's shirt. Samuel whimpered as dread clutched him. He had said he would protect her. He had failed. His wife was gone, the love of his life. One minute, alive, and in the next, dying.

The crawlers were closing in like a noose, the outer fringes of the crowd screaming as they were assaulted. The crush of people was beginning to take Samuel's breath away.

"Daddy, I can't breathe . . ."

Samuel couldn't breathe, either, but the copter was close now. The drone of the rotors drowned out all else. Samuel knew he was going to die, the realization hitting him like a hammer. He was going to die, just as his wife was surely dead or dying right now. He didn't know where Samuel Jr. was. He could only hope he had gotten on one of the copters.

So long as Samuel lived, he would do everything in his power to save his daughter. She was all he had, now.

He lifted Makara high into the air, and summoning strength from he knew not where, pushed onward. He pushed forward, even as others were crushed underneath him, just as his wife had been. He felt hands grabbing at his shins, like souls reaching from the river of the dead.

"Daddy," he heard Makara screaming, tearfully. "I'm scared. Daddy . . ."

A sob escaped his throat. The crawlers were just fifty feet or so behind. They had long passed where his wife would have been. He was too short to see into the helicopter, but he heard the crowd clamoring to be let on.

Samuel, at last, sucked in another breath, his arms on fire from holding his daughter so high.

"Daddy," she said. "They aren't letting the people on. There's no space in there."

Samuel didn't care. He pushed forward again, the violent shrieking and chomping behind him enough motivation to keep going. The helicopter was lifting off.

"No," he said. "Please, God, no . . ."

Makara was reaching into the sky. The helicopter slowed.

"The girl," he heard a voice shout from above through a loudspeaker. "Pass up the girl!"

Samuel stretched up his arms as much as he could. For a moment, there was silence, as if the crowd collectively realized what it must do. Other hands joined his, pushing Makara higher.

A soldier reached down and pulled her up and away. Makara, his angel, was ascending into heaven.

Samuel lowered his arms, feeling numb, as the helicopter lifted into the sky, soon lost to the snowy darkness. There were still screams, but it was mostly quiet, as if all recognized their fate and had embraced it. All was silent, save for the slicing and dicing of the crawlers, the whipping of their tails, and the dying screams of those on the outside. He felt the people around him shaking, heard them muttering prayers, smelt the acrid tinge of urine in the cold mountain air.

All he could do was hope Samuel had made it, somehow, some way. Makara for sure was out of this horrible place. Little Makara. He closed his eyes, mouthing a prayer for her safety. Her story wasn't over yet, but her life was still holding on by a thread.

If there was a God, he needed to watch over her. Samuel had given everything to save his daughter. But at least there was hope that she might live wherever that helicopter was taking her.

Soon, Samuel would be joining Violet in whatever afterlife awaited them.

Samuel's eyes opened to meet those of a scared teenager. In those eyes he saw his daughter a few years down the road. She *became* his daughter in his mind. She was crying.

"It's okay," he said. "It'll be over soon. You're not alone."

She sobbed and closed her eyes.

All around, the people took each other's hands. One by one, death found them.

Chapter 9

"Get a look at that, Raine."

Raine Rogers gazed out across the barren field, eyes hidden behind dark sunglasses.

"Almost hit the interstate," he said gruffly.

"Who is it, you think?"

Raine shrugged. "Doesn't matter who it is. Haven't seen a flying copter since the Chaos Years."

Captain Dan Green watched from beside Raine, shading his eyes. The tall man wore dusty military fatigues, with the badge of his office on his chest, though it had no official place in this new world. Raine was of middling height, with skin of onyx rippled tight with muscle, with close cropped hair and a face so hardened it seemed to be chiseled from granite.

From a safe distance, the copter lay on its side like a dead wasp. The crash must have been controlled, because there were no fires. Not yet, anyway.

"Round up the men," Raine finally said. "There might be salvage. And survivors."

Dan looked doubtful of that last bit, but he wasn't about to argue with Raine. Almost two decades after the fall of Ragnarok, useful scrap was becoming rarer and rarer.

As Dan radioed in the order, calling for backup, Raine held out his hand. Dan passed over the binocs.

Raine raised them to his eyes without bothering to take off his shades. He squinted as he adjusted the lenses, and the field of view homed in on the crash. It was starting to belch black smoke into the red sky. There was no visible fire, but it could have just been hidden by the thick smoke.

"Who the hell can even fly a helicopter these days?" Raine mused. "Someone with fuel, someone with a pilot who's stayed alive these last eighteen years . . ."

"Reapers?" Dan ventured.

Raine scoffed, then spat. "I've never been one to underestimate our enemies, but even *they* couldn't pull this off. This is from one of those government Bunkers, maybe. I hear 112 and 108 aren't far off."

"I thought they all went kaput," Dan said. "Raiders made sure of that."

Maybe so, Raine thought. Now, he was trying to judge whether the copter was too dangerous to scrap. It was mighty tempting to send some men to strip it before the fuel caused it to light up. It had a military look, too, and though he couldn't see it clearly anymore because of the smoke, there had to be some pretty heavy caliber armament on board.

The Reapers weren't here yet, either. Better to do it quickly, before things got too dangerous. Raine needed more men, first, to make sure the job was done cleanly and efficiently.

Raine's thoughts were interrupted when his eyes caught movement in the binocs.

Someone was crawling away from the flames, which were now visible.

"I don't believe it."

"What?" Dan said.

Raine looked again. Even with distance, he could tell the

person wasn't an adult, but a girl. She had long black hair, but he couldn't see much else.

The realization that a child was in danger kicked Raine's protective instincts into overdrive. The face of his dead daughter, Adrienne, seemed to stare out at him from the smoke. His heart started beating faster.

"Hold your post here, Dan ."

Before Dan could respond, Raine dashed forward, ignoring the captain's shouts of warning.

RAINE WAS bulky for a man of his height, but that didn't mean he was slow. That had surprised his enemies many times, much to their demise. The heat of the fire was unreal as he closed in. Raine shielded his eyes and face, even as he began to hack at the fire's fumes.

He could see the girl just ahead, lying on the ground. She was dirty and blackened from the smoke and no longer moving. She was a small thing, and Raine's heart clutched with fear. He might be too late.

Don't think of that, Raine thought. *Get her out. She might live yet.*

As if in confirmation of that hope, the girl lifted her tiny head, her black hair a mess and filled with cinders. Her smooth, olive face was smudged with dirt, while her light brown eyes were intense and arresting. No, she hadn't given up yet, and neither would Raine. This one was a fighter.

She crawled forward using only one of her arms. The other dragged uselessly behind.

The fire was visible within the helicopter chassis, and the fumes grew thicker. Raine pushed himself against the heat, feeling it crackle against his skin. If it was this bad for him, then the little girl must be roasting alive – very slowly, and very painfully.

At last, he made it, scooping her up in his powerful arms. She weighed almost nothing.

"Got you."

He ran. The heat licked at his back, and a sudden burst pushed him forward, sending him stumbling to the ground. Then there was a deafening roar, like an ancient beast from myth coming to life. The heat was incredible and gone almost as soon as it had arrived. Raine held his body protectively over the girl. Her eyes gazed at him in an effort to remain open, while her skin was splotched red with blisters. The poor thing was delirious.

"Daddy . . ." she said. "Are we there yet?"

I ain't your dad, Raine thought. *He's dead, unless he somehow got out like you.*

Looking back at the exploded wreckage, he didn't think that too likely. He'd have his men investigate once it was safe enough, and scrap whatever material was left behind, though Raine didn't suspect it would be much. He'd also try to get a body count, if such a thing was possible.

He looked down at the little girl's face. She couldn't be more than seven or eight. Though this one looked nothing like his dead Adrienne, it still seemed as if her eyes were staring back at him. Accusing him.

Raine shook the thought. With the girl in his arms, he walked toward his former position. Dan was running toward him, along with a few more Lost Angel foot soldiers, all armed with rifles.

"It'll be all right," he said to the girl. "Hold on tight. We'll get you somewhere safe."

The girl opened her eyes again, and despite her young age, there was nothing tender in that expression. She was fully lucid. Behind those eyes, which seemed hazel now in the absence of the smoke, Raine saw death. Despite the heat of the flames still present behind him, Raine felt a chill.

The girl closed her eyes and seemed to sleep. Raine

chanced a look back to see the helicopter fully ablaze now, burning through the last of its fuel. That the girl had survived was nothing short of a miracle. There might be scarring from her blisters, but she would live.

"You have no one to protect you, huh?" Raine asked, now stopping to wait for his men. "That's all right. You got me, now."

The girl seemed to sleep more deeply, her breathing becoming even. She had to be exhausted.

Raine waited, having exhausted himself from his adrenaline-fueled sprint. His strength was of a different sort, more useful for bashing a man's face in or cracking a neck. He'd done that a few times before. And now, those same hands that had brought death to so many cradled a little girl who was completely at his mercy.

But Raine swore to keep her safe with all the strength he had. Memories of Adrienne, unbeckoned, mingled in with this sentiment.

She coughed, and her tiny, cracked voice came out at a rasp. "Water."

Raine reached for his canteen. He watched in amazement as the girl downed the whole thing without pause.

He looked up as Dan walked up with the patrol. One of the two men with him had a first aid kit. All watched the little girl with widened eyes, as if they, too, couldn't believe she was alive.

He handed the girl over to the man with the first aid kit. He watched as he set to work, dressing her wounds as her eyes closed again.

Dan gazed out at the downed copter with disbelief in his eyes. The fires were low now and reflected in Dan's blue orbs. It had been twelve years since he'd met the captain. A former Marine, he and Dan had worked together for most of the past twelve years – first as cronies for the Black Reapers, and when that got bad, they struck out on their own and formed the Lost

Angels. The pairing was unlikely – even eighteen years after Dark Day, Dan was still as straight-laced as they came, more of an administrator and logistician than fighter, while Raine had run the streets and carved out a small, but defendable, territory in what used to be south L.A.

The two men had one thing in common, however: they were both hard as nails, as were all men who had managed to survive this long after Ragnarok's fall.

"You can't just do that, Raine," Dan said quietly. "You'll get yourself killed one of these days."

The girl opened her eyes again, much to Raine's surprise. Those hazel eyes were haunted, but even so, she gave a small, innocent smile, the kind only children are capable of.

"What's your name?" Raine asked.

The hardness in the girl's voice belonged to someone twenty years older at least.

"Makara," she said, her voice high, yet firm.

As the girl closed her eyes again to sleep, it was as if her life were laid out in prophecy. Raine had done well in saving her. A girl like this, if raised well, had great potential.

"Makara," he said. "Welcome to the Lost Angels."

Chapter 10

Makara was sent to the infirmary and slowly, but surely, recovered from her burns. Her arm was set and put in a sling, and she ate enough for a grown man.

Raine popped into the infirmary one day, about a week after the crash, to check on her.

"Morning, Darlene," he said.

The sixty-year-old Darlene, a redheaded nurse and the closest thing the Angels had to a doctor, looked up at Raine's entrance. She was leaning over a patient's bed, replacing an IV. "Morning, Raine."

"How's little Makara doing today?"

Darlene turned to look at him. "You don't waste time, do you?"

"No ma'am," Raine said. Darlene had told Raine that Makara would be cleared for checkout today. "Want to make sure she's set up with Isabel right away."

"That's good of you," Darlene said approvingly. "Well, she's awake. Waiting in the next room. I should warn you, though."

"What?" Raine asked.

Darlene's brown eyes became sad. "She's been through

hell and a half, Raine. I haven't been able to get much out of her. You can see pain in her eyes, though." Her voice quavered. "Just breaks my heart."

"She's said nothing?"

Darlene finished up with her patient, an old man named Jonas Stevens, who was in the last stages of his life and too weak to greet Raine. Darlene closed the door.

"You might want to sit down."

Raine swallowed, pulled up a chair, and sat. Darlene sat on the far side. Raine might have overseen the Lost Angels, but here in the infirmary, Darlene was queen.

"Haven't been able to get much out of her," she admitted. "Poor girl doesn't want to talk about what happened."

"I don't blame her," Raine said, leaning over the desk, and thinking. "She's probably in shock still. It's only been a week, after all."

Darlene looked at Raine intently. "She *is* in shock, Raine. Even if she heals physically, she'll be scarred for the rest of her life. Doesn't have parents, as far as I can tell. She keeps asking about a Sam, but I keep telling her there's no one by that name here."

"Might check with the new arrivals," Raine mused. "Family member, maybe."

Darlene looked at him imploringly. "You saved her, Raine. Maybe she'll open up to you. I know you're a busy man . . ."

"I'll talk to her," he said. The decision wasn't hard. "That's what I'm here for, right?"

"Good," Darlene said. "I know you said you were here to take her to Isabel personally, but I think she should stay here another week at least. She needs rest, Raine, and time to process things. And she needs to see Kevin."

Kevin Klein was the resident therapist for the Lost Angels. He was the only person at the base with psychiatric training, but in the absence of most drugs, he had to rely mostly on talk therapy. The poor man was probably in need of therapy himself. Everyone in Lost Angels Command had some sort of trauma, Raine included.

"I'll make sure he sees her," Raine said. "I'm ready when you are."

Darlene nodded. "I'll stand back and listen. I should take notes for Kevin."

Raine nodded, to show his agreement. He felt a nervous weight form in his stomach. It really should have been Kevin asking these questions, but Darlene had a point. If the girl wouldn't talk to her, then she probably wasn't ready to talk to the doctor, either.

Darlene opened the door, revealing the girl in a floral dress, sitting on the bed and staring out the window. She was scratched and bruised, though clean, with her arm set in a cast hanging from a sling. She didn't seem to notice the sound of the door opening at first. When Raine cleared his throat, she turned. Her hazel eyes were intense and focused, and didn't seem to belong to a child.

"Makara, Raine is here," Darlene said. "Is it okay if he visits a bit?"

Makara lowered her eyes. After a long moment, she gave the barest of nods.

"Just him," she whispered.

"What's that, honey?"

"Just him," she said, her tone taking on an edge while her eyes narrowed.

"Okay, sweetie," Darlene said, kindly. Darlene cast Raine a look, a look that seemed to admonish him to remember everything Makara said. She closed the door softly behind her.

"Morning, Makara," Raine said, after the silence had stretched uncomfortably long. "Feeling better?"

She shrugged. "I guess."

Raine swallowed. "That's good." He licked his lips. "Listen. Darlene is a little worried about you. You want to talk about it?"

Makara tensed. "No."

"I just want to help you, Makara."

She whispered something, so lightly, that Raine didn't catch it.

Raine looked down at his hands, feeling useless. "Can I sit down, at least?"

Makara nodded, and Raine took up the chair next to her bed. Raine wasn't sure what to say, and it felt as if Makara wasn't going to volunteer anything.

"I used to be married to the most beautiful woman in the world," Raine said. "Her name was Valerie." Raine paused, steeling himself to continue. He didn't much like to talk about this. "I had a daughter, too." He looked at Makara, who was staring out the window at the courtyard. "Her name was Adrienne. She was the light of my eyes and the music of my heart."

Makara looked at him, seeming to be slightly interested. "They died?"

Raine nodded. "They were killed, in cold blood." Raine shook his head, drawing from his memories, as painful as they were. "That hurt me bad. Still hurts to this day."

"Who killed them?"

"A bad man. His name's Carin Black. He's the leader of the Black Reaper gang. They're the Angels' sworn enemy."

"Because he killed your wife and kid."

It hurt, to hear it put so bluntly like that, in the way only a child could.

"That and more, Makara. Point is, I know how it feels to lose somebody you love. I loved my wife, Valerie, and my daughter, Adrienne . . ." His voice thickened, and his eyes became watery. "Loved them with everything I had. There's a hole in my heart the size of . . . the size of them both put together, I guess. But now they're gone, taken from me forever." Raine shook his head, talking as much to himself as the girl. "It's been years, but the pain's still there. It's become a different type of pain, I guess. But it's pain all the same."

Raine didn't even know what he was doing, or why he was telling this little girl about his dead wife and daughter. If Darlene were in here, she would probably smack him upside the head, talking about death to a grieving child. It felt right, though, for whatever reason.

When Raine looked up, he was surprised to see Makara had tears in her eyes. She surprised him even more when her tiny hand reached for his and was engulfed by it.

"My daddy died," she whispered.

Raine nodded. "I'm sorry."

Even quieter: "Mommy died, too."

Was there something there? Did Raine dare to ask?

Then, in the most miserable voice he'd ever heard, she said, "It's all my fault."

She hid her face and started sobbing. Raine squeezed her hand, and felt tears coming to his own eyes.

"I'm sure it's not your fault, Makara."

Makara screamed. "It's my fault! My fault! I dropped Panda! I dropped him, and Panda is gone too. All because of me . . ."

She was wailing now. Darlene opened the door with a shocked expression. Raine motioned for her to shut it, which she promptly did.

"It's okay, Makara," Raine said. "You don't have to talk about it." Then, after a moment. "Who's Panda?"

"My bear," she said, with a sniffle.

Raine figured it must have been a stuffed toy. Makara spoke again after a moment.

"The monsters killed them," Makara said. "They killed everybody. Everybody but me and Sam."

"Who's Sam, Makara?"

"My brother," she blubbered. "He's gone, too."

"In the crash, you mean."

Makara nodded, seeming to calm, if only a little bit. Her face became strangely serene as she drew a few deep breaths. She wiped her face. Her pain was bottled up, at least for now. Raine almost did a double take at the change. It was as if she had no emotion at all.

"Mommy always told me that when I'm scared, to just breathe," Makara said. "*Breathe. It will all get better.* That's what she told me."

Raine nodded, seeming to think it good advice.

"It doesn't work, though," Makara finished. "It hasn't gotten better." She looked at Raine. "When will it get better?"

Raine was at a loss for what to say. He didn't have an answer for that. He supposed no one on Earth did.

She looked back out the window. "I'm done talking now."

WHEN RAINE LEFT THE ROOM, he and Darlene looked at each other for a moment before the nurse broke the silence.

"She can stay here as long as she needs," Darlene said. "Get Dr. Klein here ASAP."

Raine nodded. "Learned a few things. Her parents are dead. You're right that she has someone close to her named Sam. Might have survived the crash, but that doesn't look likely. She had a little toy bear named Panda."

Darlene nodded. "That's good. Anything else?"

Now, for the strangest part. "She mentioned something about monsters. How they got everyone."

Darlene frowned. "Monsters. Raiders, maybe?"

"Maybe," Raine said, though he was doubtful. "She said they killed everybody. Something in the way she said it makes me think she doesn't mean just her parents, but everyone she was with. I didn't ask about those other people, though. She was distraught."

"That's weird," Darlene said. "Poor girl is rattled. I'd give her something to calm her down, but we don't have much."

"It's all right," Raine said. "I don't think it's good for her to stay in here alone, Darlene. She needs human interaction. I'll get Klein here this morning. After she sees Klein, I want her in the nursery. Maybe she can help take care of the little ones. Giving her a job might take her mind off things."

Darlene nodded. "We can try it, I guess."

"If she takes to that, well, we'll see about enrolling her in school with Isabel."

Raine had places to be. As much as he wanted to make sure Makara was okay, he had to run things. He'd have to leave Makara in others' hands for now.

Raine reached for the door and opened it.

"Raine?"

He turned, suspecting already what Darlene was going to say. "I know. Don't get too attached."

Darlene nodded. "She's a tough girl. She'll make it."

He nodded back. "Tell Jonas I'll look in on him later."

He closed the door behind him, chewing on his lip as he walked back to base. He didn't like that bit about monsters. He'd have to bring it up with the council.

Chapter 11

In the council meeting, only three members were present; Raine, Dan Green, and his half-brother, Ohlan, who surveyed him with bright blue eyes and pale skin. Lots of people couldn't imagine how he and Raine were related, and Raine could see that point easily enough. Ohlan was pale as a ghost, and for that reason alone couldn't go out on nighttime patrols. Both men listened carefully as Raine related what Makara had told him, however little that had been. Dan looked troubled, while Ohlan merely interested.

"What do you make of it?" Raine finally asked.

"Coupled with the copter, girl has to be from a Bunker," Ohlan said. "Bunker One's a likely candidate."

Both Raine and Dan looked at Ohlan. Bunker One was the holy grail, completely untapped and known to be the largest by a long shot. The amount of scrap, weapons, machinery, and medicine found within could supply the Angels almost indefinitely.

If only they knew where it was.

"How do you figure that?" Raine asked.

"Simple enough," Ohlan said. "Most of the Bunkers are too small to keep a copter. And another copter touched down not too far from here, as you well know, after running out of fuel."

Raine nodded, but that copter had been too far from Lost Angels' territory. Raine hadn't sent a patrol that way yet, but presumably, it had been picked clean by Reapers.

"This bit about the monsters, though," Dan said. "What could that mean?"

"A little girl's imagination," Ohlan said. "The Raiders out east are more dangerous. A large horde of 'em must have worked together to take the bunker down."

"Yeah, but who?" Raine asked.

Ohlan gave a superior smile, as if his brother should have known. "Char and Raider Bluff is my guess. They're the biggest thing east of L.A. and south of Vegas."

"Maybe it was the Vegas gangs," Dan mused.

"Vegas stays in Vegas," Ohlan said, in a play on an Old World expression that had no place in this new reality. "It was Bluff or nobody."

"Don't know why, but no one seems to be considering the most obvious option," Raine said. Both men looked at him. "The girl could be right. Maybe it really was monsters."

Dan looked at him, incredulous, while Ohlan guffawed.

"Hear me out," Raine said, holding up a hand. "This girl is *traumatized*. It goes beyond losing her mom and dad. She was terrified to even talk about it. And really, you think a group of raiders could have busted into Bunker One? An army couldn't force its way through a bunker door, and they were built to withstand the blast of a nuclear bomb. If it really was monsters, though . . ."

"You should listen to yourself, big brother," Ohlan said. "The girl's been through trauma, sure. Traumatic situations can cause a little girl to believe all sorts of crazy things."

Dan, who usually wasn't inclined to agree with Ohlan, reluctantly nodded.

Raine had to admit his brother was probably right. It was

far-fetched. The world was full of horrors enough without having to bring literal monsters into it.

"Did you find anything out about where it was?" Ohlan asked.

Raine felt a twinge of annoyance. "She's just lost her parents, Ohlan. She isn't a puzzle to be figured out. She's a person."

Ohlan smirked. "I thought you were stone cold, Raine. Looks like there's a heart beneath that gruff exterior."

Ohlan ought to know that better than anybody, but he had a point. Ever since Makara had been saved, old emotions Raine had buried for years were resurfacing. When his wife and daughter were murdered, he'd pushed everything down, channeled every fiber of his being toward killing the one responsible: Carin Black. Seeing Makara had caused old memories to resurface, the things that had once given Raine's life meaning.

Makara wasn't Adrienne. Adrienne, who had haunted his dreams of late. But maybe he could save Makara the way he hadn't been able to save his own daughter. Maybe if he saved Makara, Adrienne would stop haunting him and let him rest in peace.

"People are complicated, Ohlan," he said, eyeing him in a way that let him know his brother had gone too far. "You can't pick people open like they're things. We'll find out about where she's from, in due time. She's one of us, now, and we need to treat her as such."

That proclamation ended all argument and sent a clear message to his brother: don't mess with Makara.

"All right," Ohlan said, placatingly. "I'm with you, brother. You know that."

"This session is over," Raine said. "Apprise the others of what was discussed here."

Without another word from either of them, Raine left.

"Raine!"

Dan caught up with him in the hallway. Raine opened the doors and walked into the courtyard of Lost Angels' Command. Raine let Dan fall in beside him.

"He's an asshole," Dan said. "Always has been. Listen, just say the word and I'll vote that little prick off the council, and so would half of everyone else."

Raine sighed. *This* conversation again. "He's my brother, Dan. He stays. He's been with us since the beginning."

"Yeah, yeah," Dan said. "So you've told me. He owes you everything. If not for you, Black would have murdered him. Tortured him, even. He should be more grateful."

"In his view," Raine explained, "He's even with me. He saved me too, Dan. I don't want to lord my so-called benevolence over him. That's not how a good leader operates."

Dan shook his head. "I hear you, Boss, but I think you're wrong. I don't know why, but I don't trust him. You realize he's talking some of the others around to his way of thinking?"

"That's politics," Raine said. "I'm ready for him."

"He would never challenge you openly. That's not his way, Raine. He'll wait until he thinks he can win." He paused. "No, he'll wait till he *knows* he can win."

"Dan."

Raine had stopped, and Dan with him. Raine looked ahead, pulling his dark shades down. Dan just stared at his leader.

"Enough about my brother. Okay? We have our differences, but we grew up together. We share the same blood, however different we might look on the surface."

"Because of blood, I don't think you can see him in a rational . . ."

"Enough!"

Several people stared, while yet more scattered. Their leader, while slow to anger, was a sight to behold when his rage had finally built past the breaking point.

Dan backed off. "Sure, Boss. Have it your way."

"I'm going for a ride," he said. "Hold down the fort here."

"Sure thing, Raine," Dan said, his blue eyes looking stung.

DAN WATCHED as Raine fired up his custom-made chopper. The wooden gates of Angel Command opened to let him out in a roar of dust. He stood there until the gates closed again.

"Out on patrol alone again," Dan muttered. "He's gonna get himself killed one day."

Dan turned and surveyed the fourteen-story midrise building that served as Lost Angel Command, well-intact and protected on all sides by a wooden perimeter, which was always manned and patrolled by men with rifles, with guard towers protecting key points. The red sky looked especially baleful today, casting the entire scene a dreary red.

Makara, whether she knew it or not, had stirred up a hornet's nest. Dan would have to keep an eye on her, and more than that, he'd have to keep an eye on Ohlan.

Chapter 12

2048 passed into 2049 with little ceremony. As the months dragged on, Makara got better, not only physically, but mentally. Makara was questioned regularly by Dr. Klein when he deemed her mental state improved sufficiently.

One day Raine, Kevin Klein, and Darlene Sanders sat with Makara in the psychiatrist's study, and she told her tale, such as she could remember it. A lot of it didn't make sense, and a lot of it was surely blocked out, but several things were clear.

There had been literal monsters attacking Bunker One, hundreds of them, and that only two helicopters had flown free. She also said something about a spaceship, which didn't do much to add to the credibility of her story. Raine didn't know what to make of that, but he knew his brother would love it.

She couldn't say anything about *where* Bunker One was. Something about Shy Ann Mountain. Raine had asked around a bit after the session, and no one knew where it was, either. There was no mountain by that name close to L.A., Raine was sure of that. Isabel Robles ended up knowing the answer, saying it was in Colorado, and it wasn't Shy Ann

Mountain, but Cheyenne. That put Ohlan's ambitions to find Bunker One far out of reach, and Raine had to admit, learning that Cheyenne Mountain was so far away was a blow. Finding the armament to resist the Reapers was getting hard to come by.

But Raine chose to believe Makara, no matter how crazy her story. And it wasn't hard to believe her. Raine could look in her eyes and know that she was telling the truth, or at least what she believed to be the truth. She had been through hell and hadn't come all the way back.

She *needed* to be believed.

Over the following year, Raine kept a close eye on her, making sure she had everything she needed. She didn't fit in well with most of the kids, even after a few months. She played alone in the corner, and just watched her hands, as if there were something there only she could see.

She only came out of her shell with Raine, or with Isabel, and to a small extent, Dr. Klein and Dan Green. She seemed much older than her seven years in that way. That was sadly common these days, but with Makara, it was even more so.

One day, six months after Makara had arrived, she got into a fight and badly injured a child two years older than herself. That had sent her to Dr. Klein for even more evaluation. Raine worried about her, and asked Dan what he thought about Raine adopting her as his own.

"She needs a parent, a home to stay in," Raine said. "No one else will take her. She's too wild."

Dan whistled. "What about a mother?"

Raine shook his head. "Don't know about that. I got my own issues, you know that."

Dan nodded. "I know."

"As the situation stands, she has to stay in the nursery. Just locked in." Raine shook his head. "That ain't right. I've wanted her as my own from the beginning, and I've given plenty of time for others to come forward. No one's stepped up."

"They don't want to cross you, Raine," Dan said, astutely.

"Isabel doesn't seem to mind crossing me," Raine said, almost with a shudder.

"Isabel hasn't stepped up, either," Dan said.

"Yeah," Raine said. "She's pretty much Makara's mom during the day. I guess handling her at night is too much."

"My advice? Keep waiting, Raine. Someone will want her."

"Yeah," Raine said. "That someone is me. I was a problem child, too. We just want to be loved, like everyone else."

Dan sighed. "I *told* you not to get attached."

"Too late, Green."

Within the week, Raine had adopted Makara as his own.

A LITTLE OVER a year after the day she was rescued, Makara hardly ever left Raine's side. He raised her like his own daughter in that first year as she adjusted to life in L.A. It was not without its set of challenges, but she proved resilient in the way only children can be.

Raine was a busy man, but still, he always found time to spend with her, and took little Makara with him whenever he could.

Of course, the now eight-year-old girl missed her brother, Samuel, but there was nothing Raine could do about that. No one by that name had approached the Angels' base or any of their outposts.

She was a strange child, not one to fit in with girls her own age, who liked to play with dolls, or play house. She liked to tromp the broken cityscape of post-apocalyptic L.A. with the boys, who accepted her once they figured out doing so was the safer option, because nobody could easily say no to Makara. That said, she liked to sneak off on her own, too, her small frame and light foot meaning she could fool the perimeter guards more often than not.

Raine learned not to ask questions when she came home for dinner with new bruises, scrapes, or even a black eye one time. To Makara, they were badges of honor, and she would almost never go to Darlene Sanders to get her hurts patched up.

Makara hated it when the women tried to coddle her and take her under their wing, to teach her the vital skills of keeping house, sewing, cooking, and washing laundry. She learned these only because she had to, but it was clear that she'd rather be anywhere else. More than anything, she wanted to find her brother, who she refused to believe was dead. That was the real reason she snuck out so much. Samuel was out there, somewhere. She had seen him on the other copter during the journey to L.A.

Makara didn't smile often, but one of the few times she did was when Raine took her on his patrols, as a way of rewarding her when she agreed to learn from the women. Makara had become something of a mascot to the Angels, as a few of Raine's men had had a hand in her rescue.

One cool, spring day, Raine took her on one of his patrols on his chopper. The patrols that were just him and his adopted daughter were the closest he ever came to knowing peace. The women disapproved of Raine taking her with him, but as the leader of the Angels, they couldn't stop him from doing it. Makara wasn't like other children, and patrols were a good way of keeping her happy. A happy child was easier to raise, and raising Makara was often very challenging.

Over the years, the Angels' had carved out a vast swath of territory in South L.A. That part of the city had laid largely abandoned since Dark Day, and even the Reapers had trouble taming a lot of the smaller gangs that called it home. Ever since Raine and Dan split from the Reapers, Raine had used those gangs as a buffer between himself and the far more numerous and powerful Reapers. It had worked so far – but just barely. Given time, Raine feared, Carin Black would find a way to break through and end the Angels once and for all. He was not a man to forget a slight, and the founding of a rival gang was more than just a slight to the Reaper name. It was a humiliation of the worst kind that must be repaid in the harshest terms possible.

To Carin Black, killing Raine's wife and daughter wasn't enough revenge for his leaving the Reapers. He wanted to destroy Raine totally.

The Angels needed more men to resist him. Trying to recruit from the smaller gangs was hard, and that drew those leaders' ire. A lot of the local warlords resented the Angels' rise to prominence. There'd been a few turf wars, as there always were in post-apocalyptic L.A. Only the Angels' resilience had won them the right to stay. The defenses of Lost Angels' Command were strong. It would take an army to breach them, and most gangs just didn't have the manpower to do it.

All the same, the Angels weren't strong enough to defend themselves against an all-out attack from the Reapers. And Carin would never forgive Raine for his seceding, just as Raine would never forgive Carin for what he had done.

No, Raine thought. *I won't think of that today. I won't give him power over my thoughts.*

The mere memory brought the present back to his attention. Makara sat behind him, electing to let silence reign over the gray, twisted ruins of the City of Angels.

Raine pulled to a stop next to a large, open field sitting below the old Interstate. That field was full of men working hard in the cool, cloudy afternoon, harvesting potatoes. They paid little mind to the armed Angels watching over them.

Raine did everything he could to give his subjects a good

life; the Reapers often worked their slaves to death. The Angels' slaves were grateful for the kinder life Raine offered, even if they didn't truly have freedom. At least, that was what Raine told himself. As unseemly as the institution was, slavery was just a fact of life these days. There were those who had to toil in the broken fields of the city to feed everyone else.

And being a slave of the Angels certainly beat being out *there*, prey to any gang that happened along. Prey to starvation, prey to freezing in the winter, or a countless number of things that got a person killed these days. Life in the post-Ragnarok world was nasty, brutish, and short. It was impossible to support any kind of society without workers to feed the rest.

Raine had worked for Black and had seen the way his slaves lived. Many chose to kill themselves in that hell.

He knew, compared to *him*, Raine was the Angel of Mercy.

But Makara did not seem to see it the same way.

"Why do you have slaves, Raine?"

Raine blinked at the innocence of that question, one she had never asked him before. Underneath the curious tone, Raine knew that she had probably wondered it often. There was no slavery in Bunker One, where she had come from. There, they had machines to care for the people. They had farmers, at least according to what Makara had told him, that were paid a wage they could use to buy things.

This world above had been a rude awakening for her. Raine would have to tread carefully as he answered.

"We've got to eat," he said. "Without these people, we'd have no wheat, no corn, no beans, no potatoes, no cabbage . . . all those things that'll make you grow up big and strong."

"Slavery is wrong," Makara said simply. "Nobody at Bunker One was a slave."

"Nobody had to work to grow food, Mak?"

She paused as she thought about it. "My daddy did. But

he could go home, too, to me, my brother, and my mom. He could do what he wanted in his free time, too."

He had the luxury to, Raine wanted to say.

"Out here, Mak, things are a bit different." How to explain that to an eight-year-old? "The world's tougher up above. We don't have machines to help us. The ones we do have don't work half the time, or require fuel and batteries, which we just can't make anymore." He half-turned to look at her. "Make sense?"

"They taught us in school that there used to be slaves in America a long time ago," Makara said. She looked at Raine strangely, and Raine could guess the reason why she was giving him that look: he was black. Not all kids these days knew that black people used to be slaves, a long time ago in a world that was now mostly forgotten except among the old timers.

Makara had at least something of an education in the Bunker, and this brute fact put Raine in something of an awkward position, even if this present form of slavery wasn't tied to race at all. There were white slaves, black slaves, Hispanic slaves, Asian slaves. All were equal under the yoke, in that sense, and they were treated kinder than the slaves back then. At least, Raine hoped so. Makara's observation still made him want to squirm.

"This is different," Raine said, trying to sound surer than he actually felt.

"Why's it different? Even if they weren't slaves, they'd still have to eat, right? That man over there, he might have a kid, too. He might wish he could see her more, or have a day or two off every now and then."

Makara was making too much sense for Raine's liking. Kids had a way of doing that, sometimes. Questioning everything adults took for granted.

"They've got a good life here," Raine said. "They've got food, water, a place to lay their heads for the night. That's worth a lot these days. Why should it matter if they're slaves, too? Isn't that better than dying out there?"

"But why can't they be free, too? If they had freedom, my guess is they wouldn't want to run."

None of us are free, Makara. None of us. Not even me. I'm a slave to duty. I'm a slave to saving these five hundred souls under my command. How can I explain that to you, though, that sometimes I come out here and envy the lives of these people, these people who never have to make a real decision for the rest of their lives? They eat, they sleep, they make love. So what if they're ordered about here and there? Am I not the same, too, a slave to the expectations of my people?

And so, the arguments and questions ran back and forth in his mind. Raine wasn't much one for philosophy, not unless it was forced on him. And Makara was forcing it on him.

Raine finally turned, and was surprised to see she was almost crying, as if her holy image of him had been broken. That was too much for Raine to bear.

"This is really important to you, isn't it?" he asked.

Makara nodded, and wiped her face.

"It's like this," he said, trying a different tack. "This might sound kind of strange to you, but sometimes, I envy these people."

Makara's brow scrunched up in confusion. "Huh? You're saying you'd rather harvest potatoes all day with men pointing guns at you?"

"Um . . . no. That's not what I meant." He licked his lips, and tried to focus. "They don't get to worry about anything. They just wake up, work a few hours in nice weather like this, and go home. Spend time with their families, like you said. They get a day off a week, too." Raine chuckled. "Even I don't get that, and I'm the big boss."

Makara laughed, too. "So, why don't *you* become a slave, if they have it so good?"

Raine shrugged. "That's a fair question. You might be

right. It's better to be boss than a slave. There are certain privileges I wouldn't like to give up."

"Like riding the chopper."

Raine laughed at that. "Yeah. I don't think a slave would ever do that." He grew more serious. "But not everybody can be me, Mak. In a perfect world, everybody would be equal. Maybe someday, we can grow to that point. I hope so."

Raine thought she'd be satisfied with that answer, but he had underestimated the precociousness of children.

"Why can't we grow *now*?" she asked, not letting the subject drop. "Why not make them free? What's the point in even calling them a slave? Would they really run away if there were no guards?"

"They might." Raine pursed his lips, knowing he had to explain carefully. Makara was fully convinced she was right. Her hazel eyes looked up at him in challenge. A girl, no matter her age, was always dangerous in that state. He had learned that from both his wife and his daughter.

And not too many people found the courage to argue with Raine these days, but this eight-year-old sure did. Raine found the difference to be refreshing.

He also found that he didn't have a good answer for her.

"Say I free them," Raine said. "What then? How do their lives change?"

Makara thought for a moment. "They can leave, if they want."

"I can't let them leave, Mak," Raine said. "If they leave, they die. It'd be irresponsible of me. That's less food for the base, for my men, and for you, too. That's less food to give to any new members, who might want to join us."

"Then give them another reason to stay," Makara said. "If you give them a good life, they'll stay. Right? If life really is so good here, like you say, then they won't leave."

And just from those words, he saw everything laid out before him in an epiphany. The feeling was flabbergasting.

"Maybe you're right," he admitted. "It *would* change things. A lot of people wouldn't like it, though."

My brother, for one. Ohlan had always been about tighter controls for the slaves, even enforcing slavery on all new members for a few years until they'd earned their stripes.

"Who cares what they think?" Makara asked. "You have to do the right thing. We had no slaves in Bunker One. I don't want there to be slaves here, too."

Raine shook his head at her willfulness. That only made Makara smile.

But then, everything snapped into place, like a vision in Raine's mind. Makara was right. Every man wanted to be free; Raine knew that.

And that could be the key to the Angels' success.

"If we free them," Raine mused, "word will get out. More slaves will run away, coming to us from other gangs. When they do, we'll give them their freedom and they'll fight for us and die fighting for it. It's the way for us to grow, going forward."

It would also be the right thing to do. And it was rare when the right thing to do also just so happened to be the prudent thing. It wasn't guaranteed to work, of course, but already the Reapers' raids were making him bleed. The Angels had good territory and the will to survive.

The only thing they lacked was manpower. And this could be a way to get it. Maybe even *the* way.

There would be obstacles, of course. And the transition would be painful. But it could be done.

"We'll become the safe haven," Raine said, his decision fast becoming finalized. "We'll be true to our namesake. Guardian Angels of the people."

"We can save a lot of people," Makara said. "I know we can!"

After they watched the fields a while longer, meditative, Raine fired up his chopper and tore back to Angel Command.

Chapter 13

Almost all the members of the Council were present the next day for a new meeting Raine had called. Included among their number were Darlene Sanders and Isabel Robles, who represented the medical and educational interests of the Angels, along with Dan Green, head of Security, and his brother Ohlan, head of Diplomacy. Two of Ohlan's associates, Terrance Shaw and Adam Miles, were absent, which would only help in what he was to propose today. The only remaining member was Eddie Melo, who was usually more sympathetic to Ohlan than Raine.

"We're going to end slavery," Raine said, without preamble.

Seeing the shocked expressions of most of the council members, he hastily continued.

"I admit, it's a risk, but we have plenty of food stored up in case some of the slaves choose to leave. That'll give us time to find more recruits."

"Find more recruits from *where*?" Eddie Melo asked. He oversaw Inventory, including census information that kept track of all immigrants, deaths, and group membership. "Recruitment has slowed down a lot, Raine, and I don't think freeing the slaves would help. They'd band together and form their own group, last a while maybe, but eventually they'd get swallowed up by one of our enemies."

Ohlan smiled, and made a gesture with his hands that seemed to say, "There you have it."

"I disagree," Raine said. "Offering freedom to everyone who joins us is the greatest publicity we could ever have. What will slaves of other gangs do when they realize *we're* the haven?" When nobody answered the rhetorical question, Raine continued. "That's right. They flee their masters and come to us."

"Sounds like a way to paint a target on our backs," Melo said, skeptically.

Heads nodded all around. Even Darlene and Isabel, who were usually Raine's staunch supporters, were nodding.

"Let me ask all of you a question," Raine said. "Most of you have been here from the beginning. Many of you are here right now, instead of out *there* in the fields, because you have useful skills. Without that training, without that education, things could have ended up a lot differently."

"What are you getting at?" Dan asked, speaking for the first time.

"My point is, is slavery your vision for the Angels' future? Don't you want to make this city a better place? We're all equals in the eyes of God. I believe that with all my heart." Raine watched the councilors, wondering if his words were having the intended effect. "Things were rough, getting started. We needed food, and slavery was the way to get that up and running quickly. Now we're fine, and it doesn't make sense to keep doing something that brings misery to so many people." He looked at his arms. "Especially given my racial background. I'm a hypocrite if I'm not doing everything in my power to make things better."

Ohlan slammed a fist on the metal table, causing everyone to look at him. "This ain't about race, brother, and you damn well know that. It's about *survival*. I guarantee you, if you let those slaves free, you'll be condemning the rest of us to starve." Ohlan now stood, eyeing the assembly. "Now, I know it ain't pretty. But this is the harsh reality of the world we live in. There are those who have, and those who have not. You already treat those slaves better than anyone else in L.A., Raine, and all of them have the opportunity for freedom if they prove themselves."

"That doesn't happen," Isabel said. "Not anymore. The freedom clause is just a carrot we keep pulling away from them, to keep them in place." She looked at Raine. "I agree with you, Raine."

"Have you lost your mind, Isabel?" Ohlan asked, as Isabel rolled her eyes. "Am I the *only* one who hasn't lost their mind?"

"I agree, Ohlan," Eddie Melo said, stroking his goatee. "What we have, works. The harvest comes in on time, and we have a surplus. If anything, we need to be looking at expanding our slave base. That means more food, more soldiers, more scouting parties to find supplies. I know slavery isn't ideal, but they work harder than people who aren't forced to do the dirty work."

"Yeah," Darlene said. "Because our men will kill them if they don't."

Eddie nodded, not seeming to catch Darlene's sardonic tone.

Raine considered what Eddie said. It made sense, but he also thought Eddie was ignoring the advantages ending slavery could bring. "What if I told you that freeing our slaves could actually *help* us long-term? Everyone knows nobody wants to be a slave. If those other slaves hear about how *we're* the haven, that any man who comes in here walks free, what do you think that'll do to us?"

"That's dangerous," Ohlan said. "Our allies here would take that as a grave offense. You think they'd let us steal their chattel with no consequences?"

"Chattel?" Isabel asked. "They're people, Ohlan."

"You have a soft woman's heart," Ohlan said, to Isabel's reddening face. "It's just not feasible. It will ruin the precarious position we're in. Mark my words, if we go down this road, it'll be the end of us all."

Isabel was glaring at Ohlan. "I'm for it. Even you, Eddie. You can't deny recruitment has been down lately."

Eddie shrugged noncommittally.

Isabel's speech became impassioned. "If we're the *only* ones who do this, we'll start seeing the results in weeks. We keep the other gang leaders close in the meantime and divert them from what we're doing. Our line can be that it was a personal decision on Raine's part, and his vision for the Angels' future. Ohlan can do his thing, finessing the other leaders."

"So, we frame it as a personal decision," Eddie said. "One that might actually be bad for us, so they think it won't benefit us?"

"Exactly," Isabel said.

Ohlan gave him a dirty look, and Melo clarified his position. "I still think it's a terrible idea."

"We have to try something new," Darlene Sanders said. "With an influx of refugees, most can be assigned to farm work. Even if the free individual doesn't work as hard as a slave, there will be more of them. Furthermore, every one of ours can be trained to use a gun. Something you don't want to do to a slave, since he can turn it against you."

"We don't even *have* that many guns," Ohlan said, exasperated.

"Not yet," Raine said. Everybody looked at him, but he didn't elaborate on that point.

Raine looked at each person. He thought he had enough to bring it to a vote, even though his decision was final. The council was mostly an advisory body, but Raine wanted to send a message.

"We're bringing this to a vote," he said.

"Right now?" Ohlan asked. "We've barely even discussed it. Besides, we're down two members." Ohlan eyed his brother, seeming to recognize that that was exactly the reason Raine wanted to vote on it now.

"I've heard all I need to hear," Raine said. "We'll figure out the logistics later."

"Raine . . ." Ohlan said.

Raine plowed on. "All in favor of abolishing slavery, raise your hand."

Raine, Darlene, and Isabel raised their hands. Dan looked at Raine. Had Raine misjudged him? He'd been awfully quiet.

Ohlan smiled triumphantly. Without a majority, nothing would happen.

But Dan lifted his hand in the end, while Ohlan and Eddie kept theirs lowered. Ohlan's smile transformed into a grimace. Raine almost got a chill from watching the way his brother glared at him.

"Measure is approved by a vote of 4-2," Raine said. "All of you are expected to work together and come up with a plan that will enforce the measure as effectively as possible." He eyed both his brother and Eddie when he said that.

"I bow to the will of the council," Eddie said.

Ohlan said nothing.

"Meeting adjourned," Raine said.

Chapter 14

It didn't happen all at once, but it did happen.

Within the week, slavery was abolished in Lost Angels' territory. Furthermore, it was proclaimed that any slave that set foot on Angels' territory would be protected and given a place there.

For the first time in the group's history, any person could leave. And some did. But as Raine suspected, most chose to stay and keep their jobs on the farms, with less hours and more time off. As the weeks went by, Raine was surprised to find that productivity didn't fall too much. Ohlan and Eddie had been wrong about that.

One thing they *had* been right about was that the other gang leaders didn't like it. The Lobos, the Hawks, and the Krakens all saw their escaped slaves' numbers go up as many fled to Angel territory. Raine did his best to keep those leaders placated, usually by sending his brother to talk them down. Dan didn't like Raine giving Ohlan such a vital role, but his brother had a way with words, and more importantly, the ploy seemed to work. The gangs didn't raise as much of a fuss, though Raine had to give some concessions, such as allowing slave catchers into his territory, and allowing them to take back slaves if they were caught. He remained firm, though, that any slave visible from Lost Angel Command fell under his jurisdiction.

It was only a temporary measure, though. Soon enough, not even Ohlan could keep Raine's rivals placated. They had lost too many men, and enslaved people were wily enough to find a means of escape, even with tightened security.

When war at last broke out over the issue, Raine supposed it was inevitable.

IT WASN'T JUST the Angels at war at that time. The Reapers north of I-10 were the main event as Carin Black consolidated the gang's power over most of northern L.A. and its outskirts. South of I-10, the patchwork of territories and minor powers, including the Angels, fought amongst each other. The Krakens joined up with Raine, and after that, it was everybody against the Angels'.

The Slave War lasted for two years, but in the end, the Angels were victorious. All the opposing gangs' slaves were freed and ordered to join the Angels. Most of the gang leadership that had instigated the war were put to the bullet while anyone under their charge was integrated into the Angels' growing territories.

Makara during this time didn't get to go out anymore. She had to stay indoors, helping with the war effort in whatever way she could, which usually meant fetching things for the busy adults. She was something of an informal messenger between other adults and Raine, and fulfilled that role happily enough.

Lost Angel Command came under siege only one time, but its defenses held firm. One by one, the rival gangs capitulated, and by the end of the war, the Angels were twice as large as they had been before, with more resources, guns, and ammo than ever.

But the real test was to come soon, as the Reapers wrapped up their own northern wars. With their last rivals out of the way, L.A. was split in two. Anything north of I-10 was unquestionably a possession of Carin Black and the Reapers. The south was iffier, but anything firmly in or around Compton was the Angels' seat of power.

The Reapers, by far, were more numerous, even if many of their slaves sought safety in Angel territory. More people meant more hands to work the fields, more soldiers, and more specialists. Raine made it a priority for the old ones to take apprentices and pass on their skills.

But none of that mattered, not unless they could hold back the Reapers, who outmanned and outgunned them. With the Angels' newest arrivals, there weren't enough guns to go around. Some would have to fight with cruder weapons.

And so, Raine bided his time, shoring up the defenses of Angel Command and not even committing to defending the long line of the interstate, as Black seemed to be doing.

Then, one day a few months after the Angels had won their southern war, the Reapers started to advance, slowly taking territory south of I-10 with little resistance.

The First Reaper War had begun.

Chapter 15

War had been going on for a couple of weeks, and the Angels had lost most everything up to the northern border of Compton. It was bad for morale, but it was also part of the plan. Raine had to commit his men where they would be most effective. Carin and the Reapers could afford to lose three for every one of the Angels' losses.

So, Raine had to pick his fights carefully. Ohlan cautioned him to never take an open battle, but to strike from the shadows and beat the Reapers through a war of attrition, to engage in guerilla warfare. Roadblocks kept the Reapers' biker cavalry in check, forcing their slave armies to push forward, many wielding things as crude as a plank of wood as their weapon. The Reapers' slaves were the meat shield, ordered to charge in a frenzy induced from a cocktail of booze and drugs.

The real threat came from behind the slaves, the Reaper soldiers with their rifles, practiced aim, and veteran street warfare tactics. The Angels ambushed them where they could, throwing molotovs on their passing troops, sniping at their captains. Things seemed to be working for a while, but there was a major problem with the Angels' strategy.

Raine couldn't just abandon Lost Angels' Command. The rest of the Angels' army was formless, appearing where they were least expected, attacking at night, blowing up supply trucks with explosives secured from a local military base.

But so long as Angel Command was there, Carin Black could assault it and all but win the war by capturing it.

Despite their losses, the Reapers plowed forward. Carin Black would see the Angels' base in flames or die in the attempt.

~

RAINE ROARED past the open gates of Angel Command on his chopper, coming back from his patrol late one evening about a month after the start of the war.

"Close the gate!" he called over his shoulder. "They're coming!"

Though his voice was lost to the roar of the engine, the guard on duty signaled for the thick wooden barrier to be closed. Raine watched to make sure his command was followed. To his relief, the gate began rolling shut.

Now, they would see if it would hold.

A throng of people stood in the center of the dirt yard outside HQ, foremost among them Dan, who only betrayed his surprise with a slight widening of his blue eyes. Raine braked hard before he could run into them, sliding to a stop that kicked up a choking cloud of dust. Everyone stared at him in mute shock.

"Sound the alarm!" he called out. "Reapers!"

Everyone sprang into action, scurrying different directions toward their assigned battle stations. Riflemen ascended the high towers built behind the wooden perimeter.

Raine took note of the huddled group of some fifty refugees standing in front of Dan, the most recent batch of freedmen.

"Anyone who can shoot, to me!" Raine said, his voice carrying over the whole yard. "The rest of you, go inside the main hall."

The people rushed to obey, and Raine was disappointed that only four men came to join him. He supposed he should be grateful there were any refugees at all who could use a gun.

Up above, he heard his men taking shots and the collective roar of the Reaper biker cavalry. It was just a moment later that several fiery streaks streamed overhead, lighting up the late evening sky.

"Scatter!" he yelled.

The molotovs crashed in the center of the dirt yard, each one sending an explosive plume of flame that scattered hot shards of glass. Two of Raine's followers weren't quick enough in dodging, and went up like gas-doused torches.

Thankfully, the firebombs didn't catch on anything flammable, but even now, more streamed toward the main building.

No one can throw that far, Raine thought. *They're using something to launch 'em.*

Already, men and women were carrying buckets and tubs from the water pump and prepping to fight their own battle against the fires. A shed was already up in flames, being the target of several of the bottles, and a group of women were throwing as much water as they could onto it.

Raine hefted his M5, one of the few in the Angels' possession. Most had been confiscated from some Bunker survivors who had found their way into the Angels' base recently; the weapons were put to better use in the Angels' capable hands.

Dan approached, locked and loaded with his own M5.

"Orders, Boss?"

"Dan, get these men outfitted and on the east wall."

Before Raine could even see his order fulfilled, he ran toward the main gate. The Reaper bikes were still roaring outside the perimeter. There must have been several dozen of them, the same ones that had ambushed him while out on patrol. If the Reaper army was behind the bikers, Raine and the Angels would be in a lot of trouble.

They would find out soon whether this was just a raid, or whether the Reapers meant to end the Angels once and for all.

As men on the ramparts fired at the swarming bikes, Raine climbed the ladder to join them. A heavy machine gun placed in one of the towers was already under fire from below, and was the only weapon the Angels had that could make a dent in the bikes. Several of the bikers had fallen already, but it wasn't enough.

Still, the molotovs rained down. At least a third of the yard now was a roaring inferno. Reaper men waited down the street, hiding inside the buildings, lighting more of the weapons while handing them to the bikers driving by.

"Stop those damn bikes!" Raine shouted.

A heavy bell tolled from the main building, which had been procured from a local church. They needed God to save them from this onslaught. Most of the smaller fires were already dying down in the yard, aided by the endless stream of buckets entering their contents onto them. More of the tattooed bikers were starting to fall, now that the initial shock of the attack was over. The Angels were returning fire from behind the ramparts with discipline.

There might be hope yet, Raine thought. *I've still got my ace.*

But the timing was everything.

"Samuel!" a female voice called.

That voice. Raine snapped around, to see little Makara running past the flames toward . . . someone. One of the Bunker refugees they'd picked up last night, who had been under confinement.

"No!" Raine shouted, from across the yard. "Makara, inside, now!"

But she didn't even look his direction.

Raine charged forward, heedless of all danger. A molotov

fell from above, which Raine dodged just barely, skidding to a stop and backing up. The burst of flames blinded him as his skin crackled from the heat. He grunted, and all he could do was hold up a hand and hope he didn't become a human torch.

He was still safe. He skirted the conflagration, running to bar Makara's path. He blinked to get his eyes to stop seeing spots. The darkness made her hard to pick out.

"Samuel!" she cried. "Samuel!"

Samuel? Makara had told him about her big brother. But how could he be here?

Impossible. He was dead.

Makara, who was now ten, was oblivious to the danger around her. She pumped her arms, running as if she were possessed.

But Raine was just in time to intercept her, scooping her up into his arms. "You need to be inside, Mak! Now!"

"Samuel!" she said, tears streaming down her face. "Put me down, Raine! Put me down!"

To Raine's surprise, she bit him on the ear. That pain nearly made him drop her.

"What the hell! Knock it off, Mak! You trying to get yourself killed?"

He held her at arm's length, even as she flailed like a fish out of water, her tearful eyes never even looking at him. Raine followed her line of sight to see the object of her attention.

A boy, who seemed no more than fifteen years of age, was ringed by a circle of flames.

Chapter 16

Raine charged even as a thunderous crash sounded from the direction of the gate. The heat of the flames was unreal, but he didn't let that distract him. He knew he should've been up front commanding his men, but here he was instead, rescuing two kids who didn't know how to stay inside when they were told to.

Well, Makara at least. Samuel had been among the Bunker survivors, and seeing his sister had made him run off on his own. Still, for his age, Samuel was a big and strong lad, with wide shoulders and a mop of brown hair. His face was hard and square. He appeared unduly calm, as if he had seen flames before, and had survived them.

Raine did his best to ignore the sweltering heat. If either he or Samuel went through the flames, that would be a death sentence.

There was only one thing he could do. But he didn't know if there was enough time.

"Stay out of the flames, Samuel," Raine said. "I'll be right back."

Raine sprinted toward the bucket brigade. He must have been quite the sight.

"Buckets on that flame, now! There's a kid in there!"

Instantly, the civilians diverted their course. Within moments, the flames were being doused by dozens of buckets.

Raine watched their progress, even as he kept an eye on the gate rocking back and forth. They were battering it with something, probably a truck, judging by the roar of a diesel engine. The flames surrounding Samuel died down, little by little, but not quickly enough. There was some rubble feeding the flames. But the wall of fire was weaker on one side, the side Raine stood on.

"Samuel, you'll have to jump after the buckets douse it," Raine said. "It's going to keep coming back."

Samuel nodded, waiting for the splash of several buckets in tandem before charging forward and giving a mighty leap. He cried out as he fell on the other side, the hem of one of his pant legs catching fire. Instantly, he was doused with water until nothing but steam hissed off him.

By now, Makara had run up and was hugging her brother fiercely, tears running rivers down her soot-covered face. He grimaced from her touch; it would have been impossible for him to have remained within that circle without getting burned at least a little bit. But he didn't protest, and held her protectively.

"Get them both inside," Raine said, turning to a nearby woman. "Make sure they're all right. Find Isabel Robles, if you can."

"Will do, Raine," the woman said.

"Raine!" Makara shouted.

"Not now, Makara!" Raine said. "Get inside, and if you come back out here again, you'll wish you were with the Reapers!"

Makara's eyes widened a bit at that, but Raine had to say something to get her to listen.

The firebombs had mostly ceased by now, but Raine's

attention was on the gate, against which came another loud crash.

"Raine!"

Dan's voice crackled from the radio on Raine's side

"What is it?" Raine asked, raising it to his mouth.

"If we wait any longer . . ."

Dan said nothing more, just in case there were some Reaps listening in. Raine watched and considered as the gate was battered again, splintering a bit in the middle, revealing the grill of a large truck.

"Just a minute longer," Raine said. "If they bust it open, they bust it open. But this has got to work, Dan. How many hours have we spent on this? We can't just do it halfway!"

Raine's comment went unanswered. Dan might disagree, but he wasn't going to counter Raine. Not about this, when hundreds of lives were at stake.

Raine ran until he was at the gate, where several dozen men waited with their weapons; old guns, blunt instruments, even a few swords and shabby shields made of corrugated metal. Raine looked out at these brave men, hoping that they wouldn't all be dead in the next few minutes.

"We hold 'em here!" he shouted, his voice loud enough to carry despite the cacophony of gunshots and motors. "Off the wall, now! Down here! Hold 'em long enough, that's all we have to do!"

From the confused faces staring back at him, Raine knew that most of them didn't know what the hell he was talking about. They probably all thought they were goners. And they might be, for all Raine knew. But if this worked, then it would be the stuff of legends.

Raine's voice was cut off when what remained of the front gate fractured in the center. There was an odd moment of silence when the gunshots stopped, the roar of the bikes lessened, and the shouts of men and screams of women quieted.

Something big is about to happen, all right, Raine thought. *This had better damned work.*

The men formed ranks around him, pointing their guns into the breach that could fill with Reapers any minute, even as others were setting up shabby barricades to begin the final stand. The only reason they weren't pouring through, Raine realized, was because of how thick the smoke was, and the small size of the breach.

There's time yet, Raine realized.

That thought was dashed from his mind from a single, guttural yell. They poured through. First came a few long pikes, prodding for purchase, splitting the broken timbers aside to make way. A few heads appeared, along with wild, frightened eyes, with men carrying nothing more than large shields designed to cover two or more men.

The human cannon fodder came through by the dozens, a wall of shields, and in between those shields, long pikes.

"Fire!" Raine yelled. "Fire!"

Even as the Reapers' meat shield started to disintegrate, more still slipped through, engaging his men with feral tenacity. Their emaciated forms and lack of signature Reap tats told Raine that these men were slaves, just fodder to clear the way for proper soldiers.

"Hold position!" Raine ordered. "We hold 'em here!"

A large club swung toward Raine's head, which he narrowly dodged. A bullet fired from the breach, missing him by an inch.

He hastily pulled out his radio. His men were already falling. A minute more, and there'd be no way they came back from these losses. "Now, Dan. Now!"

Not a moment later, there was a deafening explosion from beyond the walls, followed shortly by screams. For those who were screaming, Raine knew there was no chance.

"Everyone get down!" Raine shouted. "Back to HQ!"

He didn't know if anyone had heard him, but they were

following. The pikemen and shield bearers remained behind, confused at the explosion and the Angels' sudden retreat.

When they turned around, they found out why.

The large, multistory building across the street was collapsing, and when fully fallen, would crush the hundreds of Reaper soldiers waiting to charge into Angel Command.

There was no sound other than that colossal crash, which was now toppling against other buildings. The screams were drowned out, as even more buildings fell, as a great dust rose into the air. The whole thing took maybe a minute, and even after that minute, there were still aftershocks of concrete continuing to fall on the street outside.

Silence reigned as a swell of dust rose over the walls, engulfing the Angels that hadn't yet retreated into HQ. Raine was among them. He covered his nose and mouth with his kerchief, wetting it first with his canteen. Even so, he started hacking, along with everyone else around him. Raine waited for that dust to clear, but it just wouldn't. It grew even thicker. He knew buildings like this had dangerous chemicals in them, chemicals everyone in this base would be exposed to now.

"Back up," he finally said, his voice somber. "We all need to get inside and assess things. We'll sweep things out there, see if there are any survivors."

Chapter 17

M akara and her older brother held each other in the dark corridors of Angel Command. Isabel Robles sat beside them, nervously staring into the shadows as the rattle of gunfire sounded outside, while the building itself shook from the impacts of God knew what.

"Don't worry, children," she said, her voice not entirely convincing. "We'll make it through all right."

Makara might have only been ten, but she was old enough to know that Miss Robles was trying to convince herself more than them.

"Maybe we should get lower in the building," Samuel said, his hand tightening over his little sister's. Makara moved closer to him, hardly believing that he was here. Despite what has happening outside, despite the death and destruction, she couldn't feel anything but elation.

It had been over three years since that day, and Samuel seemed almost like a grown man to her, looking like his father while having her mother's kind brown eyes.

There would be time for stories later, though. He had told her that their copter had run out of fuel early, but most everyone had survived the crash. He and the survivors had lived on the outskirts of Angel territory, undetected, for years.

"Raine said to stay here," Miss Robles said, in response to Samuel's earlier suggestion. "This is the back of the building. It's safer."

Makara tried to discount the fact that Miss Robles had said it was "safer" and not "safe." The teacher had always been a source of steadiness in her life. She taught her, along with the other kids, almost every single day in the school room on HQ's first floor. She had a tough job – the sons and daughters of Angel members were not an easy bunch to teach. She managed, somehow, and despite her young features, was tough as nails and respected by the children.

It was then that an explosion rocked Makara from her thoughts. The sound was deafening, to the point where it felt as if her head would split open. Samuel grabbed her, pulling her away from the blast, even as Miss Robles fell amidst the sound of gunfire.

"Miss Robles!" Makara screamed, not hearing her own voice due to the blast.

Isabel fell backward next to Makara, her face staring lifelessly at the ceiling. The first thing Makara saw was the blood dribbling out of her mouth, and only second the piece of twisted rebar, about two inches long, sticking out of the center of her forehead.

She never even screamed, Makara thought. *Why is that?*

All she knew was that her teacher was dead, and even as she knew it, she couldn't believe it. Even the vacant green eyes staring blankly at her didn't make it entirely real. And, Makara realized, if Miss Robles hadn't been sitting exactly where she was, *she'd* have been the one with a piece of metal in her skull.

Hot tears stung from her eyes, intermixed with the dust-poisoned air. Makara was aware of the sound of Samuel urging her back, and only now did she hear the tromping of boots and the screams of men and women down the corridor, where the explosion had taken place. A few gunshots rang out, and some bullets even whizzed overhead.

Samuel pulled her to the floor and threw his body on top of hers. Makara was blind and deaf to it all. Though she had seen death before, for some reason this one hit her just as hard as any of the others. Miss Robles had been her friend.

"We have to get away, Makara!" Samuel said. "This place is going down!"

Makara nodded. All it took was for Samuel's hand to pull her. They crawled on their bellies across the rubble, going in the opposite direction of the gunfire. Makara turned to look, her dead teacher already lost to darkness. The troop of Reapers was somewhere down the corridor, but they seemed to be going the other direction.

Makara allowed herself to follow her brother. Samuel pinched her shoulder, pointing to a staircase leading down into darkness.

"No," she said. "Not the basement."

She had always been afraid of the basement. Sometimes, if she walked the halls at night, she could hear screams emanating from below, so soft she could hardly know whether they were real. The other kids said it was haunted, or that they had seen people go down there in the dead of night, never to come back up.

Makara had always felt too afraid to ask Raine about it. They didn't have to tell people not to go down there, but all the same, there was almost always a guard posted.

Right now, though, there was no guard. Of course, Samuel didn't know about the basement, but Makara knew it was either that or the Reapers.

It got very cold as they went down below; nonsensically cold. It must have been seventy degrees in the building itself, but down here, it was at least sixty. When Samuel pushed open the door at the very bottom, it yowled like a dying cat, echoing in the cavernous space that was revealed. It was a large, single room, supported by a dozen or so square columns and lined with rows of boxes, shelves, scrap metal, tools, and disused machinery. After the echo dissipated, they were left in silence, broken only by the sounds of gunshots emanating from above.

"Let's find a place to hide," Samuel whispered.

Makara was led by the hand, afraid that if she let go, Samuel would lose her in the darkness. She was paralyzed with fear, and that fear culminated in a scream as a tangle of spider web stretched across her face, a scream that only became sharper as a large spider crawled through her hair.

"Get it off me!" she shrieked, punching more than brushing it off her black hair.

"Quiet!" Samuel hissed.

A door from the other side of the room slammed open. "Who's in here? Show yourself!"

Samuel pulled Makara toward a row of boxes, kneeling behind them.

They could do nothing but be as quiet as the dead that were said to haunt this place.

MAKARA HELD her breath as more footsteps entered the basement. She couldn't count how many there were because they just kept coming. After half a minute or so, the noise ceased, and she could hear the labored breathing of what most likely ten or so men.

She wasn't brave enough, or stupid enough, to raise her head above the boxes to get a more accurate count.

"Search it," a man said.

At once, the thuds of boots spread in every direction. They would reach Makara and Samuel's position soon.

"We've got to move," Samuel whispered.

He pulled her hand, and they retreated to the deeper

darkness of the basement. They followed narrow lanes, and Makara nearly knocked over a high stack of boxes as they took a sharp turn. She bit her tongue as they walked through yet more spider webs. For as long she had been alive, she hated spiders.

She chanced a look behind to see several shadows searching several rows down. Two beams of light cut through the shadowy labyrinth; Samuel pulled her to the ground just in time to miss the crisscrossing flashlight beams.

They reached the far corner of the basement, Makara fighting the urge to sneeze at the thick smell of must.

"Up there," Samuel said.

He was pointing to a line of shelves on their right, all of which were filled with miscellaneous items; tools, motors, plastic containers, metal boxes, tarps, lamps, piles of musty clothes, along with various knickknacks such as figurines, clocks, cords, and old computer towers. The Angels collected any sort of junk they could find if it was in good condition. There was no telling what could be pieced together. There wasn't any rhyme or reason to the sorting, or more accurately, lack of sorting, which usually meant these items had been down here for years, untouched, evidenced by the thick dust coating them.

Samuel boosted her up to the first shelf, and he followed soon after. The thudding of boots was getting close. Makara reached up, barely able to touch the next shelf with her fingertips. Samuel boosted her up to that one as well.

By the time they made it to the third shelf, about fifteen feet off the ground, two men rounded the corner, one bearing a flashlight. Instantly, it found Samuel, who pushed Makara forward on the shelf to hide her from view. Makara almost cried out in the following cacophony of junk that rained down from the shelf above, even as Samuel turned to the men and raised his hands.

"Over here!" the man shouted. "Found him!"

The men in the basement all converged on the source of the voice. Samuel did not look at Makara, who was now hidden, not wanting to do anything to give her away.

Tears came to Makara's eyes. "Samuel . . ."

Samuel's face tensed, a clear indication that he wanted Makara to be quiet.

"It's just a kid, Raine," the man with the flashlight said.

Makara felt her heart jolt at that voice.

A moment later, Raine's voice called out. "Samuel?"

"Yes, sir."

"I'm here!" Makara crawled toward the shelf's precipice, and together, the siblings scrambled down.

RAINE RAN FORWARD, helping Makara down first, and then Samuel.

"Where's Isabel?" he asked, once they were on the ground. "I thought she was supposed to be keeping an eye on you."

Makara held tightly to Raine, reaching her arms around his thick neck. "She died, Raine. They busted in and got her."

Raine was quiet for a moment. "You saw that?"

"Yes," Makara said. "I'm sorry, Raine."

"Not your fault," he said, his voice thick. "It's all mine."

"We had to hide down here. I hope we didn't do anything wrong."

"Good thing I found you both," he said, finally. "I was worried. We should go."

Makara and Samuel followed him upstairs silence. It took a minute for Makara to muster the courage to break that quiet.

"Raine?"

Silence for a moment. "What Mak?"

"What's going to happen now?"

Raine reached down and held her hand. "We've almost got the building back. There's just a few left inside."

"What happens after?" Makara asked.

Raine ignored her. Maybe there were things that even he didn't know.

"Stay with her," he said, facing Samuel. "The basement needs to stay secured."

"Where are you going?" Makara asked.

"Upstairs. I need to make sure everything's mopped up. Stay here with these men." He paused, then added, "And be good."

Raine ran upstairs, back into the ruin of Angel Command.

Chapter 18

At long last, there were no more gunshots, but the following quiet was not peaceful.

Raine walked through the corridors of Angel Command, surveying the damage and helping anyone he could find, and barking orders to anyone who didn't look like they weren't being useful enough. That was most people. The bodies of the injured and the dead were just as numerous as those still alive.

By all appearances, they had held back the invasion, but Raine knew they were crippled. Hopelessly crippled. Only one look at the state of Angel Command and the dead bodies was enough to know that. With all those molotovs and the Reapers' numbers, only Dan's explosives had saved the base.

If this could even be called "saved."

Raine stood at the breach the Reapers had made in the back of HQ, the one that come so close to killing Makara and Samuel. Raine wanted to curse at himself for not putting enough men to defend the back, but he had too few men as it was, and there was no way he could have known. Despite Raine putting the bulk of the men out front, the Reapers had still managed to break through there. Only a combination of luck and sheer tenacity had kept the base alive long enough for Dan's explosives to force the retreat.

It was impossible to tell just how many were dead. Perhaps as many as a hundred. Likely more. Even if the Angels had inflicted many times the casualties, they were losses Carin Black could afford.

Raine turned his head at the sound of boots crunching over rubble. He knew who it was just by the gait, and his suspicion was confirmed when a short and swarthy man, pale of skin, with shrewd blue eyes and a bald head, stood next to him. Raine didn't bother looking at him. He knew he couldn't read those inscrutable eyes, just as one can't see beneath the ice of a frozen lake.

In all his years being alive, Raine had never seen anything warm enough to thaw his brother's eyes.

They had shared the same father, from whom Ohlan inherited his ghostly paleness. Raine, by contrast, had inherited his mother's darkness. He didn't remember much of his mother; it had been their father who had raised them both. If "raised" was even the right word. Usually, it was his girlfriend of the week who was doing the raising, or their grandma, who'd had her own issues.

Ohlan stood beside him, and together, the two brothers stared out at the smoke and desolation beyond the walls. Several low fires still crackled, while the bodies of dead Reapers and their thralls littered the ground. Those wouldn't be gotten to until the Angels had taken care of their own dead.

"Remember what I told you, brother," Ohlan said, solemnly. "I'd warned you this would happen. And it did, two years later. The bill came due."

Raine didn't have the energy to argue. The slaves again. The damn slaves.

"You're trying to play games at a time like this?" Raine asked.

"I'm not playing games. I've never been more seri
my life." He could feel his brother's blue eyes on him. "ι
at me, Raine."

Raine stared resolutely ahead.

"Look at me!"

When Raine looked at him, he saw something wild and
more than a bit unhinged in his brother's eyes. They were no
longer ice, but blue fire.

"Say it. Say I was right."

"Tch. Is that all you care about? Being right?"

"Say it!"

"You were right that this would happen," Raine said.

Ohlan blinked, the answer clearly surprising him.

"I don't think your way would have been better," Raine
clarified. "We united the southern gangs, and without that, we
might have never survived this."

"Maybe," Ohlan conceded. Raine had thrown him a
bone, so he decided to throw one back.

"We don't have the men to hold here anymore," Raine
said. "That much is clear. Give me men, and I can make this
city ours."

Ohlan spat, not out of disrespect, but habit. He'd always
spat like that. Raine found the habit revolting but had long
since stopped trying to correct it. They were raised by their
father, and what mannerism's Raine earned had come from
Valerie, his late wife. Ohlan had never had a woman take to
him. Not for long, anyway.

"It's hard to find new men when everyone's dead, or afraid
of Black," Ohlan said. "Jesus, Raine. Over half of their men
had to be slaves. You think you did a good thing with that
explosion. You kept that secret from me, your own brother."
Ohlan gave a bitter smile. "No need to defend yourself. I
know we haven't gotten on all that well. Dan is your real
brother, right? The brother of your choosing."

"I can't choose my own brother," Raine said, irritated that Ohlan was picking this fight now, of all times.

Ohlan stared at Raine dangerously. "Most of those men you killed? Not Reapers. Just slaves. They'll find more, and they'll be back, mark my words."

"I know that," Raine said quietly. "You're not saying anything I don't already know."

"What's your plan? Yeah, we bury the dead. We rebuild the walls." He paused. "Or do we?"

Raine looked at Ohlan, feeling disgust. "What do you mean, *do* we? You came with me when we left the Reapers. You said you wanted revenge, like me. You swore it. We will do whatever it takes to win this."

Ohlan gave a chuckle tinged with bitterness. "I have my own secret, Raine. The question is, do I tell you?"

Raine crossed his arms. "If you intended on that, you'd have kept quiet. Out with it now. Or keep your peace."

The following quiet was icy, and neither brother seemed to want to break it.

"Father was not a good man," Ohlan said, finally. "I could have forgiven that. I don't think either of our mothers loved him much, either."

"You still loved him, though."

Ohlan smiled. "Yeah. I loved him. Even as he hated me."

Raine said nothing. He said nothing, because he knew it was true.

"Daddy's favorite," Ohlan said. "You've always had a good and kind nature, Raine. A heroic nature." He chuckled again. "Whatever was good about our father, which wasn't much, he seemed to give it all to you. By the time I was born, I guess there was nothing left."

"Goodness isn't innate," Raine said. "Goodness is choosing the right thing, even when it's tough."

"That's what everyone born good says," Ohlan said. "If it's so easy to be good, everyone can do it, right?"

Raine felt tenderness for the first time. He was cautious of that tenderness; many times, Ohlan had taken advantage of it. But searching Ohlan's face, this didn't seem to be one of those times.

"You're not a bad man, Ohlan," Raine said. "You chose to come with me rather than stay and help Black, after what he did. Valerie wasn't even your wife, nor Adrienne your daughter. You saw my hurt and chose to help me over him. You stuck with family. You've helped me run the Angels, even when you don't agree with things. You're loyal. You've done nothing to prove otherwise."

"Green would beg to differ," Ohlan said.

"Green is fooled by appearances," Raine said. "Actions matter more. You like to jibe and test me, and you're ornery as a porcupine, but you're still my brother. Always will be."

"As any good brother should say," Ohlan said. He gave a long sigh. "Enough of this talk. It's idle and does nothing. Maybe we shouldn't speak of our father again."

Raine was all too happy to agree. He never much cared for the man. "What would you do now, Ohlan? What's your read on all this?"

Ohlan stared out at the devastation. He seemed to weigh his words carefully.

"They'll be back," he finally said. "They kicked us in the dirt tonight, and they kicked us good. When they've regrouped, they'll drive in the knife. They've surely got reinforcements. If not tomorrow, then next week, or next month."

"We need more time to prepare," Raine said. "New people arrive by the day. They want freedom, Ohlan. And they'll fight for that freedom harder than any slaves that Carin sends at us. We killed five times as many as they did. At least."

"Maybe so," Ohlan said. "Except none of that matters when the numbers are ten to one. Quantity beats quality most times. That's why Stalin beat Hitler, why Rome fell to the Goths." He paused. "And that's why Raine will lose to Carin."

"Why are you giving me a history lesson, Ohlan? What good is this, right now?"

"You need to wake up, Raine," Ohlan said, his icy blue eyes becoming intense. "Wake up and see where you've gotten us."

"Every man must make a choice," Raine said. "I made mine and stand by it." Then, after a moment: "It was the right thing to do."

"That's where we disagree, brother. Most men can't make the right choice. They don't know enough. They need a strong hand to make the big decisions so that they can be safe, eat food, and pop out babies." He laughed bitterly. "The circle of life. You say new slaves will come in, wanting freedom. Well, not fast enough to replace all the ones we just lost."

"You think you can do better?" Raine shouted. "Try! Try leading for yourself and see just how easy it is!"

"I'm just telling you how it is, brother. You've changed ever since that girl came." Ohlan looked at Raine sideways. "It's good you saved her, don't get me wrong. But you treat her like she's your own." Ohlan then turned, and Raine met his eyes, as much as he resented Ohlan right now. To Raine's surprise, Ohlan seemed serious. "That girl isn't your daughter, Raine. She isn't Adrienne."

Raine pushed Ohlan. "You say this, right now? That girl is as good as mine, and you leave her out of it! This is between me and you."

"I say it because no one else will tell you. I'm making my choice, Raine. I'm making my choice to tell you that you shouldn't listen to a little girl on how to run things. She put that idea in your head, didn't she? When you'd go so soft? How many died because of that softness?" Ohlan gestured to the ruins, to the dead bodies. "Death is the harvest of softness."

"I'm not soft, Ohlan. That's where you're wrong."

"I'm just telling you what men are saying. And after

tonight, who knows? Maybe some will think they're better off elsewhere."

"If you got something to tell me, then say it straight, Ohlan. For once in your life."

Ohlan looked at him sideways, a slight smile on his lips, which was quickly erased. "They're saying we're fighting a losing war. They're saying you've gone soft letting the slaves free. They're saying we can't make it here anymore."

"There isn't anywhere else for them to go to," Raine said.

"That's where you're wrong," Ohlan said. "With enough organization, a small force could survive outside the ruins. I know L.A. is the real prize. But it's a prize Carin has already won. He has the numbers and he has the will."

Raine didn't like what he was hearing. He wondered if this so-called dissension Ohlan was referring to could be true, or if it was another one of Ohlan's games. A game that toed the line of treason.

"You listen here," Raine said, stepping closer. "As long as you're here, within these walls, there'll be no talk of that. Were you anybody other than my brother right now, this conversation would go a lot differently."

Raine didn't have to elaborate that thought. He ran the Angels like he would run any army.

Treason was a crime deserving of death.

Raine pressed his advantage. "You signed on for this, Ohlan. There is nothing more dishonorable or reviling than a man who breaks his sacred word, to a brother no less. I trust you because I have no choice. If you walk out on me, you're leaving me to the wolves. And you know what? That's something I could see you doing."

Raine waited for Ohlan to respond with some pithy remark or comeback. He didn't.

"Do you believe in God, Ohlan?"

Ohlan shook his head.

"You believe our father is watching you, then? Do you believe the possibility even exists?"

Slowly, Ohlan nodded.

"Imagine him watching you, then. Don't do this for me. Don't do it for you. Do it for your father, whom you love."

Ohlan nodded, but Raine couldn't even know was going on behind the icy surface, in the cold, dark deep of Ohlan's heart and mind.

"Try, Ohlan. Fight with everything you've got. If you don't, we're not going to make it. You have a choice, as every man does. If you do well, if you make the right choice, you are giving life. The opposite . . ."

It was a while, but finally, Ohlan nodded. "You're right. I know you're right." Ohlan smiled, but it was forced.

"Your choice, Ohlan. It's always your choice."

Chapter 19

Two months after the attack, Angel Command was unrecognizable. The walls had been rebuilt, but beyond that, everything was still in drastic need of repair. They'd hurt the Reapers far more than Raine had initially thought. There hadn't been so much as a skirmish since the siege. Maybe the Reapers were still licking their wounds, or maybe they were wary of more explosives.

Of course, there weren't any more explosives, but Raine needed Carin to believe there was. Though the siege ended in victory for the Angels, the result of the battle might as well have been a defeat. The Angels had lost influence on the South Side, and several other minor gangs had already pledged fealty to Carin, who now styled himself King of L.A.

As far as Raine was concerned, L.A. had no king, and if Carin truly wanted the title, he'd have to earn it over Raine's dead body.

～

"Raine?"

Raine looked up from the tabletop he'd been staring at.

He hadn't been looking at the council table, of course. Rather, he had been thinking. Thinking far harder than he ever had in his life.

"Repeat what you said please, Dan."

Dan nodded, his stoic face betraying no emotion. "A messenger came from the north. Carin has called a meeting between all the gangs."

It could only mean one thing. "He wants to negotiate a peace, then." Raine drummed his thick fingers on the table. "I won't go."

Several of council members murmured at that, only stopping when Raine looked up, focusing his eyes on each one in turn. Darlene Sanders. Dan Green. Eddie Melo. His eyes instinctively went to Isabel Robles' empty chair, before eyeing his brother, Ohlan.

There were several other people Raine had appointed. Kevin Klein, for one, who was now Chief Archivist, whose duty was to gather knowledge and records for the Angels to consult.

Terrance Shaw and Adam Miles were both present today, each of them being Ohlan's man through and through.

"Black hasn't won yet," Raine said. "He's ready to sign the peace when he hasn't even won the war."

At this, Ohlan smirked. It was as if his younger brother were saying that the Reapers *had* won in everything but name. Raine noticed that Shaw, Miles, and Melo were looking at Ohlan for direction.

I don't like that, Raine thought. "You have something to say, Ohlan?"

Ohlan nodded. "We've lost our ability to fight. We don't have any more explosives, a fact which is sure to leak at some point."

Raine didn't like that, either. It was to admit that there were spies in his camp running their mouths to the Reapers. So far, he had no indication the Reapers had learned anything about their lack of explosives. But Raine was a realist and knew that it was just a matter of time. He'd not only shown his ace, but he'd used it.

Ohlan continued. "We don't have the manpower for a long-term war, and Black knows it. We're running low on bullets. It might not be today, but should we refuse to negotiate with him, it'll mean worse for us down the road."

Several of the men nodded at that. Raine stared hard at Ohlan, angry, but not surprised. Ohlan was trying to paint himself as the realist, but Raine knew that Carin Black's peace might be even worse than war.

"If we go," Ohlan continued, "we may be able to secure a more favorable deal while we're still standing on our feet and coming off an important victory." Ohlan turned his cold, blue eyes on his brother. "It's a little harder to negotiate when your face is in the mud. If we take another fight, one we lose, our position will be much weaker at the table."

"He hasn't won," Raine said. "And the next person who suggests surrender will be kicked off this council."

"Isn't that a bit premature, Raine?" Ohlan asked, rising to the challenge. He'd grown bold. Raine watched as Dan stared daggers at him. "I understand that you don't want to admit some things. It's painful. Isn't the best choice the one that brings the least pain to all? Think of the little ones, brother."

By little ones, Raine had all but said Makara. Raine put that out of his mind. "We'll *never* surrender. I know these streets better than Carin or the Reapers ever will. If he wants to be king of California, let him test that claim. Here, south of the 105."

Dan nodded at that, and several others seemed to be of a similar mind. Not everyone here was biting the hand that fed them.

"South L.A. is a maze," Raine said, continuing. "No outsider knows it like us. Even *we* get lost here sometimes. The streets aren't what they used to be, and we'll make them even easier to get lost in."

"They know where we are, now," Darlene said. "They still control most of the stuff south of I-10. Our base is dangerously close to their front lines."

"We've got plenty of bases," Raine said. "Plenty of space in our territory. We'll keep Angel Command as HQ for now. But it's time to think of moving our operations further south."

Several of the men fidgeted at that. Ohlan blinked, clearly thrown off, and then frowned. For once, he had nothing to say, and Raine could see Ohlan's mind working, wondering why he hadn't seen this coming.

"We're harder to take over than my brother is suggesting, and Black knows that," Raine said. "It's easier for Carin to make us think we lost than to actually take us over. He'll lose a lot of men trying and waste a lot of bullets." Raine looked at Ohlan, who was openly scowling now. "You want to know why? Carin Black has his own enemies. It's not just us who hate the Reapers. True, we are his most powerful rival. Even now. But there are more gangs just waiting for their chance to jump him the moment he's weak or overextended. Sure, he has hundreds of lives to spend if he really wants to take us over. I say let him. As soon as he tries, we make it hell for him. Let him weaken himself, and if he does, guess what? There's the Krakens down by Long Beach. There's the Vultures up north, who Black couldn't get out of their mountains. There's the Hill Alliance, along with Last Town, Riverside, and Victorville."

"What's your point?" Ohlan asked.

"My point is, sure, the Reapers are top dog. For now. But the thing about top dogs is, they don't stay on top for long, especially when they make the other dogs mad. If anything, I welcome another attack."

"What do you propose, then?" Ohlan asked grudgingly. He was realizing that he had lost.

"We wait. We stall him. We make Black think we're actually taking him seriously about making peace." Raine smiled. "We're not, of course. We do all we can to make him think we're staying here when we're really moving. We consolidate ourselves below the 105. We make alliances. Next time he attacks, he'll find out he's made the worst mistake of his life. I'll never forget what happened two months back. I've been turning it over in my mind ever since. I may work slow, but I work hard. Black is brash. But I'm careful. And so long as I have the time, we can beat Black at his own game."

But do *you have the time?* The question was uncomfortable as it was unwelcome. But, Raine realized, the thought didn't matter. He had won the council back, and his brother had sunk into a sullen silence that he didn't even bother masking. Raine watched Ohlan closely, wondering if his brother was playing devil's advocate because that was his style, or if he truly believed the Angels should make peace. Again, Raine couldn't penetrate the icy surface of his eyes.

Did his brother want the Angels for himself? Would Melo, Shaw, and Miles back him up if it came to that? It was hard to imagine Ohlan being so bold. He preferred working from the shadows. In some ways, his brother had more power than him in that respect.

Raine realized it was possible that his home court wasn't safe anymore. Perhaps Dan had been right, after all.

He'd have to be careful. Very careful.

Chapter 20

M akara watched as the last of the trucks were loaded, signifying the end of another chapter of her life.

She had lived at Angel Command for about three years. The place had been the source of a lot of memories, both good and bad. The good ones had been good, and the bad ones had been . . . well, terrible. Makara wouldn't miss it much. Just the people who had once lived there, many now dead.

Even if it had been a few months since the attack, the building would always bear its scars. The exterior wall of the former office building had never been fully repaired. Only the wall had been built back up, and not even to its former strength. There was no point in building up what was going to be abandoned, anyway.

Raine and the Angels had found a new, better place. Almost no one knew where it was until the very day of the move; only Raine's inner circle, anyway. He hadn't even told *her* about it, and half an hour after the announcement, dozens upon dozens of trucks showed up in the night, spiriting away all the important articles in the Angels' archives, leaving the least important things behind. Such was the importance of keeping the new location secret, since an entire gang on the move was a prime target for the Reapers.

Angel scouts reported the way clear. The Reapers were involved in a turf war with the Hills Alliance, making this the perfect time to move. While they were busy killing each other, the Angels would be busy moving. Within their new home, they could lick their wounds and live to fight another day.

"We should get on the truck," Samuel said. "This is the last of them."

He was watching the line of vehicles idling outside the main gate beyond the wall. All they were waiting on was the order to get moving.

Makara nodded, then stood up to follow her brother. He had gotten tall. His height and broad shoulders made him look several years older than fifteen. Besides that, he was smart. Most of it was self-learning, and he devoured new books almost as soon as they entered the archives, and he remembered almost everything in them, too. He gravitated toward anything that had to do with science, and would speak for hours with Dr. Luken, one of the scientists who had survived the horrors of Bunker One's fall three years back.

Makara only wished she had some talent of her own. So far, the only thing she seemed to be good at was getting into trouble.

She and her brother hopped in the bed of a truck and the other stragglers piled on after them.

A few minutes later, the vehicles rolled down the dark, broken streets. They passed decrepit towers and crumbling walls for half an hour, twisting and turning at random inter-sections. Makara tried to keep track of where they were going, but before long, they were well out of range of anywhere she had been. She had snuck out of Angel Command many times before, but she had never gotten this far.

Makara fell asleep, lulled by the whine of the truck's

hydrogen-fueled engine. Before she knew it, she was being shaken awake by her brother.

"We're here."

The truck made a final turn, and they were going underground, dropping below the streets.

They were in what appeared to be a parking garage. There was a mass of people milling about between crates and vehicles, and only a small number of Angels controlling the chaos. Some of the people were exiting through a pair of doors, apparently leading into the building the parking garage was connected to.

"It's awful," Makara said.

Samuel chuckled. "It's not so bad. Being underground is much safer than being above ground."

Makara didn't doubt that, but she would miss not being able to go outside as easily as in the old base.

"Let's check out the inside," Samuel said. "This is just the entrance, after all."

Samuel hopped down from the bed of the truck. Makara followed him through the crowd, until they joined the stream of people entering through the glass doors. It was packed, but by the time they made it inside, Makara was surprised to find herself in a vast, cavernous space. Three balconies ran in a line while staircases connected all the various levels. There were little alcoves along the balconies, where people were already congregating. Plenty of sun flooded through the top of the building through skylights. All seemed to be in good condition. Raine might have repaired some of this place ahead of time, because nothing could look this intact after the madness of the Chaos Years.

"A shopping mall," Samuel said.

"A what?"

"A mall. Where people shopped."

"Yeah, I know that. It's just so . . . big. Almost as big as Bunker One."

"There were a lot of people back then," Samuel said, striding forward.

Makara wondered where he was going, until she realized he was joining a line.

"We'll get our room assignments here," Samuel said.

"Will we still be with Raine?" Makara asked.

"I don't know," Samuel said. "Maybe."

Assuming they were, Makara thought that this place might not be so bad after all.

Chapter 21

Despite Makara's first impressions, she was beginning to like the mall more than the old office building. For one, there was more room, and secondly, there were lots of places to explore.

The mall was bigger than any building she had ever been in, not including Bunker One. There were entire worlds here, and enough room to house hundreds of people. She could wander through it for hours – not just the main concourses, but all the various stores, some of which were buildings in their own right. One of these department stores had staircases and five different levels, filled with empty racks, broken display cases, and shattered tiles. This one of Makara's favorite places to go, and the fact that the lights hadn't been restored to most of the departments just made exploration even more tantalizing. Even after a couple of months of living here, there were always new nooks, corners, and secrets to find.

This department store, which seemed to be called Macy's, was where Makara headed now. It was dark inside, but Makara had excellent night vision – so long as she kept the lights from the main atrium at her back, she could find her way out. And if not, she had a box of matches she'd pilfered.

Matches weren't something to be wasted, and she'd get in trouble if she were caught using them without permission. But, one or two should be enough to find her way back in case the improbable happened. Even Makara could get lost sometimes.

She made her way to the top level, where it was almost pitch black. Only the reddish light coming from the atrium two floors below provided illumination. Makara waited until her eyes were fully adjusted, and could make out vague outlines of countertops, racks, and debris.

She explored for an hour, discovering treasures in the rubble. Jewelry, glass bottles, paper money. The last was useless, but some people liked to collect it. She found a small, thick book and pocketed it in her backpack. A gift for her brother, maybe.

It was around this time, exploring Macy's fifth floor, that she became aware of the fact that she wasn't alone.

She stood still, breathing as softly as possible while the hairs stood on the back of her neck. She was beginning to think she was imagining it, but then she heard the voices, muffled and quiet. Her first instinct was to run, but of course that was foolish. Makara's thoughts returned to the basement of Angel Command and the ghosts said to haunt it, and if there *were* ghosts, they would surely haunt this dark place, too. With as many people that died after the Rock fell, the world was bound to be covered with ghosts.

From her own experience, Makara knew monsters existed, and she felt herself starting to shake. She wrung her hands, feeling as if something were missing from between them, something she couldn't quite place.

But Makara didn't think these voices were ghosts, after listening a little while longer. Ghost voices usually faded in and out, and you weren't sure if it was your imagination or reality. These voices *were* reality, and she was definitely hearing them. If she ran, they would hear her, too, and she might even get caught. She wasn't sure *why* she thought these voices constituted a threat. Raine, after all, was still in the process of taking inventory of the mall himself, and these voices could just be men, exploring like her.

She thought about calling out, but that wasn't wise. Decent people didn't skulk around in an empty department store in the dark, and these people didn't seem to be trying to make their presence obvious. They'd be talking much louder if that was the case.

Against her better judgment, Makara crouched and crawled forward, to hear better. Makara's heart pounded; she knew this was stupid. Even with how well she could see in the dark, she might bump into something and give herself away. Even the smallest sound would betray her.

And yet, she felt herself inexplicably drawn forward. She strained her ears to listen.

"We've been waiting for months," the man said. "Now's the time."

Makara couldn't place the voice, but the next voice reminded her of Ohlan. She wasn't sure it *was* him, but she ascribed the voice to him anyway.

"It's not time. How many times do I have to say that before you believe it?"

"I wonder," the man said. "He will not be pleased with your lack of progress."

Ohlan grunted. "He'll be even less happy if his grunt tries to spook me into jumping the gun." There was a pause. "You ever played chess?"

Makara felt her skin prickle. It was Ohlan, all right. He loved chess and often talked about it. It couldn't just be a coincidence.

"No," the man said. "I don't see what has to do with . . ."

"Raine and I played, growing up. Raine is all about the short game. I'm all about the long game."

"The longer Raine's in charge, the worse it'll be," the man said.

"We're playing a game, my brother and me. Maybe it doesn't seem like that to you. But I can't have him suspecting me of anything. All he needs is a pretext. The smallest pretext. If he does that, then all this will be for nothing. If I'm hanging by my throat, what good is that to your boss?"

"You've been saying that for months," the man, so soft that Makara could barely hear. "Lord Black will hear of it."

"Lord Black must play by the rules of the game as much as any other man," Ohlan said. "Were he here, I'd tell him the same thing."

"You wouldn't kill him, then? For what he did to your brother's wife?"

On that point, Ohlan was silent for a moment. Makara waited, hardly daring to breathe.

"My brother is the one responsible for that. Only he deserves the blame. I see Raine as nothing more than an actor in this farce. Men like him come and go in a flash, like a flare in the sky. His flare is rising. But all things must fall."

"He seems like he's pretty strong to me."

"Of course," Ohlan said. "Raine isn't to be underestimated. It can't be something so simple as killing him. For all his faults, the people are loyal to him. Someone would rise to take his place. Green, perhaps. I've thought of that before. Green would make a more dangerous enemy. I can't use Green. Eddie doesn't have the gumption, while Shaw and Miles don't have the brains." Ohlan guffawed.

"Carin wants Raine out of the picture. The longer he stays alive, the more time the Angels have time to recover. Carin can't allow that."

"Your solution is to make a martyr of him?"

"Anything is better than waiting."

"That's where you're wrong, Cyrus. Most of the time, waiting is the best thing you can do. My brother doesn't make mistakes often. Just like in chess, you play a solid game and wait for the blunder. Then you strike, and before they know what's happening, things are out of their control. They are forced into a bad position, taking trades they never wanted to make. Then they lose pieces. By then, it's too late. Watching their eyes, when they realize they've been bested, outsmarted . . ." Ohlan sighed. "There's nothing like it in the whole world."

Makara racked her brain but didn't know anyone named Cyrus. With a start, she realized that they were now moving, the footsteps heading closer to her.

She backed away as quickly as she dared toward the stairway. She stopped, and there was moment of painful silence. Had they heard her?

Makara only relaxed after Cyrus spoke again.

"What do I tell Lord Black, then?"

"You tell him what I told you last time."

"He doesn't have another few months, Ohlan. He wants results."

"And so do I," Ohlan growled dangerously.

Makara didn't stay to listen longer. She headed for the steps, walking slowly until she was sure she was out of earshot.

Then, she ran.

Chapter 22

Makara ran faster than she ever had in her life. She only felt relief as she entered the main concourse of the mall, where electricity had been rigged and people milled about on each of the three levels. She felt safe only when she lost herself among the crowd.

The Angels' new location had attracted lots of people. Though it had been only a few months since the move, the number of people under the Angels' purview had almost doubled.

Makara searched the crowd for any face she might know, but everyone here was a stranger. Newer people were given homes further out from the main hub, so Makara jogged deeper within the mall, forcing herself to slow down. A few cast glances her way, but she mostly passed through ignored.

Raine was most likely in his office, which had been set up in an old department store on the opposite side of the mall. She took the steps of the defunct escalator two at a time, and within moments, she was racing toward the entrance of his office.

Or at least, she would have been, had there not been two thickly muscled guards barring her way.

"Can't let you in, Makara," one of them said. "Raine's orders."

"It's important," Makara said. "Mark, right?"

"What's this about?" the other guard asked.

"I can't tell you why, but I need to see Raine right away."

"He's in a meeting," Mark said.

"When's it over?"

He shrugged.

Makara chewed her lip worriedly. She knew Raine would want to hear her news immediately, but she was old enough to know that she couldn't even trust his personal guards with what she'd heard. There was nothing to do but come back later.

She stalked off, going to the railing and staring over the side at the concourse below. She looked in the direction from which she had come, half-expecting Ohlan and Cyrus to show up, whatever he looked like. But of course, neither did.

There were other ways to get to her destination. The mall had multiple ways in and out, so there was a chance some of the other doors weren't covered by guards. The only one she could guess would be left unguarded were some of the exterior doors that had once been fire exits. She could only hope, with the power on now, that it wouldn't trigger any sort of alarm.

Not just anyone was allowed outside, but Makara had her ways. There were way too many entrances for guards to cover them all. Blocking off the superfluous entrances was one of Raine's priorities, but he hadn't gotten around to covering them all yet.

If Makara could go back to the abandoned part of the mall and leave though one of the stores, then she could wrap around to Raine's office. It meant going outside, which was always dangerous, but it was important that Raine got the news as soon as possible.

Makara walked down the escalator until she was on the ground level. She moved quickly through the mall until the sounds of people were a low din behind her. She turned into a store which she knew would lead outside. She navigated the broken shelves and aisles of what had once been a supermarket. She found the exit easily enough; through the broken glass came the slanting rays of red sunlight. There were just a couple hours until sunset but getting to Raine wouldn't take more than fifteen minutes.

She ducked carefully through the door, which still had shards of glass sticking to its frame, and was soon outside. She looked at out at the reddened ruins beyond, and then checked in the direction of the department store in which she had overheard Ohlan. She saw nothing out that way, so she turned right, edging along the massive mall.

On her left was a vast, open space covered with dust and debris. Half-buried in the rubble were the frames of rusting cars, which Makara knew must have been sitting there since Dark Day. She couldn't help but feel exposed as the cold wind blew. She quickened her pace.

After just a few minutes, she reached the department store Raine was in, turning right through a revolving door. She gave a push, and the door spun easily enough. At least, until it got caught on something, but by shouldering as hard as she could, Makara pushed the door the rest of the way through. It spun so quickly that she tripped, and before the door could trap her, she used her momentum to dive forward into the building.

She grunted, then stood to brush herself off. A quick scan revealed no one in sight, though she could hear voices coming from the mall up ahead. Hearing that sound oriented her. There should be an escalator nearby.

She walked through the wide-open space, her boots barely making any noise on the white-tiled floor. She nearly jumped when she saw some guards sitting on some couches nearby, but they seemed to be focused on their card game. They didn't even look up as she walked by, though surely, they knew she was there. Apparently, the guards inside didn't have orders to kick anyone out who was already in.

With newfound confidence, Makara walked up the escalator to the second floor. Another guard passed her on the way down, even nodding at her as he did so. Once she reached the top of the landing, she turned up a final escalator, and upon reaching the top, saw the backs of the guards that had originally told her she couldn't enter. They were facing out toward the mall at the department's entrance, chatting away. Makara had to stifle a giggle at the thought of them turning around and seeing her.

Growing serious, she went deeper into the store, and heard Raine's voice, though it was too far for her to make out anything. She walked until she came to an open door, where inside there was a round table surrounded by chairs, each filled with a different council member.

As she stood in the doorway, Raine paused in the middle of his sentence, his eyes widening a bit at seeing her. Makara was about to speak when she noticed someone most unexpected at Raine's side.

Ohlan.

"We'll be done in a minute, Makara," Raine said. "Go find your brother."

She blinked in disbelief. There was no way Ohlan could have gotten here this quickly after she had left him there in the store. She couldn't help but stare at him in disbelief, and Ohlan gave a smirk, as if he knew what she was thinking. Did he know?

"All right," she said weakly.

She turned around and walked from the room. She didn't know whether to feel confused or frightened. She didn't know how Ohlan could possibly be there. Ohlan never really named himself, and neither had Cyrus named him. Had she just been mistaken?

No. It *had* to have been Ohlan.

She decided to ask Raine later if he had been at the meeting the whole time. He needed to know that his brother planned to betray him.

Chapter 23

When Makara got home to the apartment, which had once been a small store on the mall's third level, she immediately told Samuel everything that had happened with Ohlan, along with seeing him in the meeting with Raine not fifteen minutes after the fact.

Makara kept waiting for him to answer.

"Are you sure it was him?" he said, at last.

"I know what I heard, Samuel," Makara said. "It was him."

Samuel gave a slow nod and went right back to thinking.

"What are we going to do, Sam?"

Samuel opened his mouth to speak but stopped short. Whatever he had been about to say, he decided it wasn't worth saying. Samuel always chose his words carefully, a habit which was driving Makara crazy right now.

"I don't know, Makara. Raine must be told, obviously. What worries me most is that an agent of the Reapers got in here in the first place. Cyrus, you said? That means they know we're here already. I supposed that was bound to happen eventually."

Makara nodded impatiently. "They were talking about

killing him, Samuel!" The idea, said aloud, seemed ridiculous. But Raine was a powerful man, and he had enemies. One of which, apparently, was his own brother. "There are lots of unsecured entrances to this place. I've explored the entire complex pretty much. For all the ones Raine has blocked there are plenty more. I find new ones almost every week, and not all of them are on the ground level. There's the whole basement section that I'm still exploring."

"Maybe you shouldn't do that anymore," Samuel said. "At least, not alone. With all the ways into this place, it's a little convenient for the Reapers that we moved here. There *is* more space, and it *is* deeper in Angels' territory, but what does that space matter if it can't be controlled?"

"What about Raine?" Makara pressed. "What do we tell him?"

"Are you absolutely *sure* it was Ohlan?"

"He all but said his name. It was the same, gravelly voice. I'd recognize it anywhere."

"Then how was he able to join Raine so quickly?"

"I don't know," Makara said. "He must have while I was outside trying to get back in. If that's the case, then I barely missed him."

And if Makara was truly unlucky, then either one of them might have seen her when she left, if they also left soon after.

She pushed that thought away. "I still need to ask Raine if Ohlan was at the meeting the entire time. If so, then I don't know what to think."

"Do you think Ohlan suspects you of anything?"

Makara thought about it. He had looked at her curiously when she walked into the meeting, but there was no telling whether he thought something was off. Ohlan was an intelligent man, so Makara wouldn't put it past him to be suspicious, even when there was no real reason to be. What Ohlan had noticed, without doubt, was her reaction upon seeing him in the meeting. Makara had always been uneasy around Ohlan, so perhaps that might be written off.

Then again, her gut told her she had reason to worry.

"We should wait first," Samuel said. "Until tomorrow, at least. If we go back now and Ohlan sees either of us, it will only make him suspicious. If he suspects you, then surely he'll be making a note of your actions."

"You think he'd watch me?"

"Possibly. Not directly, of course, but he always has lackeys who follow him around. People who are more loyal to him than Raine. We can't be too careful, Makara. We'll just stay home tonight."

She hated the thought of being watched. "I was supposed to see Raine tomorrow, anyway. I thought we were supposed to be living with him."

"So did I," Samuel said. "We'll go together tomorrow. Once Raine knows, that's when we can take action."

Makara nodded. Despite Samuel's confident words, she could only wonder if it would be that easy.

Chapter 24

The next morning, Makara ran to Raine's office before remembering that running would only get people's attention. She forced herself to walk, and no one talked to her aside from two middle-aged women setting up a fruit stall in the center of the concourse for the daily market.

Makara stopped, feigning interest in the wilted fruit and vegetables being offered, but otherwise made it through the market quickly so she could get to the end of the concourse, the entrance to the command center. This early, it was empty save for a few guards making the rounds.

Samuel was going to come later. They were probably being overly cautious, but if anyone had an eye for detail, it was Ohlan. Samuel had even suggested Ohlan probably had spies working inside the mall, and if so, he was probably keeping tabs on anyone close to Raine. That would include both Makara and Samuel.

Thankfully, it was normal for her to go see Raine on her own. Makara couldn't think of a reason anyone would find it suspicious. Even so, Makara couldn't help but be nervous. She felt as if she were being watched, and she resisted the temptation to look around to see if the feeling was true.

By now, dozens of people filled the market. Some were arguing and haggling. Several people watched as she walked by, and Makara couldn't help but wonder whether they worked for Ohlan.

She was relieved to make it to the command center. As she stood in the center of the marble lobby, she looked around to make sure Raine wasn't here first. Currently, he was overseeing the construction of barricades at some of the extra entrances, so he might not even be here.

She went for the defunct escalator, allowing her thoughts to drift as she made her way up. When she was younger, she had seen Raine almost every day. Even now, at twelve years old, she still thought of him as an adoptive father. She felt guilty about that; after all, her own father had died to see her safely onto the last copter out of Bunker One. She still remembered his face on the tarmac, with the snow coming down, and the demonic screams of the monsters. It was the stuff of nightmares.

That had been the worst day of her life. The white-glowing eyes of those demons still haunted her dreams, sometimes. She could never forget them, however unreal they had seemed. She didn't even think Raine fully believed her story, despite saying he did to help her. They didn't talk about that much now. Raine didn't even come to visit her and Sam in their apartment all that often, such was his busyness.

When she reached Raine's office door, it was shut. Either he was in a meeting or he wasn't here, otherwise it would have been ajar. Raine wasn't really an office man, but he said that having an office was useful for meetings, and it gave him a place to put his personal belongings, especially the books he had collected over the years. Makara wasn't much of a reader, but she liked the stories written before the fall of Ragnarok. The Old World was incomprehensible to her, but that incomprehensibility was part of the fascination.

Makara knocked, and stood straight, military fashion. She had seen Dan stand like that.

She was just about to turn away when, to her surprise, the door opened. But it wasn't Raine who answered.

"Dan?"

His face had been wary, but upon seeing that it was her, his blue eyes softened.

"Better get inside," Dan said.

He opened the door wider, opening Makara's view until she could see Raine sitting behind his desk, his fingers steepled. His dark brown eyes were lost in thought, and his forehead scrunched deep. He broke from his reverie, his features softening.

"Makara. You all right? What's wrong?"

She walked forward, swallowing before speaking. "There's something I want to talk to you about. Alone."

"If it's about my brother, I already know," he said.

That gave Makara a start. "What?"

"My brother's gone, Mak," he said, ominously. "And some of my best men with him. Now that the deed's done, I'm just wondering how I went wrong . . ."

"Boss . . ." Dan said. "Maybe we should discuss this a bit more before letting . . ."

Raine waved one of his large hands. "She'll find out, anyway. Everyone will, eventually."

Both men looked at her, each of them probably wondering the same thing. How *she* had known. And just how much she knew.

"Do you know why he left, Raine?" Makara asked.

"He talked about starting a settlement east of the mountains," he said. "Never thought he'd actually do it."

He didn't know the reason, then. She had to tell him. No matter how much it hurt him.

"There's more to it," Makara said.

She told him, in as little words as she could, about her

exploring the old Macy's and how she'd overheard him and a man named Cyrus. After every sentence, Raine's expression grew darker. Makara couldn't bear to see him like that, but he had to know the truth.

"Ohlan did arrive late to the meeting yesterday," Dan mused. "Guess we know why, now. We can't let him get away with this."

"I know, Dan," Raine said. "I know that. He's already gone, and with him ten of my men. I thought some of them were my friends."

Raine's eyes looked lost. Makara couldn't imagine the hurt he was feeling. She wanted to do something to help, but what could she possibly do? For the moment, it seemed as if he had forgotten she was there.

"If they went with him, then they aren't your best men," Dan said, finally. Dan's face was angry, in contrast to Raine's look of loss.

"Cahors was one of them," Raine said. "So was Albright. Each one of them knows exactly where we are, our weaknesses, the munitions we have stored . . ."

"Well, there's no avoiding that," Dan said. "Give me a few jeeps and thirty guys and we can hunt them down."

Raine shook his head. "No. They'll be expecting that. Ohlan's too smart. He'd have left last night by some unused way." He chuckled darkly. "Ohlan was the one who discovered this place. Maybe he fed that to me, acting all surprised when I brought it up in that meeting six months back . . ." He shook his head.

Dan looked at Raine seriously. "Now that we know he's working with Black, it's likely he knows something we don't about this place. Some weakness." Dan shifted his feet. "Raine . . . we're going to have to move again."

"Move where, Dan? This is a good spot. If we can just close all the entrances, it'll serve."

Raine's eyes returned to Makara. There was a look on his

face Makara had never seen before. Regret, maybe. She knew she should have excused herself, but neither had told her to go.

"Thank you, Makara. You did the right thing telling me. I know that wasn't an easy thing to say since you were doing something I told you not to. But I don't want you ever going off on your own in this place again. It isn't safe."

She nodded. "Okay."

It was quiet for a moment, but before Makara turned, she plucked up the courage to ask a question.

"*Are* we safe here, Raine?"

Raine smiled, but there was sadness in the smile. "We've got a lot of good men, and plenty of weapons and food stockpiled. And we got more info on Black than you might think. In the end, they'll find out they're not as slick as they thought."

Makara didn't say it, but she knew Ohlan was slick, too, and there was a deviousness to his slyness. And deep down, she was scared. If people Raine considered friends had betrayed him, then how could *anybody* be trusted?

As that question ran through her mind, Dan was showing her the door. Makara followed his lead.

"Be careful, Raine," she said, turning to look at him.

He gave a small, almost bitter smile. "Not a day over twelve and you're acting like you're grown. I've been nothing but careful my whole life, Makara. It's one of my strengths. But even so, I have my blind spots."

Makara knew the rest, so he didn't have to finish the uncomfortable thought looming over them all; that despite Raine's carefulness, it couldn't guard him from his own brother. The brother he had chosen to trust, against his better judgment.

The walk back to the apartment was a long one, and when she was halfway there she realized Samuel had never joined her. She felt a lot of things on the way – fear for Raine's life and fear for the Angels' future, but more than anything else, anger at Ohlan's betrayal. Hundreds of people had worked hard to survive, to make this place a safe home, and all it took was one rotten apple to mess everything up.

Whatever Raine might think about it, Makara resolved in that moment to do whatever she could to stop Ohlan. And that meant finding out who was working for him here. Surely, he had left some informants behind to weave their webs. And if she was truly undiscovered in the Macy's, then they might use that as a meeting spot again.

Makara didn't like breaking promises, but Raine clearly needed help. And, Makara thought, who better than she?

Chapter 25

When Makara left the office, Raine let out a heavy sigh. He couldn't let her know how truly worried he was about Ohlan.

"What's our course of action?" Dan asked.

Raine cracked his knuckles one by one as he considered.

"You were right earlier. We got to go after him."

"If he's been gone a few hours, he's halfway to Black by now," Dan said. "He knows just about everything we do."

"Everything that matters, in any case," Raine said. "It's still a question of whether they can assault this place. We gave 'em a licking last time."

"They're warring the Hills Alliance still," Dan said. "Ohlan picked a bad time to leave."

"Someone must have tipped his hand."

"Makara?"

She had overheard Ohlan and Cyrus discussing his betrayal. It was possible that Ohlan had figured that out. He was clever, but there was no way of truly knowing.

Suddenly, Raine stood, his senses going on high alert. Raine had a way of knowing when something was off.

Last time he hadn't listened to that instinct, his wife and child had died.

Dan reached for his handgun, but before he could get a word out, Raine was out the door.

He checked both directions, but he couldn't see Makara either way. She had left two minutes ago, but Raine already kicking himself for letting her go in the first place.

He ran up to nearby guard. "Corley, did Makara go by?"

Corley pointed toward the mall concourse. "That way, Boss. What's up, something wrong?"

"Lock down Command," Raine said.

Corley's eyes widened. "Sir?"

"You want to explain what's going on?" Dan said, running after Raine.

Raine was about to when an explosion rocked him from the direction of the concourse. Raine's skin went cold even as the floor vibrated beneath his feet. He instinctively threw a hand in front of his eyes and knelt to shield himself, but it was all for nothing. The explosion had come from the direction of the market, where Makara had likely gone.

Once things settled, Raine sprinted for the escalator, taking the steps two at a time. When he reached the bottom, a cloud of dust rolled over him.

He covered his mouth with his arm, hacking and coughing even as he pushed forward. As the thunder of the explosion dissipated, he could hear the screams of both the frightened and the wounded.

The dust cleared just enough for him to see ahead into the concourse, where rubble had piled onto the floor. There were several unmoving bodes trapped beneath the concrete, and the sun shone through a large gap in the wall.

"We're being bombed!" a female voice wailed.

Someone was trying to pull up a slab of wall that had pinned an elderly man to the floor. Raine rushed over to assist.

"Let me help you with that," he said.

Together, he and the man lifted the concrete up, just enough for the man to escape, his left leg dragging behind him.

"Can you see him to the clinic?" Raine asked the man who had helped him, only now taking note of his face, since the dust had cleared a bit.

He froze.

"Ohlan?"

His brother looked back at him. "I'll get him to Darlene right away."

As he turned to go, Raine grabbed his shoulder. "Wait! I thought you . . ." Raine considered, wondering whether he should be reaching for his gun.

"It was all an act, Raine. I'm on your side. Always have been. When I learned about this attack, I was a minute too late. I rushed back to warn you, but . . ."

He trailed off helplessly. Raine just watched him, stunned.

"It was a bomb. A plot. I'm sorry I couldn't stop it in time."

Raine only now found his tongue. "Someone overheard you speaking to this man named Cyrus. I thought . . ."

"I've always been on your side, Raine. I don't agree with everything you do, but . . ." He coughed from the dust, which was still thick. "Maybe we can talk about this later. Even if I couldn't stop this, I learned a lot that will be of use."

Raine nodded dumbly. He had been prepared to go out and kill Ohlan at the first opportunity he got. But now, he didn't know what to think. There was no way to deal with this because of the current situation.

Once again, Raine realized he was forced to trust Ohlan.

"If you really were with me the entire time, why didn't you tell me any of this? Why hide this from me?"

"You would have never agreed. I had to get down and dirty." Even as Raine wanted to protest it, he realized that his brother was probably right.

"We all have our talents, brother," Ohlan continued. "If all I'm good for is sneaking, then that's what I should be doing, right? I've always worked better in the dark."

"And my men? I thought you all were deserters. Ohlan, I was about to go out there and hang you myself!"

"Well, you know now. As far as your men, they never really left, obviously. They were watching my back in case my meeting with Cyrus went bad. I can report that one of Black's top lieutenants is now dead by my hand."

"This won't happen again," Raine said. "Not ever. Even if you're still loyal, and a big part of me doubts that, you can't do shit like this and expect to get away with it."

Ohlan watched with his cold, blue eyes, even as the world around them seemed to fall away. "You have to trust me, Raine. I've got this under control."

"Whether you do, or you don't, I'm in on everything you do from now on," Raine said. "Play spy if you want to. Just let me in on what's going on."

Ohlan finally nodded, and it was all Raine could do not to heave a sigh of relief.

"Let's clean this place up. Makara came down this way. We need to find her."

Chapter 26

Raine and Ohlan ran on ahead, thinking to check the apartment Makara and Samuel shared first. It wasn't far.

They met Makara on the way, who had come out to see the disturbance.

Her eyes became furious at seeing Ohlan, but standing next to Raine, she didn't know what to think.

Her solution was to run forward and start leveling punches at Ohlan's gut.

"Makara, stop," Raine said, pulling her away. "The situation is more complicated than it seems."

"He's a rat, I know he's a rat!" she screamed.

"Get inside, Ohlan," Raine said. "You still have a lot of explaining to do."

Ohlan shrugged, and stepped into the apartment.

"What is he doing here?" Makara asked, her face red with anger. "I thought he left with ten of your best men!"

"He did, Makara. But he came back. He just went out to kill Cyrus, that's all."

She blinked at the news. "What?"

"He went behind my back, Makara. You're right about

that, and I'm very angry. But he went behind my back to help me. He got a lot of information about the Reapers, and managed to use those men to kill Cyrus. It's hard to explain, but Ohlan works like a spy for me."

"I don't believe him," she said. "He should've told you if that was his plan."

"I agree, Makara." He didn't have time for this. He needed to be at the site of the explosion, but he couldn't leave the kids alone with the likes of Ohlan. He'd have to take care of this, first.

"What a day," he said. "Let's step inside real quick."

Still fuming, Makara walked into the apartment, where Ohlan was making himself comfortable in a chair, while Samuel stared at him angrily from the corner.

"Now," Raine said, "Explain yourself, Ohlan, beginning to end. You're not out of this yet."

Ohlan looked at Makara, and then at his brother. "I went behind your back, Raine. I know. But you would have never let me deal with the Reapers the way I thought best. To do that, I had to act like I was on their side. I had to even lead them here, to show them I meant it."

"I already know that," Raine said. "I have sources, too."

Ohlan smirked. "What, the girl? We saw her. I told Cyrus I would take care of her, but obviously I didn't, since I'm on your side. I let him believe I would, though."

So, Ohlan had known Makara was there. "And after Cyrus left?"

"I took some men and followed him out. We tracked him to his campsite. We acted like buddies, so I could learn more. We killed them after they went to sleep."

"You got proof of that?" Raine asked.

Ohlan frowned. "You'll find their bodies north of here. Corner of Artesia and Cherry."

Raine made a note of it. The location was about a mile northeast. Not easy to get to, and neutral territory at best. It was far enough for Raine to have difficulty checking it out, but not too far to arouse his suspicions.

"I'll be sending Dan there, trust me," Raine said. "Until then, you're on probation until I can be surer of things. You said you came back because you learned about the bomb?"

Ohlan nodded. "I didn't know about that. Cyrus joked about it when we caught up to him. I couldn't leave right then and there, so we had a few drinks, talked a bit, until they fell asleep. We killed them. Had to wait a long time for the right chance, because they always had a couple guys on watch. Finally, I realized we wouldn't get any better opportunity, so we booked it back here as soon as we could."

"And got here a hair too late to stop the bomb, I noticed," Raine said.

"Unfortunately," Ohlan asked. "When I asked how he got it inside, he said he'd sent Reapers disguised as refugees, each of them packing a few parts. The powder was hidden somehow. They assembled it inside the mall." Ohlan nodded outside. "The rest is history."

Raine watched his brother's eyes. If Ohlan was truly betraying him, then why on Earth would he have come back here in the first place? He would have gone over to the Reapers.

None of it made sense. None of it made sense, except for the fact that his story was too incredible, too improbable, to be made up.

But Raine couldn't make any more mistakes. "Your story will be verified. Until then, I'm going to have to keep you in a holding cell."

Ohlan nodded, seeming to accept that graciously enough. "That's fair."

"He's lying," Makara said, heatedly.

"We'll find out the truth of things soon enough," Raine said. "I'm going to have to share this with the whole council, Ohlan."

"Go ahead," he said. "I'm confident that once you find those bodies everything will be exactly as I said."

Makara shook her head doubtfully, but Raine was going to give his brother a chance.

"Will you come peacefully?"

Ohlan beamed an artificial smile. "Of course."

Chapter 27

Ohlan was promptly locked in a cell. After surveying the damage of the bomb, Raine tasked his security force with finding the culprits. All of them mentioned the same four men that seemed to have disappeared from the mall, all of whom were new to the mall. Presumably, they were well on their way north back to Reaper territory.

Raine gave Dan thirty men and five vehicles, tasking him to find the escapees while checking out the site of Ohlan's fight, and to take copious notes on it. He told Dan everything Ohlan had said, and Dan assured Raine he'd get to the bottom of it.

Once Dan was gone, and the cleanup of the explosion underway, Raine sat behind his desk, shut the door, and reached for the bottle of whiskey he rarely had need of. He poured himself a double, swirling it and inhaling the fumes. He took a sip, then more than a sip, and leaned back, letting the fire burn his throat.

For his first drink in five years, it tasted damn good.

There was a knock at the door, ruining the moment. Raine downed the glass, coughed, and put the bottle back in the drawer. After taking a swig of water, he called out. "Come in."

Darlene Sanders stepped in, her green eyes worried behind her glasses. "Bad time?"

Raine shook his head. "What's the damage?"

"Not as bad as we initially thought. No deaths, though a couple of men are in critical condition. We got the supplies to treat them."

"That's good."

"Rest of the injuries are relatively minor. Most can be sent home by the end of the day."

"What's it like out there?"

Darlene took a seat. "People are scared. Rumors flying around that there are more bombs."

Raine shook his head. "I doubt that, if my brother's to be believed."

"People are saying *he* did it."

In her eyes was the unspoken question. *Did he?*

"I don't know what to think, Darlene."

He shortly told her Ohlan's version of things, and his own thoughts about it.

"It just doesn't make sense for him to come back if he's guilty," Raine finished.

"Maybe he's counting on you thinking that," Darlene said. "Your brother's a wily one."

Raine hadn't considered that option. "I just don't know what to think." He turned up to Darlene. "What would you do?"

Her nose wrinkled. "Is that liquor I smell?"

Raine mentally prepared himself for her beratement. "No."

But Darlene surprised him by smiling slyly. "What the hell. Pour me a glass, if you got any."

Raine blinked, but ended up reaching into the drawer,

pulling out another high ball glass and the still half-full bottle of whiskey."

"Mr. Jack Daniels," Darlene said. "Haven't had a taste of you since the Chaos Years."

"Sounds like you knew him well," Raine said, pouring her a double as well.

She held up her hands, indicating it was enough. "Too well. Hard to be an alcoholic these days. At first there was a lot of free booze. Not so much these days. You'd think after 99 percent of the population died, there'd be plenty left over for the rest of us."

Darlene tilted her head back and shot down the whole thing in just a few seconds. She slammed the glass back on the desk.

"That's the stuff," she said, chuckling. "I think I'm equipped to give you my opinion, now."

"I feel like I know what you're going to say, but I'll hear it anyway."

"Don't be so sure," Darlene said.

"I'm ready."

"I think your brother's a lying son-of-a-bitch." She paused. "No offense to your mother."

"None taken," he said. "We have different mothers."

"Oh," Darlene said. "That's right, I forgot that. I think he's lying but not in the way you think he is."

"What do you mean?"

"You're right about him coming back. Doesn't make sense if he's truly betrayed you. Like I said earlier, it could just be a gamble on his part, him thinking *you'll* think he wouldn't do that if he was guilty."

"I . . . follow that. I think."

"I don't think he's betrayed you, Raine, as hard as that is to believe. You did right in sending Dan to check things out. Saw him leaving on my way here. That man will do a very thorough job. We won't truly know until he comes back."

Darlene thought as she considered. "In the meantime, though, I think all this is a little too intricate, even for Ohlan. I can see him playing the double-double agent, but add another double in there and it gets to be a bit much."

That was how Raine felt. "I have to be sure, though. Hopefully Dan will come back with something definitive."

"In my opinion, we need to raise our priority on blocking all the entrances we don't plan on guarding 24/7." She eyed him appraisingly. "I'd talk to that daughter of yours. She probably knows this place better than anybody."

"I can't encourage her behavior," Raine said.

"Why not?" Darlene asked. "She'll be willful, no matter what you tell her, Raine. Might as well use it to your advantage."

Darlene had a point there. Raine had to admit that.

"Guess all there is to do is wait for Dan to get back, then."

Darlene nodded. "Just wait. I should head back to the clinic."

Darlene rose to go.

"One more thing," Raine said.

Darlene paused, and Raine reached for his drawer, and held out the bottle.

"I'll forgive myself, because today's been rough," he said. "I need you to keep this away from me."

Darlene looked at him, and then gave a bark of laughter. "It's like you're asking another robber to guard the key to the vault." She shook her head. "Keep it, Raine. We're all allowed our lapses. As long as our lapses don't define us."

Darlene turned to go, closing the door behind her. Raine sat in there a while, continuing to think.

Chapter 28

Makara lay down in her tiny bed, throwing a bouncy ball she had found in the arcade downstairs off the ceiling repeatedly. Samuel looked over, annoyed, finally closing the book Makara had found him in the Macy's, using a finger to mark his spot.

"Do you mind?"

Makara threw the ball once more, and wondered whether she should throw it again. She did.

Samuel sighed. "I know you're mad, but now you're just being immature."

Makara set up, ready to let loose her ire. "So, what if I am? Raine should've shot that lying piece of trash on the spot."

Samuel shook his head, getting his long brown hair out of his eyes. He desperately needed a haircut.

"We'll find out his guilt soon enough," he replied, coolly. "Besides, if he'd shot him on the spot, we'd still be cleaning up the mess in here."

Makara ignored the joke, or perhaps she was so rattled she hadn't even recognized it. "I *know* he's guilty. He bombed the market. It could've been you or me, Samuel. Doesn't that just make your blood boil?"

"If it *was* Ohlan," Samuel said, drily, "he had help. They're hunting down the ones responsible right now. Ohlan will have his trial, probably a week from now."

Makara growled in frustration. "I wish *I* was the judge."

Samuel, despite himself, chuckled at that. "Sorry. Dr. Klein will be presiding, if rumors are true."

Makara's mouth twisted distastefully. "I spent more time with him than I care to think about. The man's a dreadful bore."

"Is he the same one who helped you process things?"

Makara nodded. She didn't want to be reminded of that.

"I should see him myself," Samuel said, quietly.

Makara looked at him, her anger ebbing. "You okay?"

Samuel pushed the book away, all hope of reading it gone. Samuel thought in his slow, ponderous way.

"Can I function from day to day? Sure. Do I *like* functioning day to day?" Samuel shook his head. "Not really, no."

"I still think about it, too," Makara admitted, after a drawn silence. "Dream about it."

Samuel nodded, to show he was the same, too.

"I hate him so much."

Samuel rolled his eyes. "You can't stop thinking about Ohlan, can you?"

"He did it, Sam. I *know* he did."

"You just don't know how to think rationally yet," he said, in a superior tone. "You're still just a kid."

"So are you!" Makara said, feeling her anger explode again.

Samuel smirked. "This is how things are done in the adult world, Makara. People get a trial and a fair shake. You can't just kill people because you think they're lying."

"I don't think. I *know*."

"Okay," Samuel said. "What if someone told you that they

knew Raine was lying about something, and that he should die for it?"

"I'd say they're wrong, because Raine is a good man."

"All right," Samuel said. "But this person *knows*. They *know*, Makara, the same way you know about Ohlan right now." He paused, to wait and see if she understood.

Makara did understand, or at least she thought she did.

"That's a bad example," she said, lamely.

"The point still stands," Samuel said. "Maybe he's guilty. We won't know for sure until Dan comes back with the evidence. If Ohlan is telling the truth, not a boot will be out of place where he killed Cyrus and his men."

"Then a boot will be out of place, because I know that man's guilty."

Samuel rolled his eyes, and sighed.

Chapter 29

It took so long for Dan Green to return that Makara was starting to get worried. Not so much about him, personally, though she liked him. She was worried there would be no one to bring a case against Ohlan.

Anytime she had a spare moment, she went to the viewing deck on the mall's top floor and watched for his return. One day, to her surprise, the convoy actually did come back.

When Dan came in, he did not look happy. Makara was quick to accost him as something of a crowd started to gather.

"Well?" she asked.

Dan ignored her. Several guards cleared a path for him as he marched his way directly to Raine's office in the command center.

Makara trailed behind like a dog hoping for a crumb. She followed them all the way to the department where Raine's office was, but the guards wouldn't let her in.

She went her usual way around through the grocery store but was shocked to find it all boarded up.

She let out a long sigh. "Shucks."

DAN GREEN STOOD SILENTLY and at attention in front of Raine. Raine watched him, waiting for Dan to begin his report.

"You know, you don't have to act like that," Raine said, after a long pause. "All official and shit."

Dan relaxed, if only just slightly.

"What's your report, Dan?" Raine asked.

Dan cleared his throat and hesitated a moment. At a look from Raine, he began. "We found the site. It was at the corner of Cherry and Artesia, as Ohlan said. Everything was how he'd described it."

"That clears him, then," Raine said.

"All the men had the Reapers' scythes tatted somewhere on their arms. The exception was one man, whom we're assuming to be Cyrus. That's common, for their agents to have no obvious markers. Despite investigating the site for a full two days, we found no way to identify each individual."

"What're you saying, Dan ?"

"They're Reapers, all right," Dan said. "There's just no evidence that they're the *right* Reapers."

"Dan," Raine said.

Dan stiffened again, and kept his blue eyes forward.

"Thank you for your honesty."

Dan nodded. "I'll always tell you the truth, Raine. Even when it's not the truth I want."

"So, in your estimation, Ohlan is telling the truth, with the possibility that these Reapers are just some other group they happened upon that they're trying to pass off Cyrus' group?"

Dan nodded. "That's a possibility. Of course, if that's true, it means Ohlan is lying and that he knew about the bombing already."

"What is the likelihood of that happening?" Raine asked.

Dan thought for a moment. "Not too likely, in my opinion. Ohlan was gone for half the day. The odds of them finding a Reaper patrol closely matching his story would be pretty low."

"Unless Ohlan found the patrol first, and then made his story to match."

Dan shrugged. "Yeah, that's possible."

"But you don't believe he's lying."

Dan paused. "I don't trust him, Raine. His story is convoluted and seems unlikely on the surface. But everything is as he said it would be. I don't think we can pin him with this." Dan looked at him intently. "Of course, you're the boss. If you feel like he can't be trusted . . ."

Raine leaned back, looking down at his desk's bottom drawer. It would be nice right now to break out the Jack and have a drink while he mulled things over. He resisted the urge and refocused on Dan standing before him.

"Between you and me, I don't know what the hell I'm going to do," Raine said. "Not enough evidence to convict, and yet even I don't fully trust him." Raine let out a sigh. "At the same time, he does have his uses. Almost all our information about the Reapers' comes from him."

"He could be playing us," Dan said. "But like you said, this might just be how he operates."

"It is," Raine said. "His isn't a coveted role. By God, though, it's a useful one."

RAINE WENT DOWN to the security wing on the bottom floor of the mall. It had a few holding cells originally built in, Raine supposed, as a place to hold shoplifters until the real authorities could take care of them.

It was in the center of these three cells where Ohlan waited, his pale white hands wrapped around the bars. His icy blue eyes seemed to float in the darkness, and his slight smirk gave Raine the creeps.

"Well?" his voice came, gravelly.

"Dan didn't find anything that incriminates you," Raine said.

There was a moment's pause. "Really now? That's interesting. I suppose I never really did give him a fair shake."

Raine nodded toward the prison guard, who came to unlock Ohlan's cell.

"No trial?" his brother asked, as he stepped outside.

Raine shook his head. "I have a couple of conditions."

Ohlan gestured, to show he was ready to hear them.

"You're to let me in on everything you know. Otherwise, you can go right back in that cell. Kevin Klein would judge you in that case."

"Fine," Ohlan said. "I'll talk."

"Furthermore, this is your last chance to have a royal fuck up like this. You're my brother, Ohlan. When you mess up, it makes me look like a joke. When you recruit men for your own personal missions behind my back, it makes me look weak. Even *this*, releasing you early, makes me look bad."

Ohlan smiled in a way he probably thought was placating, but only looked predatory. Even his incisors were showing a bit.

"This is your last chance," Raine said. "Understood?"

Ohlan nodded. "Loud and clear. What do you want to know?"

Raine relaxed a bit. "Let's get to my office, first."

They made the short journey there. The pair of brothers passed half of the mall on the way, including Makara and Samuel. Raine couldn't bring himself to look at either of them, especially Makara. She didn't say a word as he passed. If he hadn't disappointed her beyond all hope now, he wasn't sure how else he could.

Once situated in his office, Raine did reach for that bottle of Jack. Ohlan smiled as Raine poured him a glass as well.

Raine raised his cup. "To a new beginning. And last chances."

Raine downed the glass without ever taking his eyes from his brother. Ohlan's eyes didn't move either as he finished his drink.

There was a moment of silence after, and then, both brothers started to chuckle.

"Time to talk," Raine said. "How long has this sneaking around been going on?"

Ohlan cleared his throat, and began. "As you know, I've always had my ways of getting information. You never complained of the ways I got that information. Not till now, anyway. That's beside the point, though. I've been doing this for as long as we've been down here in South L.A."

"That's years," Raine said. "How have you been able to maintain your ties with the Reapers so long without them finding out you're playing them?"

Ohlan shrugged. "Simple. They think I'm playing you."

"And are you?"

Ohlan chuckled darkly. "I feed them information. Nothing useful. Nothing accurate, but things that might seem accurate on the surface. Things they think they can make use of."

"Like what?"

"For example, in the last war," Ohlan said. "I told them when a patrol of ours would be checking on the Interstate. The Reaper patrol arrived, just a hair too late. That patrol made it back safely. Other examples include troop positions, ammo deposits. To avoid losses, I've changed orders last minute to save men's lives." Ohlan shrugged. "Of course, if my information was *always* bad, they'd get suspicious, fast. I through them some nuggets sometimes, but I always make sure what we get back makes up for it."

Raine felt sick to his stomach. "You told them where our *troops* would be?"

"I'm a gambler," Ohlan said. "Life's too boring unless you roll the dice."

"Boring?" Raine said, with rising irritation. "You're bored, so you gamble our men's lives?"

"It's worked so far, Raine. I've kept this going for years. I'm good at it. Damn good. And if you meddle with how I do things, it'll all come crashing down." Ohlan leaned forward. "You're too noble, brother. Too good. You don't have the stomach for it, and quite frankly, the intellect."

Raine opened his mouth to respond to that, but deep down, he knew Ohlan was right. His brother had always been more daring and smarter than him. The problem was, no one really liked Ohlan the way they liked Raine.

"Remember our chess games growing up, brother," Ohlan said. "Sometimes, sacrifices are necessary to attain a victory. You never wanted to lose a single piece."

"You're admitting you've let men die, then," Raine said.

Ohlan nodded. "Of course. It's all for the greater good."

"What have those lives bought us, Ohlan?"

"Something even more valuable," he said. "Information. The ability to play them, to project strength when we have none, to feign weakness when we're strong. Remember how you wanted to meet them in the field in the last war, Raine?" Ohlan laughed. "It was *me* who said we needed to be formless, to strike from the shadows, to keep them as far from Angel Command for as long as possible. That strategy gave time for Dan to set up his explosives."

Raine did remember his brother directing the Angels' overall strategy. It had saved the group, and it had given the Angels more time to resist.

"It didn't stop them from coming in the end, though," Raine said, somewhat lamely.

"All during that time, my contacts with Reapers were asking me, why can't we find the Angels? Why won't they give us a fight?" Ohlan looked at Raine, his eyes calculating. "I was playing them, Raine. I told them you were afraid to meet them in the open. That you knew you were going to lose.

That you were fleeing south, deeper into the maze of South L.A. They pushed in, overextending themselves. They lost so many men that they had to gather everything for an attack on Angel Command. Something Carin Black never wanted to do."

"You're just telling me this, now? Why keep me out of the loop?"

"Because, brother," Ohlan said, "It's like a Grandmaster trying to explain advanced chess tactics to a novice. That's not a dig on you, Raine. The point is, with your personality, you're not ready to take the risks necessary to ensure victory against a numerically superior foe."

"And you are?"

Ohlan looked away. "Yes. That's why I'm here. That's my job. To be the villain. To make the hard decisions. To be the . . . toilet of the Lost Angels. To flush all the problems away so you can keep your hands clean." Ohlan looked back at his brother. Raine thought he'd been joking, but his eyes were deadly serious. "Each of us must play our parts, Raine. You're the handsome hero, the tragic figure avenging his wife and child. And me?" Ohlan shook his head in self-pity. Raine couldn't tell if it was mocking or not. "I'm the ghost lying in wait. I'm the liar, the joker, the gambler. Formless. Unpredictable."

"That's the thing," Raine said. "You're my brother. You always will be. I demand you let me in on what you do. Be unpredictable to everyone *but* me."

"Why?" Ohlan asked. "So you can put a stop to it when shit starts to get real?"

"I need to know the risks the Angels are under," Raine said. "You need to tell me what they know about us, right now, at this very moment."

"Telling you that might ruin everything I've been working for."

"Who else is involved? Eddie? Miles? Shaw?"

"None of them know a quarter of what you know," Ohlan said. "Consider it as a token of my trust."

"You *don't* trust me, though," Raine said. "Otherwise you'd tell me everything."

"I don't tell you, Raine, because I *know* you," Ohlan said. "If I told you just how deep this goes . . ." He shook his head. "I'll tell you only if you promise to let me do my work, Raine. Swear it on the graves of your dead wife and daughter."

Raine's eyes narrowed. "I can't promise that, if you're risking too much."

"There you have it," Ohlan said.

"You're going to force my hand, Ohlan," Raine said.

"Get rid of me, then," Ohlan said. "And watch the house of cards crumble."

Raine looked at his brother closely. How serious was he? He wasn't sure how much of this to believe.

Raine reached for the bottle again, pouring two more glasses, till the whole thing was killed.

"I have the right to question you," Raine said. "You say you're the Grandmaster. Then you should know that even Grandmasters lose, given they play enough games."

Ohlan shrugged, as if to concede that point. "I haven't lost yet."

"They'll find you out eventually," Raine said. "They might already know. This Cyrus situation . . ."

"L.A. is a dangerous place," Ohlan said. "The Reapers are in a war right now. The blame doesn't necessarily fall on me for those dead Reaps."

"All the same," Raine said, "Black will be wanting to know what's happened to one of his most useful agents. The last person he met with was you."

"Green will tell you just as I will that the ambush site looks like the work of the Hills Alliance."

"All right, then. Why kill one of your most useful contacts?"

"Didn't plan to," Ohlan said. "Until I learned about the bomb. Cyrus was testing me, Raine. He wanted to see where my loyalties were." His blue gaze held steady. "I think he learned the answer to that question pretty quick."

Raine watched him for a long time, seeking some measure of doubt. Of course, it was Ohlan, so he betrayed nothing that could've given Raine a clue.

"Dan's investigation clears you," Raine said, finally. "If there's anyone who has a bone to pick with you, it's him."

"I'm a free man, then."

It wasn't a question. Raine nodded. "You're a free man. Is there anything you should be telling me right now?"

Ohlan watched his brother for a moment, pondering the question.

"There's something, I suppose."

Raine raised his eyebrows. "Well, don't leave me hanging."

"It's about Makara," Ohlan said. "You have to keep her in check, Raine. She was in that Macy's when I was meeting with Cyrus. She could've blown the whole thing up before I got the chance to finish things."

"Maybe it's *you* who should be more careful about where you meet."

"It was Cyrus who insisted on that spot," Ohlan said. "I had to cooperate. The man was marked for death anyway, so no harm, no foul."

"I thought you said you only killed him because you learned about the bomb."

"His time was already coming, Raine. He was daring too much. He was urging me to take over the gang." Ohlan chuckled. "I assure you, that's the last thing I want."

Raine shook his head. "I'll speak to Makara, then. But one thing I won't budge on: you'll never, ever to allow another Reaper into this place again. We aren't going to have this conversation again." Raine stared at him, hard. "Got it?"

"Loud and clear."

"You're free to go," Raine said.

Ohlan left, and Raine felt the buzz of the liquor, a friendly, familiar warmth. He wanted to feed that buzz, until it was a fire roaring within him that would drown out all else.

Raine cleared his throat and reached for his water.

Chapter 30

When Raine had that conversation with Makara, warning her not to stick her nose into trouble, she did not take it well. Nor did she like that Raine was letting Ohlan off easy. If anything, it only motivated her to keep her eyes on him even more.

She'd just have to be more careful. Makara didn't know *how* Ohlan had seen her in that Macy's, but somehow, he'd managed it. If she really was a loose end, then Ohlan had elected not to kill her. That didn't make sense.

She felt doubt about her conviction for the first time. If the information shared with Cyrus was as pivotal as she'd thought, then she shouldn't be alive anymore.

None of it made sense. She still didn't trust Ohlan, not by a long shot.

It needed more investigation. But how?

She lay in bed, her schooling for the day done, and threw her rubber ball at the ceiling to think. She was alone, with no Samuel there to interrupt her thoughts. No Samuel there to stop her from doing the right thing.

The dangerous thing, sure. But when had Makara ever

shied away from danger? Nothing could have been worse than that horrible night, four years ago.

Don't think about that.

Watching Ohlan was easier said than done. She had stumbled upon something last time. Ohlan would be more careful in the future. She'd never be able to get close to him again unless he was walking around in public, where everyone else could see him, too.

Makara wanted to see him when he thought no one was watching. Worse, he had his own cronies, men she was sure would obey him over Raine if push came to shove.

Maybe all this is too big for me. Maybe Raine's right. Maybe I should keep my nose out of it.

She didn't like that thought. She threw the ball harder, causing the ceiling tiles get knocked out of place. The bouncy ball rolled above the ceiling.

"Great," she muttered.

It might not be impossible get it back, though. Makara climbed on top of a nearby table, and then used that to get on top of a dresser. She had to crouch before her head hit the ceiling. She pushed the ceiling tile up, and poked her head into the darkness above.

It was cool and dusty up here. She sneezed, kicking up even more dust. Her ball was about five feet away, and out of reach from where she stood.

"This is dumb," she said.

Nonetheless, she noticed a horizontal rafter above the ceiling tiles. She reached for it, after jumping a small distance, and easily pulled herself up.

The space wasn't much. She had to crouch, but she walked another rafter over and reached down to retrieve her ball.

When she put it back in her pocket, she paused. All the hairs on her arm and neck stood on end.

Wait a sec . . .

Would it really be this easy? She peered into the distance, the space between the ceiling below and the floor above. This space extended beyond Makara and Samuel's shared room. If she could find a way to enter this space, but near wherever Ohlan happened to be, she would be able to eavesdrop on him.

If she was quiet and didn't make any missteps, there was absolutely no way she'd be detected. Even if she was, she could escape quickly and come down. The question was, if Ohlan was meeting somebody, would she be able to hear anything from above?

That answer came soon enough. She heard voices coming from a few rafters down. She creeped closer, stepping softly on each rafter as she pressed forward. The voices became louder. A man and a woman arguing.

Makara knelt, and stayed as quiet as she could. She could hear almost every word clearly, even though they were warbled through the ceiling below.

This could be it, she thought.

Experimentally, she threw the rubber ball on the ceiling above where the voices were coming from.

The voices immediately stopped.

Makara giggled and backed away. If she really wanted, she could get the ball later.

For now, though, she was too excited about the possibilities.

"I'll find him out," she said. "He'll never know."

When Samuel returned to the room, Makara was gone. His sharp eyes noticed something off immediately about the bedroom. The ceiling tile in the corner was out of place.

"That damn ball," he said.

He climbed up and set it right. He then spent the next few

minutes tidying up and putting away all Makara's books, toys, and homework where they belonged. If he didn't do it, it would never get done.

He left the room, toward the tiny kitchen. He took a corn tortilla he'd gotten from the market, and wrapped up some veggies and potatoes, and ate.

While he chewed, something tickled at the back of his mind. The ceiling tile had been in the corner, not where Makara usually threw her ball. And Makara wasn't here . . .

He returned to the bedroom, finishing his wrap. He waited.

Just a few minutes later, he heard some scratching and thuds from above.

Then, the tile moved, and a single boot lowered, then another. Makara dropped down with a thud, landing neatly on top of the dresser, facing away from her brother while she fixed the tile.

"I don't even want to ask," he said.

Makara jumped while letting out a tiny yip. She turned and immediately looked angry.

"I lost my ball up there," she said.

"I see," Samuel said, his tone skeptical.

Her face reddened as he continued to watch her. She sat on her bed and faced him.

"Where's the ball, then?" he asked.

"Couldn't find it," she said, after a moment. "Can you leave me alone, now? Don't you have stuff to do?"

"Came home to eat," he said. "I was about to head back out, but I knew something was off about that ceiling tile."

"So?" she asked, in challenge.

"So," Samuel said simply, "if you are really going to sneak around, I won't stop you. But you should consider covering your tracks a bit better."

She looked at him in shock, and that look was all Samuel needed to know he'd been right on the money.

Makara's mouth worked until she could find the appropriate repose.

"I *have* to do this, Samuel," she said. "If Raine is really going to let that criminal walk free, I have to take care of things myself. There wasn't even a trial, like you said there'd be."

"Well," Samuel said, taking a seat on his bed, "it probably wouldn't have made much of a difference, truth be told. There wasn't enough evidence. I'm sure Raine is keeping a close eye on him."

Makara sighed. "Somehow, I doubt that. If he is, Ohlan will be covering his tracks better."

Samuel had to concede that point.

He looked at his little sister, troubled. He knew it was useless to scold her. That had been Raine's mistake. Scolding her only fanned the flames of her contrarian nature.

"Well, if you're really set on doing this, then I have no choice but to help you."

Her face instantly brightened. "Really?"

Samuel nodded. "There's no stopping you when your mind is set on something. I don't think Ohlan's betraying Raine, but that doesn't mean we shouldn't keep an eye on him." Samuel paused. "As a hedge."

"A hedge? What's that?"

"It just means planning for all circumstances, in case things don't turn out the way you expect. Thinking you're right isn't the same as being right. So, you also invest energy in the opposite option. In case you're wrong."

"Raine doesn't do that," Makara said. "When he believes something, he believes one hundred percent and doesn't . . . hedge, as you call it."

"That's why he has us, right?" Samuel looked up at the ceiling. "We'll be his hedge. How quiet can you be up there?"

"Quiet as a mouse," Makara said. "Promise."

"I heard your racket coming down."

"I wasn't trying to be quiet." Makara's eyes suddenly widened. "We should practice! You try as hard as you can to hear me. I'll sneak around the ceiling, and after two minutes, you have to tap the part you think I'm in."

Samuel nodded, impressed. "That's a good idea."

The siblings did just that. After Makara disappeared above, Samuel was surprised that he heard absolutely nothing. He made some guesses, and he only got close to being right on one of them. His guessing was no better than random chance, as far as he could tell.

When Makara came down, covered with dust, the two of them put their heads together and made plans.

Chapter 31

The next step was scouting for an entry point. It took over a week to find a suitable one, in a bathroom close to the group of apartments Ohlan had a room in. The hard part was watching Ohlan's schedule over the next couple of weeks, and to Makara's disappointment, he never seemed to do anything sinister. He was almost always in the open, and he not only talked with his own cronies, like Terrance Shaw and Adam Miles, but also dealt with other Angels, including most of the Council members. Ohlan gave no sign that he knew he was being watched, but of course, that didn't mean anything. If he was trying to bait Makara, he wouldn't give away he knew he was being followed. Makara recognized Ohlan might have people watching his back, even if armed guards didn't follow him everywhere.

Ohlan was all about working from the shadows. He did meet with people behind closed doors, but Makara resisted the temptation to find a way to eavesdrop. She didn't think she was ready to take that kind of risk, yet.

Once the siblings had gotten a handle on his schedule, they began exploring the best places to enter the partitions between the ceiling and floor. Not every spot had one. Nevertheless, Makara found a lot of places she could enter, and easily memorized the points Ohlan often found himself.

On Tuesdays, he seemed to have a standing appointment with Kevin Klein, whose role had shifted over the years to be almost exclusively the Angels' Archivist rather than therapist. He met with Darlene Sanders on occasion at her office in the clinic, which Makara had easy access to. He met with his cronies, too; Eddie Melo, Terrance Shaw, and Adam Miles, but always in the open and never behind closed doors, as far as Makara could tell.

When Samuel became confident that Makara knew her away around the mall better than anybody, they were ready to begin the real work.

And slowly, over days, and then weeks, they started to learn things.

They learned Ohlan woke at almost precisely 6:30 every morning and climbed a ladder outside his apartment to the rooftop. Sometimes he waited there for the sun to rise over the mountains, sometimes he smoked a cigarette. It seemed to be the only time of day he was truly alone.

He usually ate breakfast with his cronies. Makara never dared sit close enough to him at the food court to hear what was being said.

If Ohlan was not out on patrol, he spent most of his day in various meetings. Most of them were boring, and Makara couldn't even listen in on most of them since she had to go to school. She skipped school one time just to see what he did during the day. He tended to make rounds, doing various errands for Raine.

Makara learned that Ohlan was very essential to the Angels' operations. If Raine needed something done, or someone wasn't cooperating, Ohlan usually was his guy. Usually the ways Ohlan got the job done weren't very nice. Makara wasn't sure whether to blame Ohlan or Raine for that, though Raine was surely aware of Ohlan's methods. One time, Makara had to listen as Ohlan roughed up a guy for not paying the market tax on time.

The more Makara watched Ohlan going around, doing his work, the more unsettled she became. She could barely stand to listen from the rafters above when he went to visit a lady, who let him do disturbing things to her in exchange for a handful of batts.

Worse, Makara had learned nothing that proved his guilt. It'd been weeks, and while she learned about the Angels' operations and Ohlan's role in them, she still didn't know anything about how Ohlan planned to betray Raine. She was starting to even doubt herself.

"HE'S SQUEAKY CLEAN, Sam. I feel like I'm just wasting my time."

"He's being careful, Makara," Sam said, in his quiet, considering way. They were sitting in their own kitchen, but after Makara's shenanigans, both siblings realized just how easy it was to be eavesdropped on. For all they knew, Ohlan was also aware of the partitions between the floors, and had ways of listening in.

"We need him to slip up," Makara said.

"We just have to wait him out, Makara," Samuel said.

"I'll be honest," Makara said, "I don't know how much longer I can do this. Following him around, seeing what he does. It's really depressing."

"I'd take your place if I could."

Makara smiled at the idea of him tromping around in ceiling. That'd blow their cover quick.

"Maybe it's time to consider the nuclear option," Samuel said.

Makara had been afraid he'd say that. "Yeah. Maybe."

Lost Angel

"I mean, we know his schedule pretty well now," Samuel said. "He's never in his room unless he's sleeping."

"Or with one of those ladies," Makara said.

Samuel nodded, to concede that point. "I hate that you have to see that kind of stuff."

"It's for Raine, right?" Makara asked. "He needs to be protected."

"Raine can protect himself, Makara. You don't have to risk yourself for him."

She felt herself stiffen. "I'm doing it, Samuel. That's that."

Samuel watched her, knowing that he could end all of this right now by going to Raine. Makara would hate that. And it probably wouldn't do any good unless his sister was under 24/7 surveillance.

No, Samuel could not betray her like that. He would lose trust with her for a long time.

"You will have to be very careful, Makara. More so than you've ever been."

She nodded. "I will."

"The question is, what time will be best to go in?"

"During school," Makara said. "The bathroom is on the way, so it'll be easy. It's out of sight of the concourse. If no one's in the corridor, I should be good."

And no one should enter the bathroom, either. A pre-collapse bathroom probably hadn't been working in well over a decade. Now, they mostly just served as storage space. The bathroom by Ohlan's apartment had plenty of crates and boxes, piled high enough to make entering the ceiling a breeze. Makara had already mapped everything out and knew which way to go.

The only thing she hadn't done was the final step: lowering herself into Ohlan's room.

"Let's do it tomorrow," Makara said. "If I can't find anything shady, I'll give it up."

"I don't want you taking longer than thirty minutes,"

171

Samuel said. "Don't leave anything out of place, either. It'll be bad enough that one of your hairs could be left behind."

"He won't notice that," Makara said.

Samuel had his doubts. "Maybe I should keep watch, just in case . . ."

"They'll notice, Samuel. You can't."

He knew his sister was probably right. He just couldn't stomach the idea of her doing this on her own. Staying above the rafters was one thing. Going down and poking around someone else's things was entirely another.

"He's never come home early in all the times we've watched him," Samuel said.

"That's right," Makara said. "At worst, he'll suspect some-one's been in his room, but he'll have no way of knowing who."

"He might have a camera."

"Waste of batts," Makara said. "I doubt it."

"Batts might be currency, Makara, but remember why they were originally designed. The ones made in the Dark Decade are good up to a century. Batts power things, and Ohlan has plenty of them from his position in the Angels. He might consider a camera in his room worth the cost of using them."

"I'm still going," she said.

Samuel nodded. "I guess I can't stop you."

"No," Makara said. "You can't." She reached across the table, placing her hand on top of his. "Don't worry about me, Sam. I survived alone for three years before you showed up. I know how to take care of myself."

Samuel supposed she did, at that. "Good luck, then. You can find me after at the food court. I can pick something from the market for us to eat, and you can tell me what you find."

She nodded. "Sounds good."

Chapter 32

The next day dawned, and for the first time, Makara felt her resolve waver. She went to school, as normal, and as previously planned, she excused herself at 9:30 to use the restroom. Instead of walking to the latrine built into what used to be a garden, she turned right instead. Her heart started to pound when the bathroom came into sight. She heard no one nearby. Everything was going as planned.

She quickly turned inside, making sure she was alone among the piles of supplies that hadn't been sorted yet. She started to climb, wasting no time in pushing the ceiling tile upward, lifting herself up onto the rafter. She closed the tile behind her and proceeded forward.

Eighteen rafters, she thought to herself, although she didn't really need the reminder. She just wanted to steady her nerves.

Those eighteen rafters passed as quickly as they did soundlessly. She heard a couple having conversation below, and then silence. A few rafters later, and Ohlan's room was directly below her.

The first thing Makara did was listen for a good five minutes, just to be sure. There was nothing. After those five minutes had passed, she pushed down on a tile just a bit, and peeked in the two inches or so of space she'd created. She had a view of Ohlan's bedroom below. It contained nothing more than a bed, immaculately made, a chest of drawers, with several guns mounted to the wall, each gleaming as if recently polished.

Samuel was right. He probably *would* notice a hair out of place.

Nonetheless, she was here, so she was going to make use of it. She dropped in on the drawers while stucco fell from the ceiling like snow. She'd have to clean that up.

But first, she nosed around. She started with the top drawer, finding lots of clean, perfectly folded clothes. She rifled through them carefully but found nothing of interest. The second drawer had various tools; wrenches, several screwdrivers, a hammer, while nails and screws were sorted according to their sizes and purpose. There was nothing in there, either. She pushed it back.

She opened the bottom drawer, finding it filled with papers, each organized into clean, manila folders. Most of them were labeled by year.

Makara reached for the current year, 2052.

What she found were copious notes, scrawled in Ohlan's neat, precise handwriting. Everything was dated. There were charts, hand-drawn with perfectly straight lines. Some were inventory lists, accompanied by Ohlan's notes.

Food production down since the move, clear conclusion from this graph. Will recommend Raine to upend more of the asphalt on the east side and plant potatoes. We need a couple more acres of them, probably. Will take a while for the compost to season, nine months at a guess. Will have to talk to Harvey about that.

Harvey was the head of Agriculture.

"Poop and potatoes," Makara said, shaking her head. "Where's the good stuff?"

She scanned down the notes, with Ohlan talking about trying to trade for goats with the Vultures.

We desperately need people with expertise in herding. We need more protein in our diets. Leadership does well enough, but people won't stay happy long eating stuff that grows out of the dirt. Krakens not really cooperating in letting us lease some fishing boats.

Makara skipped that page entirely. She needed to find something detailing his meetings with the Reapers.

She flipped through absolutely everything, until she saw one folder, colored red rather than manila. She picked it up. It was labeled Diplomatic Dossier.

"That sounds official," she whispered, as she flipped it open.

She found the stuff she was looking for almost immediately.

Met with Cyrus again. That man says a lot without saying anything at all. Still, some useful nuggets I can take to Raine. Makes me a bit nervous, though. We're feeding them more than they're feeding us right now. I'm having trouble allaying his fears, which could make things complicated. It's hard to convince him I'm not crossing him, but he wants information that I just can't give him. Not unless I want to tip my hand to Raine, anyway. It's difficult. Cyrus has given useful information, so he's worth keeping in my contacts. I'm wondering if it was a mistake to let him go. Maybe I really should have ended things with him for good, but of course that would be stupid. That would cut off all my abilities to gain information from the Reapers in the future.

"That lying . . ."

The front door to Ohlan's apartment opened.

Makara felt a moment of panic, and dropped the files on the floor, spreading paper everywhere. She jumped on the chest and gave a mighty leap, pulling herself up toward the rafter. Ohlan entered the room below her. She heard him chuckle.

She was in the process of pulling her legs up when she felt his grip firmly clench her shin. She kicked with everything she had, but Ohlan was securing her legs between his other arm and torso.

From there, it was a simple matter of pulling her from the rafters.

Makara felt her fingers slip from the beam above, one by one.

"Shouldn't you be in school, Nancy Drew?"

"Get off me!" she cried.

Ohlan did no such thing. Now on the floor, Makara felt his arm wrap around her neck. Within seconds, she felt the world going dark.

"We're gonna go on a little trip, Mak," he said to her, his voice fading in and out. "Maybe it'll teach you to leave the spying to me."

Chapter 33

When Makara woke up, she heard voices. She blinked a few times and her vision didn't seem to come back. She was blind.

But the air was stuffy. She felt something around her head.

She tried to scream, but there was also something stuffed in her mouth and wrapped around her eyes.

She shook, realizing her hands were bound behind her back, too. She tried to kick, but her legs were bound, too. All she could feel was the gravel beneath her and the cold air of outside.

Some of the men those voices belonged to laughed, and Makara's heart pounded. She'd never been so scared in her life.

"All y'all, shut up," Ohlan barked. "We don't have much time to make a deal before Raine comes after us. Like I just said, I'll give you the girl. You give me the information and parts I'm after."

The men quickly settled down to business. Makara whimpered, but the sound was stifled by the rag. Makara recognized Cyrus's voice speak.

"She's just a girl," he said. "What use is she to us?"

"Are you daft, Cyrus? This is Makara, Raine's adopted daughter. You have her, then you have my brother by the balls."

Cyrus chuckled. "What happens to you when your dear brother finds out you've turned traitor? Perhaps it's time you returned with us, Ohlan. If this is Makara, then she's all we need to force a deal with the Angels."

Ohlan was quiet, as if considering those words. "I have things set up the way I want, Cyrus. My game isn't with the Angels and it's not with the Reapers, either. I know you have what I need there in the truck. Just hand it all over and we can consider this concluded. You can speed off and the boys and I will give the illusion of a chase."

"The girl first," Cyrus said.

"No," Ohlan said. "The girl after. If you play dirty, Black will know you let this one slip out of your hands."

Makara heard the click of a pistol and felt the hard pressure of a gun barrel through her head cover. She squirmed to get out of the way, but two pairs of hands held her in place. She stopped struggling.

"You'd kill her?" Cyrus asked, amused.

"Don't play me false," Ohlan said. "Angels will recognize she's gone any minute, now. You realize the mall's just half a mile back that way?"

Cyrus let out a sigh. "Fine, have it your way. It doesn't matter to me."

Makara heard a car door opening, and then closing.

"Up on your feet, girl," Ohlan growled.

Makara squirmed again, and cried out, but she was forced up all the same. She tried to relax her muscles and become dead weight, but two men could still easily lift her. She stood.

The crunch of footsteps approached.

"Here," Cyrus said. "Now, hand her over."

Makara felt herself pushed. She nearly fell, but she ran

into somebody. Not Cyrus. Those hands grappled her roughly. She fought madly, but all to no avail. Her tears were staining the band covering her eyes. She felt herself led away.

I'm so stupid, she thought. *So, so stupid. I'll never see Sam again. Raine. Dan. Nobody. I'm all alone, now.*

She should have died four years ago.

It was quiet one moment, and in the next, the sound of gunshots rang out. Makara fell to the ground instinctively, crawling forward and keeping her head down. The storm of bullets seemed to never end. Men screamed and died around her; a body thudded to her right. She stayed put, pretending to be dead in the crossfire.

She didn't know how long that madness lasted. Two minutes? Ten? How many bullets had been fired?

Once it was all over, she heard footsteps approach her.

"Get up, Makara," Ohlan said.

Makara stood. Her legs were shaking. She felt her hands untied first, then the sack was lifted from her head. The gag was removed and she sucked in a deep breath, and then sobbed. She removed the band herself, to see that it was late evening, almost full on night. Four of Ohlan's men stood in front of her, with Ohlan himself at the fore. His pale skin made him look ghostly in the darkness.

Makara bunched her fists and screamed. She ran forward and started throwing punches. Ohlan let her, while his men watched. After half a minute of this, Ohlan nodded to his men, who restrained her.

He watched her for the next few minutes, waiting for her to calm down. Makara only calmed down on the surface. Beneath, she was volcano still in the process of erupting.

"Cyrus is dead, Makara," Ohlan said. "We're about to head back."

"You're a traitor," she spat. "I don't care if you killed him, I read your files, I know what you are, Ohlan."

He gave the ghost of his smile. His teeth, unnaturally

white, gleamed in the night.

"You don't know what you're talking about, Makara. You're just a little girl who got yourself caught up in the adults' world." He brushed himself off, exactly where she had been wailing on him. "Not to say you don't have your uses. Have to say, the boss's adopted daughter makes a pretty good bargaining chip." He chuckled darkly. "Well, I think it's safe to say my bridge with the Reapers is burned for good."

She bottled up all her emotions. All she wanted to do was cry. And scream. And punch Ohlan some more. None of those actions were practical right now.

"When we get back to base," Ohlan said, "you're going tell Raine you were exploring outside and got kidnapped. You're going to tell him that I saw it and came after you."

"I'll never say that," Makara spat. "Why would I help you?"

Ohlan smiled. "Simple. You like your brother, right?"

Her eyes narrowed. "You leave him out of this."

"Afraid I can't," Ohlan said. "You have a simple choice, Makara."

"What's to stop me from saying all this to Raine when I get back?"

Ohlan shrugged. "First, you'll have to admit you've been sneaking around, something Raine told you not to do. Second, I will hurt Samuel. Badly. Don't test me on that. You saw what I just did to you. How much more will I do to someone who Raine doesn't care all that much about?"

"Raine cares about Sam, too," Makara protested.

Ohlan shrugged in a way to show he didn't give much credence to that. "Make your choice."

Makara stared at him angrily, but she neither wanted to tell Raine the truth about her extracurricular activities, nor place her brother at risk.

She nodded. "Fine."

Ohlan turned to one of his cronies. "Let's pack up and head back."

Makara got into the back of the truck with the rest of the men. The ride back was silent.

Chapter 34

"And that's how it happened."

Makara had just got done explaining events in the exact way Ohlan had ordered. Makara's only hope was that Raine would pick up on the way she said it and realize something was off. It was hard to give hints with Ohlan standing right next to her.

The entire mall had been in an uproar looking for her, and when the news of Makara's abduction reached Raine's ears, he was about to head out into the city himself after she hadn't been found after a few hours.

That was when he'd learned that Ohlan was gone, too. His mind had thought the worst. But Ohlan had come back, together with his men, thinking quickly to track her down while everyone else was panicking. They picked up the trail of Reapers and caught them in the open, saving Makara in the process.

After all the hugs and tears, Raine wanted to hear a full report from both.

Raine looked from one of them, to the other, until his eyes finally settled on Makara.

"Maybe a bit of it is my fault," he said. "I haven't really

been around much. I know that, Makara. I'm sure you're probably wanting some more time with me. Things have been hectic, but that's no excuse." His expression became more severe. "That still doesn't excuse what you did. You *know* you're not supposed to go outside. And you went out of sight of the mall, too." He shook his head. "You would be a Reaper slave right now if not for Ohlan."

Raine noticed a bit of stiffness in her posture. The girl was as stubborn as she was wild. In the end, though, she lowered her eyes. "I know, Raine. I'm sorry."

The words seemed to be choked out of her. Ohlan looked at her sideways, his light blue eyes amused.

"I thought the worst when you were gone too, Ohlan," Raine said. "I apologize for that. You've proven yourself beyond all doubt to me, now."

Ohlan nodded graciously. "I know you don't always agree with my methods. One thing I can guarantee, though, is that I'm always effective." Ohlan considered a moment. "I've proved that tonight to you, I hope."

"You did," Raine said. "I'm glad that conversation we had seemed to take."

"It grated on me a bit then, but I can see the sense of what you said. Open and honest will be my modus operandi."

"I hope so, Ohlan."

Makara felt as if she wanted to barf. Ohlan had ordered her to keep her cool, but it was hard. Raine looked at her a moment, and then back at his brother.

"Leave Makara and me for a minute, Ohlan," Raine said.

"Of course." Ohlan looked at Raine. "Stay out of trouble now Mak, you hear?"

Makara made a fist. *Only* friends and family called her that. "Whatever."

Ohlan smirked before leaving Raine's office.

Raine watched Makara for a long moment, either waiting

for her to cool off, or to ensure Ohlan had gained enough distance from the door not to overhear.

"What aren't you telling me, Makara?"

Makara did her best to keep her face neutral. If she told Raine the truth, she had no doubt that Ohlan would make good on his word. Maybe he wouldn't outright kill Samuel, as he'd threatened, but he'd do something almost as bad.

"That's everything. I'm sorry, Raine. I was being stupid. I won't go outside anymore."

Raine steepled his fingers, and seemed to think things over a bit. "I wouldn't say anymore. You're getting older, Makara. You'll be twelve, soon. Too young by far to be going out on patrols, at least without me as an escort. Samuel will be starting to do that soon enough. In fact, it's past time he did."

"I thought sixteen was the cutoff age," Makara said. "I won't be there for years yet."

"Things can change," Raine said. He cleared his throat. "Now, how are you doing? Okay? Do you want to go see Darlene? Kevin?"

Unbidden, hot tears sprung to her eyes. Raine stood, and helped her sit in the chair. All Makara could manage was to shake her head.

"We dodged a bullet," Raine said, handing her a tissue. "If they'd gotten you, there's a good chance you'd never have seen daylight again."

"It was horrible," Makara said. "Horrible."

There was a knock at the door. Raine, annoyed, looked up at it. Before he could ask who, Samuel's voice resonated from the other side.

"It's me."

Makara shook her head. As much as Makara wanted Samuel's comfort, she didn't want to put him at risk.

"Wait just a minute, Samuel," Raine said. He turned his attention back to Makara, gesturing for her to continue.

"I don't want to talk about it, Raine."

He nodded. "I understand. I want you to head to the infirmary, all right?"

"I'm fine," Makara said. "Just a few scratches."

"I insist," Raine said. He looked at her in an appraising way. "I guess we're lucky Ohlan was in the right place at the right time."

Makara's face twitched, but for the most part, she thought she did well in keeping her face neutral.

Raine stood. "Come on. I'll walk you there."

"It's okay," Makara said, rising from her chair. "I know the way."

"Makara . . ."

"I said I know the way, Raine."

His brown eyes became hurt. It was strange to see Raine like that – it made the hulked-out, battle-scarred veteran look as fierce as a giant teddy bear.

"Okay, Makara," he said. "Just take it easy the next few days. Take off from school. I'll try to cut back here where I can."

"It's all right," she said. "Sam's waiting for me."

"All right. See you soon?"

Makara nodded, and left his office.

Samuel was leaning against the wall outside. He rushed forward and held Makara close. She wanted to cry, but all she felt was numb.

"He walked out of here like nothing happened," Samuel said. "He abducted you, didn't he? Why didn't he sell you out?"

Samuel had already guessed almost everything.

"Don't talk about that," Makara said. "Not here."

Samuel's eyes widened. "Yeah, okay. Sorry."

"And don't tell Raine what I was doing. Keep your mouth shut. Please, Samuel."

"But . . ."

"No buts. Do it for me."

And for you, too. But Makara didn't want to tell him about Ohlan's threat.

Samuel swallowed. She could tell from his eyes that he didn't understand. He could never understand. Ohlan had won. Raine had said it himself. Ohlan had proven himself beyond all doubt.

There was nothing left to be done on that front, and even Makara now had to recognize that her own doubts about Ohlan had been misplaced. Ohlan was ultimately a cruel, manipulative, and recklessly calculating man. He wasn't afraid to gamble big, and doing so had won him something big. Makara didn't know what that was, nor did she care, but it was clear Cyrus had given him something, and Cyrus was now actually dead. Apparently, whatever Ohlan had gotten from him had been worth burning his bridges with the Reapers forever.

Didn't that prove he was with the Angels through and through? Makara just didn't know anymore.

She was just tired. She'd had enough of this cloak and dagger stuff.

She wasn't cut out for it.

WEEKS PASSED, and then months, with little deviation. Makara tried her best to put Ohlan's betrayal behind her, but that was difficult when she was having nightmares about the abduction. She'd wake up, gasping for breath, her heart pounding so fast that it felt it would leap out of her chest.

She kept it all to herself, though. It was horrible having no one to confide in. Well, there was Samuel, but she left out the worst bits. Being blinded, gagged, kicked, powerless. At least in Bunker One she could run, at least she'd had her dad to protect her.

She had no one to protect her. And worse, the one who

had betrayed her was being lauded as the hero who had saved her.

Ohlan seemed to forget about her, at least. She no longer bothered to keep track of his movements. In the back of her mind, she wondered whether if this would be the best time to watch him, when there was no suspicion on him at all.

One thing she kept wondering; how had Ohlan known she was in his room? She kept thinking about what Samuel said about a camera. As far as she could tell, Ohlan never returned to his room once he left it. The fact that he *did* return this time meant it was very likely he was keeping track of her. She hadn't been in there fifteen minutes when he'd come barging in.

Makara didn't want to think about it. She'd been outplayed. She was foolish for thinking she could go toe to toe with the Ghost.

She went about her day, hiding her true feelings and struggles in plain sight. Not even Raine knew something was bothering her. He at least started spending more time with her and Samuel, and she was good at pretending everything was okay. It hurt to pretend around them. Every time she thought about telling Raine the truth, her thoughts returned to Samuel. If she told Raine, he would never be able to treat Ohlan the same way. That was something Ohlan would pick up on.

There was no winning.

Makara's birthday passed. She turned twelve, but she felt twice as old. Whatever joy and happiness she had seemed to be completely gone, now. Even the truce between the Reapers and Angels didn't do much to help her spirits.

The weeks went by in a blur. All the main entrances to the mall were closed, more farmland was cleared, and even water was restored to the mall, though it wasn't potable. That had been Raine's biggest accomplishment since the move. He was focusing on building up the mall, trying to restore it the best he knew how, even as the Reapers expanded their reach in the north. The Hills Alliance lost their war, at long last, and all too soon, Carin Black had no more easy targets to bolster his army of slaves.

It would only be a matter of time until war broke out again. Skirmishes between south and north resumed on the eve of Makara's thirteenth birthday. Samuel was seventeen, now, almost a man, while she was going through her own changes.

By now, though, she was good at bottling up her emotions. She had learned to channel her latent anger and aggression into becoming an expert shot at a variety of armaments, while being a fierce fighter without any weapon but her hands and feet. Raine had noticed, and even started letting her go on patrols early. When the war with the Reapers finally kicked into high gear, they'd need every able person on the front lines.

And that next war would be the last one, the one to decide who would control L.A. — the Reapers and their vision of slavery, or the Angels and their vision of freedom.

Chapter 35

One day, Makara woke up to some news she wasn't quite sure how to process, that had the entire mall in an uproar.

Ohlan was gone.

One day passed, and then a few more. The entire surrounding city was scoured for a trace of him, along with the twenty men who had decided to go with him.

I was right all along, Makara thought.

On the fourth day of his absence, she was pulled into Raine's office and asked if she knew anything about his whereabouts.

She told him then, everything Ohlan had said not to tell, feeling as if a weight was being lifted. At the same time, though, she hated seeing the look of hurt in Raine eyes.

"Why are you just now telling me this, Makara?"

She lowered her head. "I was ashamed. I did wrong, and I was afraid of what he might do to Samuel. If he's gone, though — really gone — then he can't hurt any of us."

Raine leaned back in his chair. He was quiet for a long time, seeming to mull things over. "We don't know what's happened to him, Makara. He could back any day, now. You were right about one thing, though. If you'd told me that, I couldn't have treated my brother the same, and he would have known." He looked at her seriously. "You have no way of knowing this, but I had a conversation with him, after the first Cyrus incident. I told him he had one more chance."

Makara felt as if she had been punched in the gut. For all these months, she'd kept the secret for nothing. He could've been gone this whole time.

"I'm sorry," Makara said. "I should have been honest. I was stupid."

"You were scared," Raine said. "I knew something was wrong."

Makara nodded, lowering her face. "There was. It's not your fault, though. I just couldn't tell you."

"Well, whether Ohlan comes back or not, he's gone from the Angels for good."

"Where do you think he went?" Makara asked.

Raine heaved a sigh. "Beats the hell out of me. It makes a little more sense, now, after what you told me. Cyrus was never actually dead that first time. If he killed him more recently, that means he was still talking to the Reapers the entire time. He led me to believe the trickle of information had slowed because of the whole Cyrus incident."

"Do you think he's working with the Reapers now?"

Raine considered. It would be the ultimate betrayal and spitting on the graves of his dead wife and daughter.

"There was something he told me, after the fight at Angel Command. It's probably nothing, but . . ."

Raine trailed off, and Makara watched him with interest. "But what? It could be the key, Raine."

"He sort of . . . implied that I'd made a huge mess of things, and that it might be better to pack up and head out past the mountains. You know, to that place raiders call the Wasteland." He paused, recalling the conversation as clearly as he could. "He thought L.A. was a lost cause. I told him *no*.

He respected my decision. Or, at least he gave the impression he did."

"Why leave now, though?" Makara asked.

Raine was sharing more of his innermost thoughts than he ever had. Though she was all of thirteen years old, barely even a teenager, he was treating her as if she sat on his council. Maybe one day, Makara realized, she would.

"I don't know," Raine said. "Maybe that thing you talked about Cyrus giving him. Maybe that was what he needed to make his move. A few more months of preparation, and the rest is history."

Raine was quiet, and so was Makara as she thought it through. There had been no sign of Ohlan in the city, as Raine had said, and no news of Ohlan on the Reapers' side of the highway.

The longer things went without news of Ohlan, the more likely it was that he wasn't in L.A. at all, or dead.

"Thank you for being honest with me, Makara. You can return to your duties now."

She waited a moment before nodding her understanding and leaving Raine alone in his office.

RAINE WAITED a few minutes for Dan Green to arrive for his scheduled appointment. Dan had just returned from a multi-day recon that had taken he and his men over most of the southside, and as far west as the ruins of San Bernardino.

"Make your report, Dan," Raine began.

Dan shook his head. "No sign of him, boss. We followed the tracks the Recons made, but we lost them after being forced to turn south. The last direction the Recons went was east." Dan frowned. "There isn't anything east, Raine. There's Last Town and then a whole lot of nothing till Raider Bluff."

Raine was now surer of his theory. "Ohlan told me something after the fall of Angel Command that I didn't put much stock in. Not till now." Dan waited for Raine to collect his thoughts. "If it's true, it means we're probably never seeing Ohlan again."

"What did he say?"

"Something about my incompetence as a leader, and how it would be better to pick up again out in the Mojave. He said L.A. was all but lost to the Reaps."

Dan's frown deepened. "He'd always talked more about eastward expansion, but we never really had the water sources to make it feasible."

"All the same, looks like he's figured out a way to make it work. And it seems like he no longer wants to do what I say, even in name."

"Should we go after him? If you're right, Raine, we might be able to catch him and put an end to his schemes."

Raine waved his dismissal. "If he's talking about setting up east of the mountains, then he won't be bothering us much."

Both men were quiet for a while, each of them trying to puzzle it out.

"Well, good riddance is what I say," Dan said.

"He was useful, Dan. His information always came when we needed it. It was the key to holding on as long as we have."

"We can manage without him," Dan said. "Who knows? We might be wrong about him leaving. Another one of his projects. For all we know, he could be showing up tomorrow."

"If that happens, I won't take him back. I can't go back on what I told him."

Raine then told him about what Makara had said, and Dan listened attentively.

"It makes a lot more sense, now," Dan said, finally. "The question is, what will we do about it?"

"The better question is what *can* we do about it? And even if we could do something, would it be worth it?"

"It's a slap in the face," Dan said. "If we take no action . . ."

"Whatever action we take will require time, men, and resources. That's less we have to defend against the Reapers. As soon as Black catches wind of this, he'll see it as an opportunity to pounce."

"He might know already," Dan said glumly.

Both men were quiet, considering the ramifications. If Ohlan's own reports were to be believed, the Lost Angels were outnumbered and outgunned by a factor of two. Even the few men Ohlan took would make a dent, and those numbers included Terrance Shaw and Adam Miles, two members of the council.

"We need alliances," Raine said.

"There aren't many independent gangs anymore," Dan said. "We'll have to go out east, get everyone from Fullerton to Last Town on board. Maybe then we'll be a match for numbers."

"I see no other way, Dan," Raine said, finally. "This is Ohlan's arena. The only way we can survive is by taking the fight to the Reapers, hitting some of their biggest settlements before they can reinforce them."

"Their bikers are fast and there's a lot of them," Dan said. "They've converted most of them to hydro fuel by now."

"The longer we wait, the worse the position we'll be in," Raine said. "How much longer till we're ready?"

Dan shrugged. "A year, at best. And it's not likely our plans wouldn't be made clear to Black at some point. There are too many people we have to let in on it. One of them is bound to squeal."

"The options seem to be attack on our own with the element of surprise, and then ask for help," Raine said. "Or to make friends first and risk tipping our hand, but potentially strike with greater strength."

Dan was quiet; he as well as Raine didn't know which

option would be better. As much as Raine sometimes disliked Ohlan, he knew his brother would have had some useful insight unforeseen by either of them.

"I see no other way," Raine said. "We strike, and we strike hard. Someone has to lead." He looked up at Dan, his best friend, and saw those blue eyes looking back at him fiercely.

"Let it be us, then," Dan said. "Let the strongest take the first step."

Raine nodded. If the other groups didn't pick up the slack, then the Angels would most likely lose the war. And if the Angels lost, all of L.A. would, too. They wouldn't like that they're hand was being forced. But they, too, would want to rid themselves of the Reaper oppressors. Half of them already paid Carin Black tribute.

"The Krakens should have our backs," Dan said.

Raine was confident of that, too. The Angels were the only thing that stood before the Reapers and Long Beach, where the Krakens had their main base.

Raine leaned forward. "We should let the Krakens, along with anyone else, know that we plan to attack the day before it happens. Give them at least some time to mobilize."

"That'd tip Black off," Dan said.

Raine nodded. "Likely, it would. But I won't have our men fighting alone. By the time news of the war reaches the others, it might be too late. Better to get ahead of it, let them know the exact reasons we're fighting, before Black has the chance to frame it as aggression on our part."

"That makes sense," Dan said. The captain put out his hand. "Are we agreed, then?"

Raine took the hand. "It's the only way forward. We have to make our move, before it's made on us."

Chapter 36

The Angels didn't have the chance to build up for a year.

The Reapers poured south over I-10 within a couple of weeks, overwhelming the Angels' positions. There were hundreds of them, and they overran the empty streets, the only thing slowing them down were the substantial roadblocks the Angels had set up from before. Every man and woman capable of firing a gun was organized into squadrons and led into the fray. Dan took control of the logistics of the Angels' forces.

Makara, like everyone else, reported for duty on the ground floor concourse. There, she was handed her rifle and handgun, while Dan himself assigned her and Samuel to Scouting Squad D. It wasn't much of a squad, since she and Samuel were the only members.

Maybe Raine was just testing them and seeing how they did. If successful, he would probably assign more troops to Samuel's squad.

Dan told each of the squad leaders their orders, and they set out into the city.

He came last of all to Samuel, giving him orders quietly. Samuel nodded as Dan said, "Good luck," the only part of the order that Makara could hear. Samuel saluted, fist over heart, as the now General Green withdrew.

"What was that about?" Makara asked.

Samuel motioned her over to a nearby table. Makara hung her rifle by the strap over her shoulder.

Once seated, Samuel spoke. "Our task is a little different from the others."

"How so?" Makara asked.

"We've been ordered to head toward San Bernardino. Raine wants to know if the Reaps are pushing into the eastern groups as well. He wants us to get there first and convince them to join us."

"We're the diplomatic corps, basically," Makara said, distastefully. She'd hoped for an assignment of being sent to the front lines.

"This task is important," Samuel said. "Securing alliances will be the key to winning this war."

"I thought Raine had tried that already."

"If the Reapers' aggression hasn't changed the eastern cities' minds, then nothing will," Samuel said. "Raine must want to take one last shot."

Makara nodded. "All right. When are we headed out?"

"Right now."

Her eyes widened at that. Things had gotten very real, very fast. "It's almost night."

"Exactly," Samuel said. "If we walk fast, we'll be most of the way by morning. We need to pack up. There won't be much chance to refresh our water until we reach the Santa Ana."

THEY WERE out of the mall within the hour, the blood red sun setting behind them over the dilapidated buildings of southern L.A. They heard the roar of motorcycles leaving the parking garage in the distance, the Angel cavalry going to meet their enemy on the front lines. The sound quieted until there was nothing but the wind and the cold, dry air. The occasional crack of a gunshot split the evening silence, but those shots were distant. Most of the fighting was due north, and Samuel plotted a course east northeast.

Samuel knew they couldn't be complacent, though. The Reapers might think to approach the new Angel Command from the east, the direction they were headed. The going was slow, since they stuck to the shadows or even walked through buildings themselves in order to be out of sight. Both wore dark clothing, and the atmosphere above, eternally dusty from the impact of Ragnarok, meant the darkness was almost complete.

Makara had no idea how Samuel could make his way forward. She would have lost all sense of direction by now. Still, every half hour or so he found a dark corner in a building, knelt, and shone the pair's single flashlight on a compass and map that was provided to all the scouting teams. Once done, Samuel put the flashlight up, and they were on their way again.

The passed through Anaheim first, climbing a tall fence and finding themselves on the other side an overgrown theme park. Most of the signage was faded, or even spray painted over.

"What was this place?" Makara asked. "Why would they have built train tracks that high?"

"It was for entertainment," Samuel said. "People would come to this place and ride trains on them, going down those hills and back up." Samuel paused as he gazed up to look at it. "It was called a roller coaster."

Makara's eyes popped. "Why would they risk their lives like that?"

"I assume it was safe if people did it."

Makara felt it was anything *but* safe. The wide promenades

were lined with rubble and trash. Some of the train tracks had even collapsed, and at one point, they had to climb over a small mountain of wood barring their path. There was a large sign that had landed fallen sideways over the path ahead, with the faded face of what looked like a mouse. His comically happy face looked deranged surrounded by such destruction, as if he had been the cause of it.

They made the rest of their way through the park, passing deadened flower beds, wilted trees that had been long dead, and several dried lakebeds and ponds. There were skeletons, most half-buried in the debris.

"People tried to shelter here," Samuel said, breaking the silence. "Hard to tell just how long ago these communities fell. My guess is they tried to make this place work sometime in the Chaos Years. A theme park this size would have had a lot of amenities for taking care of a lot of people." He paused, as if considering the problem. "Of course, the food runs out eventually. A place like this, with its surrounding walls, might have been a nice shelter once upon a time. Now, there's only ghosts."

Neither of them said anything more, and Makara felt she could breathe again once they'd passed through to the other side.

"We should find some shelter before morning comes," Samuel said.

Makara nodded. She was starting to feel tired, too.

When they reached the Santa Ana, little more than a trickle running from the north, they crossed a bridge quickly and refilled their water after filtering and sanitizing it. They found shelter in what used to be a large grocery store. The shelving was still there, all of which had been picked clean years ago.

They hid behind some boxes and slept the day away.

Chapter 37

That evening, they picked up where they left off and headed west through the bare hills, following the line of the highway. The cars had been mostly cleared by this point, even if the pavement and supports were cracked in many places. Few trees were still alive. The lack of rainfall and sunlight meant few things could survive into the new Ice Age.

"How much farther?" Makara asked.

"It's still a hike," Samuel said. "We should be at the first settlement in a few hours."

Makara resisted the urge to complain. Her legs were sore, but if she complained too much, Samuel might tell Raine, who would be all too happy to keep her back home, cooped up and no help to anyone.

"It's quiet," Makara said. "No Reaps. No gunshots, even. I thought people lived out this way."

Samuel paused for breath; the highway was climbing in elevation. He took a swig from his canteen. "Beyond these hills are the last settlements before the San Bernardino Mountains. First one on the way is Riverside." He took a few more puffs. "Might try there first."

They continued, pausing briefly for a lunch of jerky

wrapped in flatbread. Then, they were on their way again, using the highway to travel more quickly. There was no sign of any other person. The ruins of L.A.'s suburbs were all but deserted.

"Gives me the creeps," Makara said.

Samuel motioned down suddenly, and instinctively, Makara fell to the ground. Both siblings crawled forward until they reached the railing of the highway and peeked over. Samuel raised a pair of binoculars to his eyes.

"Reaps," he said after a moment. "Seems they're setting up an outpost on the highway."

"Pass that over."

After a moment, Samuel obliged. Makara peered through the lenses, counting four or five Reapers, but seven parked bikes, all lined up in a row.

"At least seven of them," she said. "That tower they're in is high. You don't think they can see us, do you?"

It took an uncomfortably long time for Samuel to respond. "It's possible. Whatever the case, we can't approach any closer. Dawn will be coming soon, and they'll surely see us then."

"Failed," Makara said. "And we haven't even made it, yet."

"All the same, we've gotten valuable intel," Samuel said. "Come on. Sooner we get back, the better."

HALF AN HOUR after they'd turned back, they heard the roar of an engine behind them on the highway.

"Guess that answers whether they saw us," Samuel said. "Down that ramp!"

They both sprinted down the off-ramp as the sound of the engine approached. They ducked into the first building they saw, a gas station, to make their stand.

They set themselves up behind the counter and poked

their rifles out through the shattered glass. Shell casings littered the dirty floor. There had been a fight here before.

"Stay calm," Samuel said. "There's only one engine I hear, so we can take him."

The bike thundered down the ramp, turning into the gas station. The headlight remained on but was pointed toward the street. A man's bearded face looked toward them, lost in shadow.

He didn't seem to know for sure whether they were in there, and Makara was reluctant to take a shot in the darkness. Besides, shooting him would only give away their position if there were more.

The man killed the engine, and she heard the cock of a handgun. His boots crunched over the pavement to their position. The man paused, and shortly after, Makara heard him retching. He straightened, and then swayed a bit, as if he had difficulty keeping his balance.

Was the man drunk? Was he even coming after them?

Samuel held up a hand and raised his rifle slowly. He hesitated, watching intently before relaxing and allowing the barrel to drop.

The man was sitting down now and groaning.

Samuel slowly stood. Makara shook her head vehemently, but he motioned her to stay put. He walked, without fear, out into the gas station. He reached the man, and Makara heard him talking. The man just groaned some more.

What is going on? Makara thought.

She followed her brother out onto the pavement. She stood a few feet behind him.

"Olson," the man growled, in a deep voice. "Name's Olson." He coughed violently a few times, then spit on the ground next to them. "They thought I'd get them sick. They told me to go this way. To not come back. I took my bike. They told me to leave it." Olson looked up at Samuel. "Say. Take me back, patch me up, and there's a lot I can tell you about the Reaps." Olson coughed into his hand violently, while both Makara and Samuel took a step back.

"We can take you back to base and help you," Samuel said carefully, after a moment. "We have medicine. You'll have to give us information, though, like you said."

"I'll do whatever," Olson said. "Whatever you want. They don't want me anymore."

"He'll just get us sick, Samuel."

Samuel stood. Even in the darkness, Makara could see the frown on his face. "Maybe, Makara. But he has the Reaper tats and I have no doubt he knows a lot. He insists he wasn't sent out here by them. His face is burning up. He needs medical attention immediately if he's to survive long enough to give us information. Information that could be the key to winning this war."

"Why should we waste our stuff on the likes of him?"

Samuel inclined his head toward her. "I wouldn't want to, either. But we've been sent to get information, and if we save this man's life, he'll give it to us."

"What about San Bernardino?" Makara asked. "What about our mission?"

Samuel shook his head. "He told me there are ten guys in that outpost. Their only purpose is to block envoys from coming this way out of Lost Angels' territory. We're not going to get through that, and we don't have the supplies or the time to sneak around. Olson here is a good consolation prize for Raine."

"He's just a grunt," Makara said. "He probably doesn't know much."

"I know a lot," the man said. "Carin's getting the eastside gangs on his side. He plans to surround the Angels. Should be ready for the final assault inside a couple of weeks."

The man hacked again, and said nothing else, as if speaking was too much effort for him.

"What do we do, Sam? We can take his bike back, but I say let's leave him."

"The bike's big enough to carry all three of us," Samuel said. "Not fast, and not very safely. I have some rope and can tie him to the back. You can hold on to me, and I can drive."

"You know how to drive one of these?" Makara asked.

"A little. Dan showed me a few things."

"I . . . I can help," Olson said. "Just get me back."

"Let's tie him up, then," Makara said. "If you're really set on doing this."

This was done quickly. Olson groaned as he was rigged to the back of the bike. Samuel sat in front and turned the key in the ignition. He pressed the throttle and the bike rolled off. He did a testing loop, and came back.

"You'll have to sit right behind me, Mak," he said. "I won't go more than twenty miles an hour. This set up isn't safe."

"What if those Reaps behind hear us?" she asked.

Samuel frowned as he considered. "Let's hope they think it's Olson still. They haven't come after him yet. If they do, then I guess we'll just have to speed up. No choice in that. I'd like to know what he has to say. And he won't say much unless we can get him better."

Makara pursed her lips. "Okay. This is probably the stupidest thing we've ever done, but . . . I'm for it. Information could be useful."

Space was tight, and Olson was none too comfortable, Makara was sure. His boots even dragged on the ground as they set off, returning to the highway and heading west to the Lost Angels' turf.

Chapter 38

Makara was shocked at how fast the landscape rolled by, even at the tame speed of 20 mph. They did in several hours what had taken almost two days before. By the time the sun was rising behind them, they were pulling inside the parking garage and getting help pulling Olson to the holding cells.

Raine was there, and gave the order for the man to be transferred to the infirmary and placed under Darlene's care.

"I hope we did the right thing," Samuel told him, once they were alone in his office.

Raine nodded. "That man can never leave this place alive. Still, he might be useful. What he said about Black corralling the eastern gangs . . . that worries me greatly. He seems to be in a bad spot, though."

Olson's condition had worsened considerably on the ride home. He was breathing, but his head was burning up. Makara could see clearly that none of it was faked. Makara was just relieved for the ride to be over.

"Both of you get some rest," Raine said. "I'd say you both earned it."

Makara and Samuel left the jail and went back to the apartment.

～

OLSON AWOKE LATER but was catatonic. An IV full of precious antibiotics seemed to be doing no good. Could it be that they had weakened over time? Raine knew the day would come when most medications would start to lose effectiveness. Or maybe this man had something that couldn't be cured by the Angels' medicines.

"Not much else I can do," Darlene said, shaking her head. "I'm no doctor, even if I'm the closest thing you've got to one."

"I understand," Raine said. Olson's eyes were wide open, his pale face full of scars beneath his yellow beard. A thin line of dribble ran out of his lower lip, while his body shook in tiny tremors. Raine remained half an hour longer, enough time for the man to fall back asleep.

Raine left feeling disappointed. "Tell me if anything changes."

He went about his day, letting the kids sleep. They'd performed well, and he was relieved for them to be home. He had also misjudged the eastern groups terribly. Both Makara and Samuel could have gotten in big trouble if the Reapers had gotten a sight of them.

He needed to see Dan. Raine saw the reason why the assault from the north had stopped.

Carin Black meant to seize control of the east, first.

～

ONCE RAINE HAD FINISHED EXPLAINING what the kids had told him, the general thought it over for a moment.

"The strategy I've laid out becomes almost pointless if

you're right," Dan finally said. "I need to talk to this Olson guy myself."

"Well, he may not last the night if what Darlene says is any indication."

"Let's hope he does," Dan said. "I hate to admit it, but this is where Ohlan would have come in handy. If he were here, we'd have half of our forces on the eastern front right now."

"The kids said the main attack would come inside two weeks," Raine said. "If he doesn't get better by then, then we need to go ahead and shift some of our men over there."

"We're holding in the north," Dan said. "Just holding. Right now, the strategy is just to take good, clean fights and drop back when things get too dicey. We still have plenty of space to retreat into, and I've rigged some booby traps at important crossroads."

"What are the total casualties so far?"

"Maybe a hundred on both sides, more theirs than ours," Dan said. "They can afford the losses, though."

"That they can." Raine let out a sigh. "We have to work with what we have."

"If we pull men from the north, then we'll be forced to retreat at least half the distance to the mall," Dan said. "That means giving up a few outposts."

"Outposts make little difference," Raine said. "We just have to make it hurt. Any word on the Krakens?"

Dan's mouth twisted distastefully. "They say they're mobilizing, but they have yet to send a single one of their bikes up this way. They're already overdue."

"What about our main strike force?" Raine said. "Are they ready to go?"

"They were. Until I heard about the east side attack that might be coming. Carin Black hasn't shown himself yet. If we can get a clean shot at him . . ."

Raine shook his head. "I don't think that's coming. He'll show himself when victory's assured."

There was a knock at the door. When Dan opened it, Darlene stepped in. "Sorry to interrupt. Olson's awake, and seems to be lucid."

Raine stood immediately. "All right. Let's go."

RAINE AND DAN walked together to the clinic, where they found Olson sitting up in his bed with a spaced-out look. When the Reaper's eyes went to Raine, Raine wondered if he even knew he was there.

"Was he like this before?" Raine asked Darlene.

"No, he was talking and everything," she said. "I'm sorry, I guess maybe . . ."

"I'm here," the man said, speaking as if he had phlegm in his throat. He didn't bother to clear it, making his voice gravelly. "What do you want to know?"

Raine looked at Dan sideways, who seemed tense. Raine focused his attention back on Olson.

"Why are you helping us?"

"They cast me out," the man said. He started coughing, and Darlene brought a bed pan over. The man hacked into it while Raine turned his face away. Once Olson had some water, he cleared his throat.

"They kicked you out for being sick?" Raine asked.

The man nodded. "That's right."

"They must be low on medicine," Dan said. "We shouldn't be in here with him. He's probably contagious."

The man shook his head. "Just a bad fever. Nothing serious."

Dan shook his head. "Boss. We should be wearing masks at least."

"I'll get some right now," Darlene said. She seemed a little sulky, as if disappointed she hadn't thought of it first.

It was only when Darlene returned with the masks that Raine began his questioning again.

"What kind of sickness do you have?"

"Beats me," the man said. "I feel hot. And cold. Nauseous. Dizziness."

"Sounds like a nasty case of the flu," Dan said.

"That's my thought, too," Darlene said, watching from the doorway.

"It'll pass," Olson said. "Lots of Reapers are sick. That's why . . . advance has slowed. But the war is still on."

"Might be the time to strike," Raine said.

"Or sit back," Dan said. "Let sickness fight for us. If a lot of them are getting sick, we're risking ourselves just by being here. How many people have exposed themselves to this guy?"

Raine frowned. "You and me. Sam and Mak. Darlene, some of the guys in the garage who helped move him here."

"I feel fine," Darlene said. "For what it's worth."

"All right, then," Raine said, turning his attention back to Olson. "So, there's sickness in the Reapers' camp."

"That's right," Olson said. "Hard to say how many. Any of the sick are rounded up in camps in the mountains."

"Are they killed?" Dan asked.

Olson shrugged. "Some say that." A small smile tugged at his lips, but his pale pallor made it look corpse-like. "Guess I got of lucky. They just told me to scram."

"What else can you tell me?" Raine asked. "The kids mentioned that the Reaps plan to surround us on all sides."

"They do," Olson said. "That plan is on hold though. For now."

That wasn't what he'd told the kids. In truth, this sickness worried him almost as much. There was no one here showing symptoms, as far as Raine knew, but that could change quickly. All he could hope for was that the outbreak of war had completely stopped people from traveling between Reaper and Angel territory.

"What else?" Raine asked.

"I want . . . guarantees."

"We're healing you up, ain't that good enough for you?" Darlene asked.

"I need safety," he said. "I'll renounce the Reapers. They cast me out, anyway."

"Don't worry, you're safe here," Raine said. "Whatever you tell us will be used to protect you."

"Tired," he said. "Told you most of what I know."

"We need numbers," Dan said. "Troop positions."

"Our orders were to build an outpost on the highway outside Corona," he said. Olson seemed to be struggling to speak, his voice raspy. "We were a forward base, meant to keep watch . . . to keep the Angels . . ."

Olson settled back against the pillow propping him to the wall, his muscles slackening while his eyes went up into his head.

Darlene stepped forward. "He's fading."

"Fading?" Dan asked. "What's that mean?"

"Going catatonic again," Darlene said. She put a stethoscope on Olson's bare chest. She frowned.

"Lot of fluid. It's like the flu and pneumonia are having a battle in there."

Olson suddenly convulsed and gave a great hack, spraying Darlene with copious amounts of dark, dripping fluid. It stank like rotting meat.

"You rat bastard," Darlene said, after she'd recovered.

"Wash up, Darlene," Raine said. He noticed a fleck of the horrible stuff had gotten on his finger. Dan checked himself and seemed to be clean. Raine wiped the finger on a clean part of the bedsheet.

Darlene left, cursing, while Dan pulled Raine out of the room.

"I'm no doctor," Dan said, "but I know that isn't the flu."

Chapter 39

Makara and Samuel woke up sometime the next morning, and both were surprised to see Raine sitting at their kitchen table. His large frame looked almost comical at the tiny table and small chair. Some fruits and bowls of oatmeal were laid out.

"Picked this up from the market," he said. "We have stuff to talk about."

The siblings sat, the table crowded with the three of them.

"What happened with Olson?" Samuel asked, broaching the subject, even though Raine was the one who wanted to talk.

"He told us some interesting stuff," he said. "Worrying stuff." Raine looked up at them both. "Either of you feeling under the weather?"

Both shook their heads.

"Is he worse?" Makara asked.

Raine nodded. "Yeah. Real bad. Darlene thought he had the flu, or maybe pneumonia, but then he hacked up all this . . . *stuff* . . . on her. Now this morning *she's* feeling sick. Got me worried, is all."

"He's been around her more than us by now," Samuel said. "You said he coughed on her?"

Raine nodded. "That's right."

"Was she showing symptoms before that?"

"No," Raine said.

"May be communicable through the discharge," Samuel said. "Both should be separated while it works through them."

"Darlene runs the entire infirmary," Raine said. "If we have wounded soldiers, then we'll have to take care of them without her leadership."

"That'll be tough," Makara said.

"Did he say anything important?" Samuel asked.

Raine nodded. "That's what I was trying to get to. Apparently, a lot of these Reaps are having the same sickness. They've been rounded up in camps in the mountains."

Samuel's eyes widened at that. "We should have never brought him back."

"Well, might be too late for that," Raine said. "Him and Darlene are being confined."

"Poor Darlene," Makara said. "How is she?"

"Just came back from there," Raine said. "Seems in good spirits and is determined to get better. She more than anyone understands the need for stopping whatever this is in its tracks."

"Still . . ." Makara said.

The three of them were silent for a time, finishing their food. When Raine was done with his, he continued.

"Olson said the Reaper advance will slow down because of the disease."

"Sounds serious, then," Samuel said. "Black wouldn't stop for just anything."

"Assuming this guy is reliable," Makara said.

"I think he is," Raine said. "That's a consideration, though."

There was a sudden knock at the door, which opened

before Raine could even stand to answer it. Dan Green stood at the door, his stern features on high alert.

"What's going on?"

"Reaps," he said. "They're pouring in from the north and east."

Raine nodded darkly. "Bad information, then."

"False information," Dan said. "I've ordered everyone to fall back here."

All Raine could feel was numb. Was this how it was going to end?

Just when the news couldn't get any worse, Dan laid another bomb on them. "Their numbers are too great to be just Reaps. Seems the eastern gangs are helping, too. By the time they push back the barricades, the mall will be under assault."

Raine stood and looked down at Samuel and Makara. Makara thought he looked sad.

"We've been setting up the defense here ever since we arrived," he said. "Now's the time to see what it's worth." He turned back to Dan. "I'll be out there in a minute, Dan. I have some things to tell these two."

Dan nodded respectfully and withdrew, closing the door behind him.

Raine turned to face them both. "Things are going to get very serious, very soon. Both of you will have to fight. If I give the order, though, I want both of you to get out of here."

"No," Makara said, immediately. "I could never do that."

"It's an order," Raine said. "I hope I never have to give it."

Samuel stood to face him. "Raine . . ."

Raine cut him off. "No excuses, Samuel. I give the word, you get her out. Find Ohlan out east. He's my brother and he'll protect you both."

"No," Makara said. "We'll fight with everyone else."

"We will," Raine agreed. "We'll fight together. I hope the alternative doesn't become necessary."

"What do we do in the meantime, Raine?"

"Report to your battle stations," he said. "I have things to take care of."

Without another word, Raine left them behind while Makara shouted his name.

~

RAINE HATED to leave her behind like that, but he had to command. The first order of business was following Dan to the infirmary to enact his retribution on Olson. It was obvious now that the Reapers had *wanted* Olson here, to infect the base before Olson himself could die.

He had already infected Darlene, and perhaps others, too.

Raine and Dan raced across the concourse, a controlled chaos of people gathering their weapons and heading to their preassigned positions. Raine opened the infirmary door to find a scene of madness.

Darlene sat slumped in a corner, completely still, her neck and clothing completely soaked with blood. Her green eyes stared lifelessly ahead.

"Darlene!" Raine said.

Raine's attention was drawn to the door to Olson's room, which was open. Within, there was no sign of the man himself.

"He'll die for this," Dan said.

They left the infirmary, running in the direction of screams. They saw Olson's back facing toward him and shambling forward, as if Darlene had injured him in the fight. He lunged toward a group of women, biting one of them on the arm while the others pushed him away.

Dan ran ahead, raising his gun all the while.

"Move!" he called out. "Move away, now!"

The women scattered, leaving Olson standing alone. His face was pale, while a mixture of blood and purple fluid dribbled from his gray lips. The man looked all but dead as he shuffled toward Dan and Raine, arms extended.

Dan unloaded the entire clip of his handgun into the man, pelting him in the chest and legs. Despite stumbling, Olson continued. Was he wearing body armor under those clothes? Raine didn't see how it was possible, but it was the only thing that made sense.

"Raine!" Dan called. "I need backup here!"

Raine walked forward calmly, pulling out his own handgun. At Raine's approach, Olson stumbled forward more quickly, barely remaining upright.

By Raine's reckoning, the man had lost all right to life. Darlene was dead and he had hurt one of the women standing to the side, who was now nursing her arm. Had the sickness driven him mad, or had this all been a part of the Reapers' plan?

Raine would never know that answer. Just a few feet away from him, he raised his handgun and aimed directly at Olson's forehead.

One shot, ringing out loud and echoing throughout the concourse, and it was over.

Olson tumbled forward stiffly, landing flat on his face. A mixture of blood and purple fluid oozed from his mouth, pooling on the floor beneath.

Raine went over to the woman who was holding her arm. He almost told her to go to the infirmary, before remembering what had happened to Darlene.

"Go get the cleaned up," he said. "The rest of you head to your assigned posts."

The women scurried away, a couple of them crying. Dan caught up to Raine. "First casualties already, and they haven't even opened fire on us yet."

"This needs to be contained before it gets out of hand," Raine said. He shook his head. "This body needs to be burned."

"I'll find some men and see to it."

Dan was already raising the radio to his mouth and calling for backup.

Raine just couldn't stop himself from looking down at Olson. How had they been so easily fooled? Why would Olson have risked himself coming here if he knew he was going to die, anyway? He must have been Carin Black's man through and through to be willing to die to get at Raine and the Angels.

This type of fighting was dirty, even by Black's standards. Raine supposed that this time, the lord of the Reapers was leaving nothing to chance.

When backup arrived, Raine helped load Olson onto the stretcher. They headed off with Dan to oversee them and Raine following behind.

When they reached the infirmary, Raine called a halt and took a couple of the guys to help get Darlene loaded onto a stretcher as well, covering her with a bedsheet. Normally, they'd preserve the body long enough to give it a proper funeral, but with the coming invasion and the risk of contagion, there was nothing else to be done. It felt disrespectful to Darlene in the utmost. But Raine couldn't call off the defense, even for a few minutes.

The Reapers were pushing south, and there was no time for anything. He wouldn't even have time to watch her pass out of this world and into the next.

"We have to make sure she's burned, too," Raine said. "I hate to do it like this, Dan, but I see no other way."

He nodded. "I understand, boss. I'll inform everyone on what's happened after the fact. We need to let people know they're safe from him, now."

Raine nodded. "I agree. We'll just say Olson was a plant and that he took Darlene down with him, which is true, and that he was stopped. We'll say nothing about his sickness. Don't want to cause a panic."

Raine watched sadly as Darlene was wheeled away. Darlene, who had overseen little Makara, made her feel at home in a strange new place. Darlene, whose wisdom had helped the council break deadlock countless times. Darlene, who had healed countless sick and injured people, doing as well as a doctor or even better, despite her lack of pedigree.

She would be sorely missed, not only by him, but by the rest of the Angels. But she would only be missed if they survived the coming storm.

Raine headed down to the first level. It was time for his part in leading the defense.

Chapter 40

Makara and Samuel had made it to the main concourse on the ground floor when they heard gunshots ringing out from the upper tier. Both looked up to see Dan firing at a man stumbling toward him.

Makara took off, but Samuel grabbed her by the shirt, keeping her in place.

"Let *go* of me!"

Samuel didn't let go. The gunshots ceased, as the two siblings watched Raine approach the man. Another shot rang out, and then silence.

Several people were running up to the third floor, where the fight had taken place, but most remained in place, watching the proceedings from the safety of the ground floor.

"Let me go up there, Samuel," Makara said. "Raine might be hurt."

"Raine is fine," Samuel said. "See? You can see him walking around up there."

Makara saw that he was right. Raine, along with Dan, were moving with a group of soldiers toward the infirmary.

"Looks like somebody got hurt," Samuel said.

At that moment, Makara felt a rumbling from the floor

beneath, shortly followed by the sound of an explosion coming from outside. Some of the people on the concourse ducked, but Makara didn't bother.

She felt fear for the first time, though, a reminder that the actual fighting would be starting all too soon.

"We should take up our positions," Samuel said.

Makara nodded, glancing worriedly at the third tier. Raine was no longer in sight.

"Okay," she said. "Let's go."

RAINE WATCHED as the flames licked away at Darlene Sander's shroud. The smell was something awful, but he wouldn't dishonor her by standing aside.

He heard artillery in the distance, mortars whistling and falling on their outer defenses set up to the north. Those defenses would not last long.

"Boss," Dan said. "We should go back in."

Raine nodded. "You're right. We'll focus on the ones we can save."

Raine leaned aside and coughed, the palm of his hand covered with some nasty looking mucus.

Just a coincidence, he thought, but he hid his hand before Dan could see it.

"Let's head back in," he said. "I need to get on the P.A. to give a few last orders."

RAINE HEADED TO THE ANGELS' command center, not far from his office. That was where the mall's old security office had been located, and the Angels had restored the P.A. system during their time fixing up the mall. Any message relayed in here would play out of every speaker in the complex.

Raine reached for the handheld mic now, holding it up to his mouth. Dan pressed the power button.

What, already? Raine thought. He'd barely had time to gather his thoughts.

"Lost Angels," he said. "This is Raine. If you've followed orders, you're already well on your way to your battle stations, or already in place. We still have some time before the main attack begins, but the Reapers are coming. They're already bombing our northern outposts, which we don't expect to last long."

Raine paused to gather his thoughts. What should he talk about first? The Angels' overall strategy? His own thoughts on the matter? What about what to do with the young ones?

There were so many things to cover.

"The defensive strategy General Green and I have outlined has shored up all of our defenses here, in the mall. Every entrance has been closed but two, both of which are well-defended and reinforced."

That won't matter if they shell us to hell, Raine thought. He'd leave out that detail, though.

"This place is our home," Raine said. "Home is a rare thing for most folks these days. We worked hard to build something, a society where all men and women are free. We're the only ones in all L.A. who have outlawed slavery. We are the example, the future for everyone to aspire to. This mall is *more* than home to me, for that reason. It's worth defending with every drop of my blood. My friends are here, and so is a future that'll shine brighter because of our actions today."

He looked to Dan for support, who gave a nod for Raine to continue.

"We've been on a course for confrontation with the Reapers for a while, now. Carin Black's way is different from our way. Many of you came to us after escaping his slave camps. You know what the city will be like if he wins this battle. His members fight out of fear, while we fight for freedom and our homes.

"Our strategy is two-fold. Most of you will be staying behind to help with the defense, while a smaller, handpicked force will be on the attack. If you're part of the attacking force, head to the garage, and defending force, head to the concourse if you haven't already received your assignments.

"Both of our forces have to find success today. We depend on each other. Defenders need to keep out the invaders until their dying breath. Do not surrender, never accept surrender from the Reapers. Nothing but death or slavery awaits you at their hands. Fight to your last, and don't show the enemy mercy. They will show you none.

"Makara, Samuel. If you're listening to this, come join me now in the command center.

"Children under thirteen years of age and their designated guardians; seek shelter now on level B1."

Raine thought things over, wondering if there was anything he had left out. When Dan said nothing, he thought of his closing statements.

"The sun will rise on a new future for L.A., one where freedom will banish the darkness caused by Ragnarok. Fight for that future, as surely as you fight for yourselves and your loved ones. That's all. Good luck."

Raine put the receiver back and waited.

Chapter 41

Makara and Samuel left the crowd of people heading for the barricade located on the mall's north side, and turned back to head into the command center. When they arrived, out of breath, they found Raine waiting for them.

Before either of them could ask what was going on, Raine spoke.

"You're both with me."

Makara blinked in surprise. "Wait. We're part of the attack force, now?"

Raine nodded. "Yes. I'll be leading that personally, while Dan is going to be overseeing the defense."

Makara felt her chest swell with pride. "I won't let you down, Raine."

"What's the plan?" Samuel said.

"Simple," Raine said. "Carin Black will be behind enemy lines. We're to take our force, punch a hole in the Reapers' eastern lines, and find him and settle the score once and for all."

Makara felt her eyes widen at that. "What . . . how are we to even . . .?"

"I know," Raine said. "It's a long shot. But it might be the only shot we have. We're outnumbered three to one at least, and when the reinforcements arrive from the eastern gangs, the odds will be even worse. We have to end this quickly. If the mall goes down before we take out Black . . ." He looked from Makara, then back to Samuel. "Remember what I said earlier."

"Raine . . ." Makara started.

He shook his head. "Remember. If you don't agree, then you're off the attack force, and I'm sending you both on your way right now."

"We agree," Samuel said, before Makara could say anything more.

Raine arched an eyebrow at Makara, and she let out a huff. "Fine."

"You can take one of the bikes with a sidecar," Raine said. "Samuel drives, Makara shoots."

"What about you, Raine?" Makara asked.

"Me? I'm leading the attack. About fifty of us in all."

Fifty. Would that be enough to break the Reapers' line and find Black at the same time? Makara realized that the majority would have to stay behind and defend the mall.

"All right," she said. "Are we doing this?"

Raine nodded. "One more thing. That guy you brought back . . . he went crazy and attacked Darlene. She's no longer with us."

Dan nodded to confirm this fact while Makara processed the news.

"I'm sorry," she said. "It's our fault we brought him back . . ."

"You couldn't have known," Raine said. "I'd have done the same myself. Both he and Darlene were burned out back. There was no time for a proper ceremony."

That hurt even worse, but Makara couldn't find fault with it. "She'll be missed, Raine."

"You should get going, Boss," Dan said. "The attack force should be assembled by now."

Raine nodded. "Good luck, Dan."

The two men shook hands. Makara knew as well as anyone else that this could be the last time they ever saw each other.

They headed out the door for the parking garage.

WHEN THEY ARRIVED, they found all the Angel bikers with their guns at the ready. They cheered Raine as he came forward, but his serious attitude caused them to go quiet and pay attention.

"This ends today," he said. He paused a moment, coughing into his shoulder. He took a swig from his canteen to wash down the phlegm that had collected in his throat. "We have no choice but victory. If we lose this battle, it'll be the end of the Angels. We have one mission, and one mission only. Kill Black. He's out there somewhere, behind enemy lines. We'll find him and end this war for good."

"We'll find him, Raine," a gruff, bearded man said. Other Angels shouted their agreement.

"Let's ride, then," Raine said.

He went to his chopper, parked at the forefront of the rest, its pair of silver angel wings covering the handlebars. The others mounted up, but Raine was the first to start his engine, the roar echoing throughout the confines of the garage. Others started up their bikes until a great din filled the interior of the garage.

Makara and Samuel headed for one of the nearer bikes with a sidecar, given to them by the garage head. Samuel climbed on and started it up while Makara entered the sidecar, hefting her AR-15.

The bikes were heading down the exit ramp, now, and Samuel pulled out after them.

The attack was on.

Chapter 42

The Angels rolled north in a single mass, across the parking lot and onto the streets north of the mall. The sounds of explosions were barely discernible above the collective roar of the engines.

It did not take long to meet resistance. They came upon a group of ten or so Reapers, off their bikes and setting up a barricade on the road. Raine surged on ahead, taking the first shots as his chopper approached. The Reapers dove for cover, but it did them little good. The skirmish was over in a matter of minutes, with all the Reapers dead and only one fallen Angel.

The men raided the bodies for more ammunition and pressed on. Raine turned north and the Angels followed him. The sounds of the bombardment were getting louder. Makara realized that Raine was following the sound.

And before she knew it, they were rounding a corner and straight ahead was the Lost Angels' old base, filled to the brim with Reapers using it as a fort. Raine charged ahead, to catch them unaware before they could set up a proper defense.

As the Angels neared the old walls, still mangled from the siege two years ago, they received some sporadic gunfire, but there was no gate to keep them out. The Angels opened fire, downing multiple Reapers before they even had the chance to return fire.

Reapers were shooting from the windows of the old base, down on the Angels below.

Raine parked next to the building and shot his way up the front door, with others close behind.

We're up to our necks in it now, Makara thought.

She followed Raine into the building, where Angels were already securing the place floor by floor.

The numbers were about even, but the Angels had surprise on their side, killing at least ten Reapers within the first couple of minutes. Now, the Reapers were setting up defensive positions within the building. Raine and the Angels knew the building, and used that knowledge to their advantage, coming up on defensive emplacements from behind and taking Reapers out who were hiding.

Makara stayed with Samuel the entire time, her heart pounding madly. They joined several Angels at a corner, and took turns taking shots down a hallway. Makara reloaded her magazine, and fired again, scoring a hit on a Reaper's shoulder.

After thirty minutes of fighting, the gunshots were lessening. What Reapers were left were rounded up and executed in the yard.

There was no Carin Black, though. Raine was fuming, but already, the Angels were gathering in the yard around him, waiting for the next move.

"Where to, Boss?" one of them asked.

"Word will get to Black that we're here, if it hasn't already," Raine said. "We have to keep moving."

Raine didn't look good to Makara. There a hazy look in his eyes, and she didn't like the way he was coughing. He suddenly gripped his stomach and threw up on the yard. As the men stepped back, Makara could see whatever came out wasn't normal upchuck. It was dark, and smelled vile.

Some of the men turned aside to throw up themselves, while Raine stumbled for his bike.

"Raine!" Makara ran up to him. "You're sick. You can't fight like this."

The roar of engines filled the air. The sound was coming from outside the base.

"They're coming, Boss," one of the men said. "What do we do?"

"Black," Raine said, half-delirious. "We have to get to Black."

The men looked at each other, unsure of what to do.

"We ain't finding Black if you're puking your guts out," the same man said. "Help me load him on his bike, Mike."

"There's no time," Mike said.

Makara saw that he was right. The sounds of the approaching engines were louder, now.

"Man the walls!" Samuel called out, taking charge since no one else wanted to do it.

The men exchanged glances at being told what to do by a sixteen-year-old, but none of them could argue against the sense of that order.

The Angels hurried to man the walls. If they didn't set up their positions as quickly as the Reapers, they'd meet the same fate. Makara and Samuel, meanwhile, pulled Raine inside the old base, despite his protests and struggles. It was a testament to his weakness that he couldn't break free of their grip.

"We'll watch over you," Makara said. "Don't make this harder than it needs to be, Raine."

Raine was all but crying now. "I need to avenge them, Makara. I need to avenge my wife and daughter."

"It's not over yet," Samuel said. "You might get your chance, Raine."

Gunshots sounded from the ramparts as Makara and

Samuel dragged the Lost Angels' leader up the stairs. Reapers on bikes poured through the open gates. The Angels concentrated their fire, knocking a few of the Reapers off their mounts. They leaned Raine up against a wall, going to the window to add their own fire at Reapers pouring in from below. Angels started to go down in the crossfire.

Raine was already standing up, and stumbling towards the stairs.

"Raine!" Makara called.

He lost his footing and tumbled down them. Both siblings abandoned their positions and came to help their leader. He groaned as he crawled toward the wall, as Makara and Samuel helped him up. He had a nasty gash on his head.

"Raine, can you hear me?" Makara asked.

He spat, and blood came out. "For it to end like this . . . this disease will get me, sure as it got him . . ."

"Don't say that," Makara said. "It's not over yet."

"Makara," Raine said, his eyes glassy. "You have to go. That's an order."

Makara was about to protest when a mortar whistled overhead. The entire building rumbled from the impact, while bits of wall and ceiling rained from above.

"I'm not going anywhere, Raine."

"This was . . . a last-ditch hope. Dan and I . . . we knew this would be over unless we somehow killed Black." He coughed again, the liquid staining his hand a mixture of blood and dark fluid. "The mall is going to fall, Makara. This is the Angels' last stand. I don't want you to die in it. You're a survivor." His dark eyes met hers. "Keep surviving."

"No, this isn't the end," Makara said, voice rising. "Don't say that, Raine."

"Samuel," Raine said, his eyes seeming to get lucid for the first time. "Remember what I told you."

Makara looked at her brother in horror. That horror was realized when her brother nodded.

"I'll do it, Raine."

More gunshots from outside. Makara ran up the stairs and took up her position again at the window. Angels were falling now, and fast. A few bullets whizzed by, so she ducked and crawled back to the stairwell.

"In the basement," Raine said. "There's a cellar door that comes out the back. If the Reaps don't know about it, you might get out alive."

"I will *not* run!" Makara said. "I'll die here before I do that."

"Take her, Samuel," Raine ordered. "Makara . . . find Ohlan. Your purpose isn't over. You must survive. You *must* survive."

Raine closed his eyes, as Makara shook him by the shoulders madly. "Raine. Raine! Don't you die on me. This isn't over."

Tears streamed down her face, washing the dust of the bombardment away. Another explosion rocked the building from the south.

"This place is gonna come down," Samuel said. "We got to go, now."

Even Makara had to admit it was over. Even if Raine were to survive whatever sickness was taking him, they'd have to carry him out of the building, causing their progress to be slowed.

"Thank you," Makara whispered, to Raine's quiet form.

His lips tugged upward in a smile. His eyes opened halfway, but only halfway.

Samuel reached for his neck and waited.

"Nothing," he said. "I'm sorry. We can do nothing else." His eyes were watery, too.

He stood and started to pull Makara downstairs. They needed to make it to the basement before the Reapers started getting into the building.

Makara resisted at first, not wanting to leave Raine

behind, the man who had saved her and kept her safe. It was all gone, now. There would be no vengeance for him, no justice for Adrienne or Valerie.

"I'll finish what you started," Makara vowed. "I'll kill Carin Black for you, Raine."

Samuel pulled her downstairs, rushing her through the back of the building as the storm fell upon them.

Chapter 43

Raine's eyes fluttered open. He was alive? How was he still alive?

The world was gray, and shapes blurred into one another. The sound of gunshots and artillery fire was muffled, seeming to come from another world.

Raine forced himself to focus. Someone was coming up the steps. His consciousness faded and all went back. The blackness was momentarily forced aside when he felt a stinging shock of pain on his cheek. Raine was powerless to resist it.

It's over, he thought.

When Raine opened his eyes, he saw a face floating in front of him. A terrible face. Raine's eyes narrowed to see Carin Black's gloating features and dark, beady eyes boring into his. Was this real, or a vision?

Black spoke, but the voice was warbled. Raine could hardly follow the words.

"We finally meet, Raine Rogers. I only wish it could have been in better circumstances."

Raine tried to respond, but ended up only grunting.

"None of that, now," Black said, with a chuckle. He held

out a copper flask. "Here. This is good Kentucky bourbon. Just like we used to drink together."

Raine wanted to spit, but only succeeded in drooling.

"Should back away, Boss," a nearby crony said. "He's got the Red Sickness."

Carin turned to him. "Why don't you fuck off, Nathan, huh? Raine and I are having a moment. Two old buddies catching up." He turned his gaze on all his subordinates. "That goes for all of you. Scram."

Carin's cronies vacated the stairwell, leaving the Reaper's warlord alone with Raine. Raine felt the blackness taking him once again.

"Nothing, huh?" Carin asked. "Well, this has been disappointing. I was itching for a good fight." Black touched Raine's face almost tenderly. "You fought all these years like a cornered badger. In the end, though, you fell into the trap."

Carin pinched his cheek roughly as Raine slipped further from reality. His arms, which had once been so strong, were no longer under his control.

"Say hi to Valerie," Carin whispered. "I'm sure she misses me."

Those were the last words Raine Rogers heard before the darkness took him forever.

Chapter 44

The basement was completely empty, save for the shelving. Almost everything had been taken with the Angels to the new base. For the first time, Makara would see what was beyond the door that was the subject of so much speculation and fear during her time living here.

When Samuel reached it, the door opened easily enough with a creak. What they found inside was a series of doors lining either side of a short hallway, at the end of which was a short set of stairs leading to the cellar door Raine mentioned. Samuel ignored the side doors, forging ahead, while Makara paused, unable to resist the pull of her curiosity. She reached for the first door, finding only an empty room and a bucket.

A jail cell, maybe.

"Come on!" Samuel called from ahead.

Makara hurried after him, his flashlight beam leading the way. Samuel pushed the door open, and she could see red daylight pouring in from outside. Makara was out the door first, just as a mortar whistled overhead and rocked the building behind her.

Makara screamed as she was knocked off her feet, scrambling forward to avoid getting crushed by the side of the

KYLE WEST

building coming down. Everything was falling, the crumbling of the building drowning out all other sounds.

When things finally calmed, Makara got up with nothing more than a few scratches and bruises, a large piece of masonry having mostly shielded her from the collapse. She crouched as she walked forward through the dust, back to the cellar entrance.

It was completely buried in rubble, and there was no sign of her brother.

"Samuel?"

He didn't respond to her call.

"Samuel!"

A few gunshots rang out from the front of the building. Makara held her rifle in front of her, trying to dig at the rubble. Even the smaller pieces were incredibly heavy. She strained to lift one of them, but it was wedged in tight.

Makara sobbed, falling onto the pile. Samuel was buried under there, either suffocating or dead. The late afternoon light was fading into evening.

What was she supposed to do now? Where would she go, back to the mall? The mall was going to go down, anyway. Their only chance had been to find Black and kill him.

Was that what she should do? Find Black?

Raine told Samuel to get me out. Well, Samuel's not here anymore. So, what do I do?

She dried her tears, pushing down all her pain and sadness, forcing herself to go numb. She wasn't going to be any good if she was a blubbering mess.

Raine, dead. Samuel, dead. What was to stop her now from ending it all, or suiciding herself for a chance to get at Carin Black? She was just going to die out here in the open, anyway, or be taken a slave.

Might as well try to get some revenge in the process.

She made her way out of the compound and started climbing a stack of rubble to get on top of the wall. She edged along the rampart, which was still in decent shape, and set up a position near the corner of the building, where she would be well-hidden from the yard, where Reapers were on the prowl.

In the gathering darkness, though, it was impossible to tell which one was Black, or if in fact *any* of them were.

She wanted to cry in frustration. She should just try to kill as many as possible before they got to her?

She was about to do just that. She lined up the sight of her AR-15, concentrating to make sure her first target went down. Her aim would be true, but after that first shot, what then?

Raine's words ran through her head.

Your purpose is not over. You must survive.

She could not disobey Raine's dying wish. He wanted her to survive. He'd given everything to let her go on.

"I can't," she whispered.

Killing herself would be the easy way out. Why had Raine cursed her with the hard way?

Makara backed away from the precipice, lowering herself to the ground below. She would try to make it out, as impossible as that would be.

She had to do it, if not for herself, then for Raine.

Chapter 45

Now that she had decided to try and get out of L.A., Makara had to figure out the best way to go about that. Stealing a bike would be too risky, and all the Angels' bikes were controlled by Reapers in the yard now, anyway.

Makara quickly saw that the only she could escape was on foot. First, she'd to wait for the full cover of darkness. She hid behind the rubble of Angel Command until the darkness was absolute. Only then did she make her way forward, down familiar streets and through buildings she knew like the back of her hand. All those years of exploring the surrounding territory was paying off. For a moment, it felt as if she had returned to those more innocent days; at least, until the crack of a gunshot interrupted the night, or the howling of a flying mortar made the hairs on her neck stand on end.

The whole time she made her way east, it felt like the wrong decision. But Raine's instructions had been clear: to get out of L.A. and to find his brother. Makara didn't relish the part about finding Ohlan, but Makara felt she couldn't disobey Raine's dying wish. Raine wanted his brother to know about his death as soon as possible, for whatever reason.

So, she resolved to make it to him, or die trying.

The ruins of L.A. were empty and forlorn. Makara ran when she felt she was far enough from the fighting to go unnoticed, with a goal of reaching the Santa Ana by daybreak to refill her canteen. She took a more northerly route than she and Samuel had just a couple of days before, to avoid the Reaper outpost on the highway.

As much as she tried to push thoughts of Raine and Samuel from her mind, she couldn't help but blame herself for their deaths. It was she and Samuel, after all, who'd brought the sick man back to the mall on the bike. If they hadn't done that, Raine would still be alive, and maybe even Samuel would be alive.

It was useless to think about, now.

When Makara became too tired, she found a building to hide in for the night. She didn't dare build a fire, instead eating some of the food from her pack. There wasn't much; she hadn't planned on being out for the long haul.

She had her blanket, though, so she took that out and wrapped herself in it. The nighttime quiet was often broken by the sound of cracking gunfire and the whistle of mortars. They were miles southwest. Makara seemed to be well out of range of the fighting.

Those sounds would signify the mall going down. It was hard to believe without seeing it with her own eyes. She shook at the thought of all the names and all the faces that she would never see again. Lives destroyed in a single night, and those who weren't killed would be made the Reapers' slaves.

Makara could still suffer that same fate, if she were unlucky.

She didn't see the point of going on. Coldness clutched her heart as she thought of Samuel, dead beneath the rubble, of Raine, expiring from his sickness. He hadn't even had the chance to go crazy, like Olson. Something was off about that disease.

For some reason, it reminded her of that terrible night, long ago. Why was that?

The bile, she realized. The stuff Raine had been hacking up looked like the purple fluid from the monsters that had attacked Bunker One.

Makara shivered. That means that whatever disease those things were carrying had made it here, all the way from Colorado. The further she went east, the closer she got herself to ground zero.

"There's no way I'm surviving," she said. Though she spoke quietly, her voice sounded loud in the room she was in.

Your purpose is not over. You must survive. Your purpose is not over. You must survive. Your purpose is not over . . .

Raine's words ran over and over in her head as the tears sprung forth, no longer able to be contained.

MAKARA SLEPT FOR A LONG TIME, fading in and out, though the red daylight shone through the open window. She slept, seeing no reason to get up and face the day.

She wanted to lie there until she was dead.

But it seemed that she wouldn't even get the choice to die on her own terms, for she heard voices coming from the floor below. Two men were talking, and she heard boots on the steps.

Quietly, she shifted position until she was waiting behind the door with just her handgun. She left all her stuff in the open, including her rifle. There was just no time to hide it.

The men reached the landing, and their footstep rounded the corner and came to a pause before the door of the room she was in.

"In here," a voice said. "Told you she went this way."

"Careful, Devon," the other one said.

"Now, where is she?" He stepped into the room, but didn't check behind the door, where Makara was hidden. "Window's open. Think she jumped out?"

The man went to stand by the window, and looked down. Makara waited. She wanted the second man to come in to get a clear shot at both.

Come on, she thought. *You come in, too.* Her hand shook as she pointed her handgun.

As if answer to her though, the other man stepped inside the room, just as the first turned toward him.

His eyes widened upon seeing Makara behind the door, but already, several shots rang out, deafening in the confines of the room. Hardly anyone could have missed at that range. Both men went down. Makara watched them twitch until they both had bled out.

Instead of moving, Makara waited and listened. When no help seemed to be coming, only then did she stir from her position.

Coolly and mechanically, the thirteen-year-old girl rifled the contents of their pockets for anything useful, finding some 5.56 rounds for her AR-15 as well as a butane lighter, still half full. Both men had packs, and she rummaged through them, taking all their food and water. She also found a half bottle of rum and a carton of cigarettes. Both would be useful for trade.

Everything was done in a matter of minutes. She wiped her hands clean. The men didn't have Reaper tattoos, so they must have belonged to one of the other gangs. Still, the other gangs were helping the Reapers, so Makara didn't regret their deaths in the least.

Have I really become so cold? Makara asked.

She would have to become even colder to survive this city, and after that, the Wasteland. If she even made it that far.

She judged it was dark enough to move on, which she

promptly did. The main bulk of L.A. had been left behind with the passing of the hills. If she got through the next few settlements, and finally, Last Town, she'd be well on her way.

Chapter 46

Those two men were not the last of Makara's victims.

She killed another she happened upon at night on the highway, an old man who thought she wouldn't have the stomach to kill him. He came forward with groping hands that meant to disarm her and then do far worse. She fired and left him for the carrion birds, after taking away his food and cigarettes.

She avoided fights where she could, and bigger crowds. It seemed a lot of folks were on the highway these days, all heading west. It wasn't just soldiers and bikers, but chain gangs of slaves, too. Makara veered north, out of the way of the highway settlements.

Makara was fast realizing that the era of the Reaper had begun. Makara knew that without having to be told. Raine and the Lost Angels were no more. With Raine gone, all the Angels' former territory would be gobbled up by the jackals.

She skirted the southern part of the mountains, running into few people up that way. The path was longer, but safer. When she reached San Bernardino, the town was practically empty. Makara was almost tempted to walk through it, but she knew that would be foolish. A girl on the road was a target, and people would always think of her as someone to be taken advantage of unless she made them think otherwise. Better to avoid confrontations, where possible. If she was forced to fire her gun, it was not just a waste of bullets, but a broadcasting of her position to any creep in a two miles radius.

When she reached I-10 again, she had no choice but to follow it east out of San Bernardino. She walked on an empty highway until the outskirts of the greater L.A. metropolitan area was replaced by dry desert and a smattering of crumbling buildings. The monotony was broken when, between two ranges of mountains, she reached the wooden walls of Last Town. When she stood before the gates, which covered most of the highway, an armed guard hailed her from above.

"Lost your daddy, girl?"

The barb did not hurt Makara. Her skin was thicker than rawhide by this point.

"Just a traveler seeking passage through," she said coolly. "I'm bearing a message for Ohlan Rogers."

That erased the man's quippy smile. "Ohlan? He's not here. What's your business with him?"

"My business with him is none of yours," Makara snapped. "Open the gate or you'll never hear the end of it when I reach him."

"I can't open the gate," he said. "Do you have the Red Sickness?"

Makara frowned. "What's that?"

"Don't play smart with me, girl." At Makara's lack of response, the guard continued. "All right, hold your horses. Stay put and I'll have someone come over."

Makara didn't have to wait long. The guard came down and opened the gate. Before Makara could enter, he held up a hand, along with his gun. Another old man stood beside him, with a thick, white mustache and wild, snowy hair.

"This is Doctor Evans," the guard said. "He'll need to examine you before you can enter."

Makara immediately raised her gun. "No one's touching me."

The old man looked appalled and held two hands up. "Don't worry. I just need to have a look into your eyes and mouth, if you can stomach that much."

"No," Makara said. "I just need to pass through. I don't have to stay long."

The old man blinked. "There's nothing out there in the Wasteland, child. Nothing but death for one such as you."

"I'll manage," Makara said. "I made it all the way here from Compton on my own, I think I can manage the rest of the way to Ohlan." She eyed him critically. "Any news of him passing through here?"

Dr. Evans looked even more shocked, if such a thing was possible. The gate guard watched the interaction with interest.

"Young lady," Dr. Evans began, "we're not going to let you pass through here until I deem you to be of good health. After that, well, I suppose you can ask around for news about Ohlan. I know nothing about that, but perhaps Mayor Bliss will know something."

Makara nodded. There seemed to be no other way. "All right. Let's get this over with."

Makara condescended to have her mouth and eyes examined, and the whole process was over in less than thirty seconds.

"All right," Dr. Evans said, pulling back. "She's clean."

"Looks like you can pass through," the guard said to Makara. "Don't cause any trouble."

Makara didn't give any response to that. "Should be out of your hair soon, don't worry."

Despite her tough words, she was nervous about walking through the town on her own. She'd never been in a proper town like this. Raine and Angels had more souls under their care than a town this size, but this was a community she knew nothing about.

Makara wasn't sure how it would differ from the mall, exactly, but she supposed there was only one way of finding out.

Feigning confidence, she stepped through the gate and walked down the highway, on either side of which were shabbily assembled buildings of wood and corrugated metal. People either worked in the fields of growing crops on the highway's sides or sat on their porches. Almost everyone looked up at her while she passed. A girl with a heavy pack, a handgun, and an AR-15 was quite the sight, but no one made a move to deprive her of her possessions.

That alone seemed noteworthy to Makara. There was law and order here, unlike the ruins she'd just come from.

She walked up to the largest building she could find, made from two floors rather than one, and looking less shabby from the rest. A sign was painted over its front door: Town Hall.

Makara opened the door and walked inside.

THERE WAS no one inside as Makara walked up to the empty desk ahead of her. She began rummaging through it, seeing if there might be anything useful to pilfer.

A throat cleared from behind her.

Makara turned to see an old lady with a bun and faded floral dress looking at her severely.

"Can I help you with something, dear?" Only now did she notice Makara's armament. "Dear heavens!"

"Don't worry," Makara said, feeling bad for giving the old lady a scare. "I won't shoot you as long as no one in this town tries to hurt me."

"I see," the woman said, leery. "Well, Mayor Bliss does well in keeping the rule of law here. You don't have to walk in here guns a-blazing just to defend yourself."

"Huh," Makara said, as if the concept were foreign to her.

"I've been told that a Mayor Bliss can tell me where Ohlan Rogers went. I have a message for him."

"Ah," the old lady said. "I'm his secretary. Ohlan passed through here a few months back. He took some of our folk with him, to start a new settlement in the Wasteland." She shook her head disapprovingly. "Mayor Bliss will not remember him too fondly."

"I need to find Ohlan," Makara said. "It . . . it was his brother's dying wish."

"Oh, dear. Well. Have a seat there and I'll go fetch the mayor for you. I'm sure he'll appreciate whatever news you have of what's going on out west."

Makara just did that, settling down in the chair to take a load off, while not totally letting down her guard. The old lady left, and a few minutes later returned with a middle-aged man wearing glasses and a gray mustache.

"This is her, then?" he asked.

The old lady nodded. "Yes. I didn't catch her name."

"Makara," she said, simply.

"Makara," he said. "You look a little older than my daughter." He looked at her guns cautiously, but didn't ask her to hand them over, for which Makara was thankful. "I hear you're asking after Ohlan Rogers."

Makara could see the mayor didn't like Ohlan very much just from his tone, which immediately raised her opinion of him.

"I'm not doing it by choice," she said. "His brother wanted me to pass on the message that he had died. For that, though, I need to know where Ohlan headed."

"Well, I wouldn't be opposed to telling you what I know if you can let me know what's going on in L.A."

Makara shrugged. "Sounds fair."

The mayor gave a satisfied nod, at last taking up a spot behind the central desk across from Makara. "Oh, I'd say he passed through here several months back. Persuasive fellow.

We had to kick him out, but that didn't stop a lot of our people from following him. Why they'd follow him out into the Wasteland, I don't know. Said he'd found a good water source, well-hidden. Don't know how he knew that. Apparently, they've set up quite the town out there."

"Where did they go?" Makara asked.

"From what I gathered, they found a source of water to the northeast, at a place they're calling Oasis," the mayor said. "Said he had some schematics and parts to get an old machine there working again."

"Why would people follow him in the first place?" Makara asked. "This place doesn't look half bad."

"It wouldn't be half bad, if it weren't for those Reapers," the mayor said. "People are scared of them, and Ohlan said they'd lick us if we didn't follow him out there and start fresh."

Makara nodded at that. When the time came, she had no doubt that Carin Black would crush this place like a bug. She didn't express that opinion, though.

"Now, I wouldn't mind pointing you in the right direction," Mayor Bliss said. "If you give me some information as well."

"A nice meal, too," Makara said. "And maybe some supplies to make the journey."

"Sure, sure," the mayor said, amiably. "Jaz, why don't go find this young lady a warm lunch?"

"Sure," Jaz said, after a moment's hesitation. She was probably wondering why she had to cater to a teenager, but she wasn't going to disobey the mayor.

"Now," Mayor Bliss said, sitting down behind the desk finally, "you came from the west, that much I can see. What's going on that way?"

Makara told him the news, such as she figured it. She left out the parts about Raine and her brother, of course, but basically communicated that the Lost Angels were all but done for. She was surprised how cold and controlled her voice was as she related it. It scared her, even, but she couldn't allow any of those feelings to get in the way. She didn't want the mayor to think she was an Angel, too. She didn't want to volunteer any information about herself.

The mayor listened with a scrutinizing expression, twisting his mustache while his thick brows scrunched up in the middle of his forehead. To Makara, he looked soft and intellectual. She didn't know how a man like him could survive so long. There must have been something about him that she just wasn't seeing.

When Makara's food came, she ate it ravenously: chicken, corn, and beans, all covered generously with a spicy gravy. Within minutes she was full and licking her plate clean. Prosperous place, too, if they could afford to feed a stranger such rich fare.

"Guess they don't cook like that out west, huh?" the mayor asked.

Makara nodded, eating until while gesturing the mayor to continue talking.

"Well, I'd say you earned it," Mayor Bliss said. "The news you shared has me worried, to say the least."

"What about Ohlan?" Makara asked, wanting to get down to business.

"You don't waste time," the mayor said. "Well, some of the men are saying he was headed due north of here, once you got past the mountains. Say, you don't intend to go out there all on your own?"

Makara felt a sliver of doubt, but then she remembered what Raine had said: to find Ohlan. He would have never told her to do that if he thought the task impossible. "I've got no choice, Mayor."

He leaned back in his chair. "I see. Well, at least stay the night, Makara, and I'll even make sure you have a good breakfast to see you on your way."

"I'd like that," Makara said.

Mayor Bliss invited Jaz back in, who had been waiting outside during the meeting.

"What's the verdict?" she asked. "If she's to stay here, I wouldn't mind taking her down to the schoolhouse. Penelope should still be there."

"She's heading to Oasis," Mayor Bliss said.

Jaz looked at him as if he were crazy. "Mayor, that's got to be a hundred miles, and that's supposing the fools aren't all dead by now. How do you expect a young girl to make it all that way?"

"I get the feeling Makara here won't take no for an answer," he said. "I would honor Raine Rogers' dying wish."

"But for a girl to go out there, with the cold and the raiders and the dust storms . . ."

"She won't go alone," the mayor said. "I'll send Jack and Elliott with her, good men both. They'll see her safely there."

Makara cringed at that, and felt a bit of a panic. "There's no need for that, Mayor."

"Nonsense," he said. "I'd be remiss."

"I can do it on my own," she said, dangerously. "I won't take anyone with me."

The two adults shared a troubled glance, but they saw that she really meant it.

"Stubborn child," Jaz said, crossing her arms. "You'll die out there on your own."

So be it, Makara said, but Makara didn't trust having anyone she didn't know coming with her.

"Well, it's improper," the mayor said. "But if she's made it all this way on her own . . ."

Makara hadn't mentioned the three men she'd killed just getting here. She had hoped she wouldn't have to.

"I can tell she's tough," Jaz said, uncertainly. "Certainly, she's that."

"I'll have my breakfast at six a.m., if it please you,"

248

Makara said, standing up. "Do you have a place I can lay down and catch some sleep? This porch would do just fine."

Both adults seemed aghast at the suggestion.

"You can stay with me, dear," Jaz said, in a tone brooking no argument "I can't stop you from heading out and finishing your errand, but the least you can do is get a good night's rest in front of a fire."

That sounded good to Makara, even if the old lady wanted her to stay behind and not finish her mission.

"I'd feel better about that, too," the mayor said. "If you must do this, Makara, then neither of us will stop you. Just remember us when you're done. You'll have a safe place here. I don't much trust that Ohlan, even if some of our own were foolish enough to follow him."

"I'll remember that, Mayor," Makara said. She would have liked nothing more than to stay on a little longer. Misguided as they were, both the mayor and his secretary seemed to be good people. Last Town might be a place she could let her guard down a bit, but that could only come after she delivered her message to Ohlan.

Makara was led out of the town hall and set up in Jaz's home, a wooden cabin that was well-made on the east side of town. It was humble, being only a couple of rooms, but it was far more luxurious than anywhere Makara had ever lived. She plopped her pack in the corner and sat in front of the fire, warming her hands.

"My husband's name was Edgar," Jaz said, once both were inside. "Built this cabin with timber from the mountains, and helped James build the town and its walls."

"James?"

"The mayor." She smiled down at Makara. "It's been lonely without my husband, so it'll be nice to have company."

Makara felt nothing at Jaz's sentimentality. She didn't know how to handle it. "I think I'm going to sleep now."

"All right," Jaz said. "I'll come back around nightfall. Might make a warm, nice stew."

Makara nodded, and Jaz closed the door behind her.

She stared into the flames for a while, seeming to see in them the destruction of Los Angeles, a city already destroyed. This new reality she found herself in, this peaceful cabin, seemed like another life. Something unreal. She held her hand in front of her and was surprised to feel it shaking.

Samuel. Raine.

She pushed their names from her head. They were dead, now. There was no use mourning what you could never get back.

She closed her eyes, but sleep wouldn't come, not for a long time. She saw them both and felt the guilt that she had been the one to get away.

Your purpose is not over. You must survive. Your purpose is not over. You must survive. Your purpose is not over . . .

Makara slept, the refrain resonating in her mind.

Chapter 47

Jaz returned that evening and fixed up the stew. Makara had been facing the wall and crying but stopped almost as soon as she heard the old woman's steps on the porch.

She dried her face and pretended to be asleep. When Jaz called her to dinner half an hour later, the old woman could tell that something was wrong.

"Your face is all puffy, dear. Have you been crying?"

Makara shook her head vehemently. "Just tired."

She accepted a bowl of potato soup and began eating gratefully. It had good flavor, with bits of bacon, onion, and garlic in it.

"Soup's always welcome on these cold evenings," Jaz said, making conversation. "When I was your age, it was never cold like this here, especially this time of year. But of course, after the Rock fell . . ."

Makara nodded. She'd heard it all before. The meteor dust would keep it cold for decades more. To this day, Makara had never seen the full brightness of the sun, and none but the brightest of stars and planets shining at night. The dust wasn't expected to settle for decades at least, and more likely centuries.

By then, she figured, what was left of humanity would be dead. She ate another mouthful of stew.

"I'm here, if you need to get anything off your chest, Makara."

Makara shook her head. "I'm fine, Jaz. I don't want you to think I'm ungrateful. I am. It's hard to talk about stuff and I don't think it'll help, to be honest."

Jaz considered for a moment. "I understand. Remember what James told you. There's a home for you here. You can stay as long as you like."

Makara nodded, and tried not to let her emotions show. "I'll remember that. I have to do this, though. For Raine."

Makara left it at that. She helped Jaz to wash the bowls and stoke the fire, and after that, Jaz read out of a book for her. Makara listened to a story from a time she would never understand or know, something about a group of kids trying to solve a crime. It was hard for her to believe that those kids were the same age as her. The way they talked about death made it seem as if they had never actually experienced it first-hand. The concept was foreign to her.

She fell asleep a few chapters in.

WHEN MAKARA AWOKE, it was still dark outside. She got up quickly, started to pack, and heard Jaz stir in her bed in the corner.

"Leaving already? At least stay for breakfast, I'll have something ready in a jiff."

Makara nodded, and Jaz set to work, cooking some pancakes on a cast iron pan set over the coals. Makara ate while Jaz cleaned up.

Jaz packed a few more supplies in Makara's bag, including some homemade granola bars and sandwiches, and made sure her water was topped off. She even gave her a few extra bottles, with the admonition that she should return them one day, so she'd see her again. Makara wanted to refuse, but Jaz insisted, so she promised to bring them back, even though she knew it would probably never happen.

Last of all, Jaz gave her a heavier coat, dug from deep inside one of the old woman's drawers. She looked at the coat longingly for a moment, and then gave it to Makara.

"This belonged to my daughter, Catherine," she said. She smiled wistfully. "Don't know why I kept it all these years. She didn't survive long after the fall. She was about your size." As Makara looked at it, Jaz said, "Try it on."

It was a little loose, but it came with a belt that made it easily cinched up. The extra size would allow Makara to grow into it, or even to store things hidden from others.

"I don't know what to say," Makara said. "Thank you."

"It's dreadfully cold out there," Jaz said. "Remember to wear layers and to take shelter when a storm comes a-blowing. Grown men die out there from nothing more than the weather. I still have half a mind to stop you, but I can tell you'll get out of here all the same, lest we tie you up."

Jaz smiled to show that this was a joke, but Makara didn't find it funny.

"Will the guards let me out?" Makara asked.

"I can walk with you to the gate," Jaz said. "In case the mayor hasn't given the proper orders."

Once Makara's new coat was secure, and her boots laced up, she shouldered her pack and walked out the door.

Together, they passed through the dark town toward the east gate. Makara could see gray tinging the sky above the wooden walls. Daybreak would come soon, and with it, she could hopefully put a lot of miles toward Oasis.

Once they reached the gate, Jaz gave some last-minute advice.

"Be sparing with that water, now. You'll find a few towns between here and there, mostly safe, if not as safe as here. If you tell them your mission, I'm sure they'll let you pass on through. Ohlan's respected out there, so you'll be under his protection. No one will want to cross him."

Makara felt a tinge of fear. Her journey to here from southern L.A. hadn't been voluntary. Now, though, she was making the choice to leave. If Raine knew that she could have a safe life here, would he have wanted her to stay? Makara pondered the question, but ultimately, she didn't know the answer.

All she knew was to honor Raine's last wishes. Her future, if she had any, was in Oasis. Despite her misgivings about Raine's brother, she had to deliver the news.

"If you can find a caravan, join up with it," Jaz said. "You'll find them in the towns sometimes, and they'll let you come along for a few batts or offering your security services, or maybe grooming and taking care of their livestock."

Makara nodded. "Got it."

"Remember what I told you, child," Jaz said. "Come back. You're welcome here and we'll find a place for you."

"Goodbye, Jaz," Makara said. "You be careful, too. The Reapers are not just going to stop with the Angels."

Jaz's eyes became worried for a moment, but then it was erased by her smile. "Don't you worry about us. James is a smart man, and I'm sure he knows how to handle the Reapers."

Makara felt sorry for her. If Raine and the Angels hadn't stood a chance, how much worse off would Last Town be?

"I should go," Makara said.

Jaz hugged her, which Makara wasn't ready for, but she let herself be held for a couple of seconds before wrangling herself free. Jaz signaled the gate guard, and the wooden door rolled back, revealing the dusty road leading into the red desert pockmarked with mesas and hills. Several dilapidated buildings littered the scene, but otherwise, there wasn't much else besides a whole lot of nothing.

But it was the start of the Wasteland, and once Makara entered it, little did she know, she would not be returning to this side of the mountains for many years.

Chapter 48

Makara had never felt more lonesome than at that moment. She felt stupid, too, for having left. How could Raine have expected her to survive out here? He probably hadn't counted on anyone showing her kindness and mercy, but Makara owed it to him to finish what she and Samuel had promised to do.

Samuel was no longer here, too. That meant it fell on her shoulders and her shoulders alone.

The burden was a heavy one.

When she circled a hill, aiming north, she was out of sight of Last Town for good. She started crying. The frigid wind blew, kicking dust into her face. She wrapped everything below her nose in a scarf she'd packed in her bag.

Get a handle on yourself, she thought. *Tears are a waste of water.*

The thought made her laugh manically for a good minute, to the point where she wondered whether she was going crazy.

"Don't go crazy yet," she thought. "Wait till we get there. *Then* we can really go crazy."

The sun rose, shining red on the wasted surface of the horizon. She passed through empty ghost towns, the buildings decaying, and windows empty of glass. Half-buried rubbish lined the streets. The paint was faded, and the letters of signs were nearly illegible. Almost as soon as she entered these places, she was passing through. No one lived there anymore. There was nothing left in them.

She realized, after the second small town she passed in the early afternoon, that it probably wasn't a good idea to head into these places. There could be people lurking within the buildings, as uninhabitable as they seemed. This suspicion was confirmed when she came across the remains of a campfire in an alley that appeared fresh. It was the first sign of life she'd seen all day out here.

Like the ruins of L.A., people would be best avoided. This certainly didn't look like a land of plenty, so she was sure people would try to nab whatever they could from her.

She ate while walking, trying to close the distance to Oasis as quickly as possible. She followed the road north and didn't come upon a single soul.

When it got too dark to keep moving, she went off road, climbing under some desert scrub that would provide at least some protection from the wind and prying eyes.

It was cold. Very cold. Makara longed to start a fire, but she didn't dare do it. She ate under the brush, and tried to use some of the scrub and her backpack to keep her off the cold ground. It helped, but her thin blanket wasn't enough to keep the cold at bay.

Nonetheless, she was so exhausted that she fell into a fitful sleep, with dreams full of Samuel, Raine, and Reapers.

～

WHEN MAKARA WOKE, she was so stiff she could hardly move. She forced herself to get up, and did her best to brush the brambles off her coat and hair. She had a few nicks and scratches, but that was the price she had to pay for safety.

There was no one on the road, so Makara followed it

north. All she knew was to go north, but unlike what Jaz had told her, she passed through no occupied settlements.

That would change later in the afternoon, when she came to a small town with dirty and ragged buildings with several fields of crops growing next to a small stream.

When Makara entered, she was stared down by a few of the town's shabby, thin denizens. This town was clearly far less prosperous than Last Town and didn't even have a wall. Makara got a bad feeling from the place, but she needed information to know whether she was on the right track.

She was quickly approached by a tall, thin old man wearing a wide-brimmed hat and patchy overalls, so ratty that they were almost falling off his boney shoulders. "Who are you, and what brings you here to New Barstow?"

A woman, similarly thin, along with another man, this one the oldest of all with a dirty face, gathered around. Their eyes looked unnaturally large in their sunken faces.

Makara did her best to project confidence. "I'm looking for Ohlan and Oasis. I've got a message for him from Raine in L.A."

The first man smacked his lips a few times. "I can help you with that. It'll cost you, though."

The others nodded their agreement. "What've you got in there, love?" the woman asked, her eyes beady and hungry.

"None of your business," Makara said, reaching for her handgun. The others backed up as she did so. It didn't seem any of them had weapons.

"She's bluffing," the old man said. "She ain't got nothing in there."

"I don't want to use it," Makara said. "I've killed three men on my way here, and I don't want that number to go up six today."

The warning was enough. They made no further move to try and reach her bag.

"Now, where can I find Ohlan?" Makara asked.

"We want food first," the woman said, spitting on the ground.

"I need my food," Makara said.

"I guess we won't tell you nothing, then," the old woman said. "Be gone, brat."

The woman turned away, and reluctantly, the two men followed her.

Makara waited a moment, and then called out. "Fine. I'll give each of you a sandwich if you tell me where he is."

The woman stopped and turned around. "You'll have to do better than that, love."

"I got something I can give her," the skeevy old man said, licking his lips. His teeth, Makara saw, were yellow and rotting.

"Shut your trap, Clarence," she said. "She's a child." She looked at Makara, appraisingly. "Still, we would need more than just a sandwich. Give us whatever food you've got, and we'll tell you where to find him."

"I'm not giving everything I have," Makara said. "How else would I make it there?"

"The girl has a point, Marnie," the old man said.

Marnie narrowed her eyes. "What've you got besides sandwiches?"

"I'll throw in some jerky, one stick for each of you. That's my best offer. And I only give it to you if I like what I hear."

The three conferred for a moment. After half a minute, the old woman, who seemed to be the ringleader, nodded. "All right. We accept that."

Makara reached into her pack, keeping her eye on the three old people, trying to push down her disgust. They seemed to be the town's only occupants. Where had everyone gone?

"Hand us that jerky first," the woman said, wetting her lips. "Then, we'll tell you everything. After we're done, you give the sandwiches." She held out her hand. "Deal?"

Makara ignored the hand and backed away a few steps, keeping her hand on her holstered handgun. "Sounds good to me."

Once Makara had the three sticks of jerky, she showed them, and handed them to the man in the overalls, who seemed a safer bet than the depraved old one.

The three tore into them like coyotes in a chicken coop while Makara watched, equal measures disgusted and feeling bad for them.

"All right," she said. "Tell me all about Ohlan."

The woman was done eating first, smacking her lips. "We don't much like him. He left us behind. Promised to bring us to his new town. Took the rest of the town with him, but left us three behind." She spat. "Said we were too old, a drain on resources." The old woman eyed Makara from head to toe. "Oh, he would like you enough, though. Don't you worry. Maybe you can put in a good word for us." She cackled madly.

That sounded like Ohlan, leaving behind the old folks to starve. Makara felt sorry for them, despite their rough appearance. Hunger had a way of twisting people into the worst version of themselves.

"Where did he go?"

The woman pointed with her chin. "Not far. Twenty miles that-a-way. The road leads right to it."

That was it? Makara could have just kept walking up the road, as she would have done originally, and saved herself the food. She could keep moving on herself, now. Didn't look like any of these folks had a gun, either. She might just keep those sandwiches.

But, despite knowing these people would have taken advantage of her if they could, Makara decided not to do the same. She reached into her pack and passed out the sandwiches.

"Thanks for the information," she said.

The three starving people tore into the food while she went on her way. She glanced back every half minute to make sure she wasn't being tailed, but the old folks were already back inside whatever building they had come from. The road went over a barren hill, after which New Barstow was thankfully out of sight.

Chapter 49

The old ones' information seemed to be correct. Makara passed a couple of folks on the road. One old man led a couple of laden pack mules, and was armed to the teeth, but seemed cordial enough, tipping his Stetson to Makara while he passed. The other one she passed was an old woman in rags, who crossed her path, mumbled something, and wandered out into the desert with nary a glance her way. She had made Makara more nervous than the man with the guns.

By late afternoon, she was making good time. By the onset of evening, she rounded a hill and the road took her directly ahead to a large, walled settlement, with thick wooden gates with manned turrets on either side. Makara jogged up to those gates, and the guard from above hailed her.

"Who goes there? State your business."

"I'm here to see Ohlan," Makara called up. "I have a message from his brother, Raine."

The man stared down at her for a long moment, as if trying to guess her game. After half a minute, he responded.

"All right. Let me talk to someone, I'll be right back."

Makara waited for well over ten minutes before the gates started to creak open, revealing a prosperous town within filled with people. Either side of the street was lined with wooden buildings, recently constructed, while the street between them forged ahead to a body of water.

This was Oasis, Makara had no doubt about that. Makara stepped inside, and was met with the guard, as well as a couple of men bearing rifles. One of them she recognized; he was one of Ohlan's cronies back in Lost Angels' days, though she didn't know his name.

Lost Angels' days. It still felt wrong to think of that in the past tense.

"That's Makara," he said. "Raine's adopted daughter."

He frowned at her. "You made it all this way on your own?"

Makara nodded. "I have a message for Ohlan, and Ohlan alone."

"One thing first," he said. "Open your mouth. You don't look sick, but we got to make sure."

Makara rolled her eyes, but knew there was nothing she could do about that. The process was mostly painless, and she was cleared, just as she had been in Last Town.

"Ohlan will see you now," the man said. "This way."

Makara followed the man and another guard through the street. People watched her pass from the stoops of buildings. There were dozens of them. She could easily tell that this was a town of at least two hundred people. As she approached the oasis itself, she could see that there were more buildings and homes on its other side. From somewhere in the town, she heard the ring of a hammer on metal. A smithy, maybe.

This is what Ohlan had wanted, then. A community that he could control and not be second. It looked like he had gotten what he wanted.

There was a central building, larger than the rest, built of wood and completely circular, that looked to be about two floors. It was into this building that Makara was led by the two guards. Its interior was lit by blazing torches. No power out here, then. At least the Angels had managed that much.

They took Makara to a back room, where Ohlan sat eating with two women. It looked to be a rich feast; a whole cooked chicken over potatoes, onions, and garlic, with a large bowl of mixed salad, and even a dish containing what looked like pudding. Ohlan gestured toward an empty chair.

"Have a seat, Makara." His voice was gruff, but amiable. The two women, both pretty, looked at Makara curiously at first, and then with suspicion. Makara did her best to push down her anger and hatred of him. Something of her mood must have showed to the women, who were both staring daggers at her.

"Don't be mean, ladies," Ohlan chided. "This is Makara, my brother's adopted daughter." He flashed a yellow smile. "Sit down. I don't like repeating myself."

Makara sat, but didn't help herself to the food, even though she was hungry.

"I won't stay long," she said. "I've come to deliver a message."

Ohlan nodded. "I have a feeling I already know what it is."

"Raine is dead," Makara said. "He wanted you to know that."

Ohlan paused midbite, and then swallowed after a moment. He cleared his throat with a glass of beer. "Leave us," he said.

The women, without a word, stood up and left Makara alone with him.

Ohlan's sharp blue eyes looked up and regarded her. "What's the manner of his passing?"

"The Reapers attacked," Makara said, quietly. "He actually died of sickness, though. The Red Sickness, I guess they're calling it."

Ohlan nodded. "Yeah. That's been going around out here,

too." Ohlan ignore his food, turning his full attention to Makara. "How are you feeling about it?"

"Fine, I guess," Makara lied. "Raine just wanted you to know. Whatever his reasons."

"I'm sure he did," Ohlan said, his voice lowering. "Well, I guess that means I have to take care of you, now."

Makara's eyes popped at that. "What do you mean, take care of me?"

"Raine made me agree," he said. "If anything happened to him, I'd look after you."

Makara felt shock. Could Raine have said such a thing?

"I don't need taking care of," Makara said. "I made it all the way out here on my own."

"Yes, I'm sure you did," Ohlan said. "A promise is a promise, though. You might not think much of me, Makara, but I did love my brother. Our methods were different. But I never betrayed him. Not once." He paused thoughtfully. "Well, except when I struck out on my own. But that couldn't be helped."

"You used me," Makara said. "You'll do the same thing again. How could Raine ever make you promise such a thing? How could he ever trust you?"

"The world is tough," Ohlan said. "It's better me watching over you than for you to be on your own, with no one to protect you or Samuel." Ohlan eyed her. "I don't see him here, so I have to assume that he died somewhere along the way."

Makara nodded. "He did. Back in L.A."

Ohlan nodded, as if he had suspected that. "Well, Raine made me promise that I'd take care of you if something happened to the Angels. I knew it would, eventually. I suppose I just didn't expect to see you so soon."

Makara could hardly even process this news. Raine had never let her know. If he had, she might have never come out here in the first place.

"I don't need you, Ohlan," Makara said. "I met a lady in Last Town. She said she'd take care of me."

Ohlan gave a bark of a laugh. "Last Town? I hope you didn't get too attached to anyone there. They won't last the year."

Makara blinked. "That soon?"

"Last Town controls the main way into L.A. from the east," he said. "Black will want to control it eventually. It forms a perfect eastern border for his territory."

"We have to warn them," Makara said.

"I did," Ohlan said. "Anyone smart enough to see the writing on the wall came with me."

Makara remembered Mayor Bliss mentioning that.

"You can't stop people from digging their own graves," Ohlan said. "All we can do is stop ourselves from digging with them." He frowned, considering. "Just take my brother as an example."

Makara jumped out of her chair and started throwing punches at Ohlan. He easily held her back while the two guards came into the room. They pulled her away from their master.

"You take that back!" Makara said. All the emotions she had been bottling up burst forth, like too much water behind a damn. She feebly attempted to punch Ohlan some more, but was restrained. Ohlan was brushing off his pants, where some cornbread had fallen on him.

"I don't blame you for being angry, Makara," Ohlan said, signaling for the men to let her go. "I'm angry, too. I tried warning him of what was going to happen. Many times. But you know how Raine is. He likes to deal with things directly, and wouldn't let me do anything too dirty go get ahead."

"You could have gotten me killed, Ohlan," Makara said. She still wasn't calm, but she could at least keep herself from punching him.

Ohlan shrugged. "Those were desperate times. The

Angels needed a leader to take aggressive risks to win an unwinnable war." Ohlan shook his head sadly. "Raine was not that leader, as good a man as he was."

"You don't seem sad he's dead," Makara said.

"Don't let my looks fool you. I've never been one to show emotion. People always joked I'd be a serial killer someday when I was a kid." Ohlan laughed humorlessly. "I don't know. Maybe they were right. But hey, look where I am now. I'm warlord of Oasis, with two hundred souls under my charge. I got a wife and a mistress, and neither of them seem to mind."

He laughed again, as if this were a great joke, but Makara was just thinking about how she could get out of there. She'd forgotten just how much she hated him. It seemed as if getting even a little bit of power had just amplified all his worst qualities.

"Well, I'm sorry about Raine, but truth be told, Makara, he was practically dead in my mind the minute I left. I knew that'd be the last I saw him. Everyone who followed me out here saw much the same."

"You're a coward," Makara said. "A disloyal traitor."

"Nah, I'm neither of those," Ohlan said. "I'll take shrewd and insightful, though. And realistic. I'm nothing if not realistic."

Makara found she had nothing else to say. She had come here for Raine, and maybe Raine had thought she'd be best in Ohlan's hands, but Raine had been delirious at the end. If Raine could see his brother now, then Makara had no doubt that he'd want her to head back to Last Town.

Who knew? Maybe she could convince Mayor Bliss and the rest to strike out into the Wasteland on their own, just as Ohlan had.

"You ever want to know what Cyrus got me when I was using you as a bargaining tool?" Ohlan asked.

Makara felt disgust at the question but couldn't help her curiosity. "What?"

"Information," he said. "And tools. That information came in the form of a map that led me to this place. And the tools were specifically ordered to get the water pump here working again. Essentially, for gambling your life and my place in the Angels, I won freedom, and saved a couple of hundred lives. Including yours, Makara."

"What do you mean, including mine?"

"You don't see it yet? Well, Oasis is your only chance at growing up in a safe place. There aren't any real water sources for fifty miles all around. For that reason alone, we're pretty safe from attack, and even if raiders from Raider Bluff made it out this far, they'd be met by the walls manned by my men, who have plenty of ammunition. In the space of a year, we've gone from nothing to being top dog. Or close to it."

"I don't want to grow up here," Makara said. "I'll take my chances back in Last Town."

"The choice is out of your hands, Makara. I won't let you out. And if you think you can *sneak* out, well, you'll be surprised at how hard that'll be. Besides, why would you want to leave? Last Town is toast. Where else are you going to stay, New Barstow?" Ohlan laughed at that.

"Shame on you for leaving those poor people behind," Makara said.

"They're dead weight," Ohlan said. "No one really liked them much, anyway. You have to pull your weight to live here, of course. You can join the kids at the schoolhouse tomorrow."

"No," Makara said.

"Come on, Makara. Be reasonable. Where are you going to go?"

Ohlan waited for an answer, and Makara found she didn't have one. Where *could* she go? She was all alone in the world.

All alone, with only Ohlan for protection. It was her worst nightmare. She might as well have died on the way here. That probably would have been a kinder fate.

How could you do this to me, Raine? Did you even know what you were getting me into?

She wanted nothing more than to run, but she knew that was impossible. She imagined they'd probably be confiscating her weapons, too. What was the other option, trying to shoot her way out? If she managed that against all odds, *then* what?

Death, Makara thought. *Starvation and death.*

Raine had wanted her here because he saw it as the best chance for her survival. Oasis would have to do, at least for now. She'd live here, contribute however they told her to, even go to school, as Ohlan had said.

None of that meant she had to stay forever. An opportunity would present itself to leave. And, it would give her time to plan her revenge. Revenge for Carin Black for what he'd done to Raine and the Angels.

"All right," Makara said. "I'll stay here."

Ohlan nodded. "That's what I thought."

"Not because I want to," Makara said. "For Raine."

"The reasons don't matter," Ohlan said. "My oath is fulfilled." His cold blue eyes went to her weapons. "You'll have to give those up, of course."

Makara nodded. "I know."

"You'll get them back as soon as you prove yourself," Ohlan said. "Might be sooner than you think."

"If I kiss your ass, you mean."

Ohlan smirked. "Well, a lot of people around here seem to think that's the way to my heart. I don't care much about that. I care about results."

"Where will I stay?"

"Well, since it's late, we have a boarding house near the gate you can stay in. I'll have one of my guys lead you there. Someone will get you tomorrow. Give you a tour of the town, drop you off at the schoolhouse." Ohlan smiled. "The teacher, Emelia, followed me from Last Town, like a lot of the others. Maybe it's her I'll send to fetch you tomorrow." Ohlan nodded toward the food. "Help yourself. Me and my ladies were done, anyway. If there's nothing else . . ."

Makara shook her head. "Not that I can think of."

"Let my guard know when you're done."

Ohlan retired, leaving Makara alone in the dining room. She ate until full, not really relishing the food. Makara didn't complain, though, even taking some of the food to bring with her for later.

When she was ready to leave, the guard asked for her weapons. This was the true test. After a moment, she reluctantly handed over her AR-15, handgun, and the ammo in her pack. The guard eyed the carbine approvingly, as if he himself might take it.

"At least wait till you're done with me before admiring your new weapon," Makara said, with a growl.

The man just laughed. "I'll take that pack, too."

He opened the pack, and only took a few seconds to sort through it. He handed it back to Makara, after determining nothing inside could be construed as contraband.

"Follow me," he said.

Makara followed him down Oasis's dark main drag. Most of the people were indoors by now, but she spied a few heads looking at her from the interior rooms. It felt as if she were being watched by ghosts.

"The warlord must think a lot of you," the guard said. "Did you really know Raine?"

Makara nodded. "I did."

"Lucky you," he said. "Ohlan isn't taking on anyone knew here. We turn away at least a dozen folks every day."

He said nothing else, until Makara was brought to the boarding house, a log cabin with a single entrance. When she was led inside, there were twelve bunks on one side with a small wooden table and hearth on the side. There were only a few logs in the fireplace, and Makara would have to light it herself. Looking around, all the bunks were empty. At least she'd have the place to herself.

Without so much as a goodbye, the guard shut the door behind her. Makara was left in silence.

She got a fire going soon enough, and brought in a few more logs from outside. Makara wondered where Ohlan was getting the wood. Trade caravans must already be passing through Oasis and dropping off their wares. She hadn't seen so much as a tree on her way here, except in the mountains by Last Town.

Once the fire brought some warmth and light, Makara lay down on the nearest bunk, kicking off her boots. Now alone with her thoughts, she found that there was nothing comforting in them. She started to shake, and once again, the tears came to her eyes.

She was alone again, and being stuck in Ohlan's town where everyone worshipped him was practically her worst nightmare. She would live, but she didn't know what the point of living was.

First, she had lost everyone in her family but Samuel. Then, she had lost her second family with the Angels and Sam, too. Everyone she'd come to know, trust, and love was dead.

"What's the point?" she asked.

She stared into the flames for what seemed hours, despair making her go cold. She didn't want to do this anymore. With her guns gone, the easy way out was, too.

There was nothing but to sleep and see what the morning brought.

Chapter 50

A knock woke Makara up, and by the time she opened her eyes and was shielding herself against the red morning light, a young woman wearing a long green dress with long sleeves entered and stood next to the table, watching her. She had shoulder-length black hair, along with a pinched, but pretty, face.

"Hello," she said, pleasantly enough. "My name is Emelia. I teach over at the schoolhouse?"

She said it as a question. Makara coughed and took a swig of water she kept by her bed.

"Oh yeah," she said, groggily. "Ohlan said he might send you."

Makara got out of bed, still fully dressed from the day before. Emelia frowned at her dirty state.

"He didn't even have a *bath* brought? Well, there's no time for that, now."

There was no time for Makara to sit at the table and eat, either. She had to take the leftovers from last night and eat on the way. She stuffed the food into her mouth while Emelia gave her the tour. The exterior farms, the shops, the trading square where the caravans came two times a week, the homes, the blacksmith. Though Makara tried not to show it, she was impressed. Everything in the town looked fresh and new, and the people milling about on their business were laughing and joking with each other. It looked like there was plenty of food to go around.

"When Ohlan told me where you had come from, I could hardly believe it," Emelia said. "You'll be safe here, and you should have a permanent home, soon."

"Why did you leave Last Town?" Makara asked, suddenly.

Emelia paused. "I followed my boyfriend, George, out this way. He was convinced Ohlan was right about Last Town. That one day, the Reapers would get to it."

Makara could hardly blame her for that.

Emelia pointed at a building on the left, where children were walking in. "That's the school."

When Makara went inside, she found she was joining twenty other kids of all ages, from six to nearly Sam's age. She was one of the older ones, and everyone looked at her curiously as she took up the only empty desk, which was in the back.

She endured the lesson, about English and history, things she didn't really see the point of learning. Emelia taught out of a ratty old textbook that was clearly from before the fall of Ragnarok. Makara couldn't focus on a thing. Yesterday she'd been out in the Wasteland, trying to survive. Today, she was sitting in school, as if nothing had changed from her life in the mall.

During the lunch recess, several of the kids tried to talk to Makara, but she brushed them off. A couple of older boys tried to pick a fight, one of them trying to force a kiss out of her. Makara kicked that one hard in the balls, and he ran of squealing to Emelia. Even though she got in trouble, his friends backed off, too, and after that, no one dared talk to her.

After school was out, Emelia came up to her and asked to

go on a walk. They walked to the oasis together, around which several people were drawing their water for the evening's cooking and cleaning.

"I can tell you're not a happy child," Emelia said.

"Geez," Makara said to herself. "What gave that away?"

Emelia seemed to swallow her first response. "I want you to have a happy life here, Makara. It's the best shot we have in this world."

"What a sad thought," Makara said, not censoring herself.

"I don't know what you went through back in L.A. I'm sure it was truly horrible."

It was, Makara said. That thought she did keep to herself.

"I want you to stay with me and my boyfriend," she said. "We have a nice house, and an extra bed and blanket."

"No," Makara said.

"Makara, I know it's hard to accept help . . ."

"You don't know anything!" Makara said. She felt as if all the anger of the last couple of weeks, all the sorrow, all the injustice, was just about to make her go crazy, if it hadn't already.

Emelia was watching her sadly while Makara started crying. Emelia held her.

"Ohlan is a bad man," Makara said. "He left Raine behind to start this place. He let Raine die."

She probably didn't even know Raine was, but Emelia rubbed her back all the same. "There, there."

Makara wriggled free of her, at once wanting her comfort while wanting to lash out at her. "If only you knew what he's done . . . how he used me to get what he wanted . . . you wouldn't think so much of him."

Emelia looked back at the water, troubled. Several people were looking their direction. "I know he's not a good person, Makara. That's why I have George to take care of me. A lot of the other women . . . aren't so lucky."

Makara looked at her. She realized, for the first time, that she wasn't the only one Ohlan had hurt. Ohlan had hurt people back in L.A., so of course he was bound to hurt more here.

"We have safety. Food. Water. Items to trade to the caravans for what we can't get here naturally." Emelia shook her head. "Unfortunately, Ohlan knows that and takes advantage of his station. Anyone who doesn't agree with him doesn't have a place here for long." Emelia looked at her, her brown eyes wet with unshed tears. "I know it's not your way to keep your head down, Makara, but you're going to have to if you're going to live here. There's no way around that."

"I can't ignore who he is," Makara said. "Anyone who does is a coward."

Emelia nodded. "Fine, then. I'm a coward. We become who we must to survive, Makara."

"*I* don't," Makara said.

"You're doing it now," Emelia said. "By being here."

"*Raine* told me to come here," she said. "If I knew he meant me to live here, I would have never come."

"Maybe you're right," Emelia said. "What do you say, then?"

"To what?"

"To staying with me. I'll let you have a bed if you agree to help around the house. I won't suffer insolence, though. Save that for the ones who deserve it, not me."

Makara looked at Emelia, and immediately felt guilty. "I'm sorry. You're only trying to help me."

Emelia nodded. "I accept your apology. Come on. George will be hungry and the fire's not started yet."

Emelia walked off, and Makara hesitated only a moment before following her.

Chapter 51

S lowly, Makara settled into life at Oasis. It wasn't easy, and every day she was still mourning the loss of Samuel and Raine. She kept ruminating about the things she could have done differently, but no matter how she thought about it, she couldn't think of a way she could have saved them. She could have never known Raine would get sick from the man they'd brought back, nor could she have predicted the mortar that would cause the cellar to collapse on Samuel.

At least Raine was with his daughter and wife now, while Samuel was with their parents. All Makara could do was push down the feelings of grief and sadness until they were so small that they were barely noticeable.

There was little time for grief, anyway. Emelia didn't much ask about her past, while George was even quieter. The bearded man was gruff, and the opposite of the daintier, more gregarious Emelia. He was probably just too tired to talk much to Makara after working the fields all day. He and Emelia seemed to argue sometimes, and Makara got the feeling it was about her. She caught something about "the girl being a drain," but Emelia never asked Makara to leave. Makara did what she could to pull her weight, forcing herself to focus at school, despite her lack of interest in any of the subjects, while working hard to keep the little cabin clean.

Inside, though, she felt as if she were going crazy. Anytime she saw Ohlan, strolling around or joking with his men, she felt barely controlled fury. If he hadn't come here, Raine might still be alive today. Only Emelia's admonishment to behave kept Makara from doing something stupid. The more she saw Ohlan around, the more she thought of how she couldn't stay in Oasis a day longer.

And yet, she did stay. For weeks, and then, months. She stayed so long that her birthday passed, and she hadn't bothered to tell a single soul.

The one thing she liked about living in Oasis was talking with the caravan merchants and their guards. She got to know a lot of the regulars who passed through, and some had even ranged as far as San Fran or Mexico. They had stories of those places, about an army called the Legion to the south and the empire it was carving out, or how the winter ice was advancing in the north and making it harder to find salvage there. Some of them had even gone to Raider Bluff, on the Colorado River, which had the best stuff for sale in the Wasteland.

That was what Makara wanted to be. A raider. Joining an outfit out of Bluff, ranging far from all known territory to find the good stuff, then bringing it back to Bluff to sell to the caravans and make a mint in batts. That became her goal, but none of the caravans would agree to take her on. As she saw it, joining a caravan was the only way out of this town.

No one seemed to believe she was as good with a gun as she said, and that was practically a requirement. Besides, she was a girl, and girls were supposed to stay in the house and do what they were told.

Makara didn't care about any of that. Being a raider was her best chance at becoming self-sufficient and not depending on Ohlan for anything.

Once she was a raider, she'd be free.

~

MAKARA NEVER FORGOT HER GOAL. Everything she did, from being forced to go to school, to doing chores for Emelia and George, to even helping other townsfolk with their problems, was all for the eventual aim of becoming a raider.

One day, she was given her chance.

"I'm low on guards," Daryl Lapin said, a merchant who led the Desert Foxes caravan. "If you can outfit yourself, including your own gun, I'll give you a chance."

"Where are you bound this time?" Makara asked, feeling excitement build in her chest.

"Northbound," he said. "Gonna try to make it to San Fran, and we need all the bodies we can get. Survive the journey, well, you might have yourself a permanent spot on my team."

"I will," Makara promised. "I'll be back tomorrow morning at sunrise."

Daryl nodded, then shooed her away.

Now, for the difficult part. Finding a gun.

As much as she didn't relish it, she knew she needed to talk to Ohlan. She went to the town hall, where she would most likely to find him, assuming he wasn't out on patrol.

Luckily for her, he was in, and he had a moment to talk to her.

"Makara," he said, beaming a yellow smile. "To what do I owe this honor?"

Makara swallowed, trying to force all the animosity out of her voice. "Ohlan," she began. "You know I've been doing a good job since I've come here. I've been studying hard at school, helping Emelia out with whatever needs. I even helped build that fence for Mr. Norris on the northside."

Ohlan nodded. "That's good. You have been a willing hand, and don't think I haven't noticed that."

Makara nodded. It was going well so far. "Well, I thought I was ready for a bit of extra responsibility."

Ohlan arched an eyebrow, an invitation to continue.

"I want to be a wall guard."

Ohlan had a chuckle at that and shook his head. "You're not ready for that, Makara. A woman's place is in the home, anyway. Raine spoiled you."

"Raine let me fight in the final battle," Makara said, trying her best to keep her voice reasonable. "I even killed a few men. That extra ammunition I brought you all those months back. I won that defending myself in L.A. If anyone has won the right . . ."

Ohlan cut her off. "You're too young, Makara. I know you've proven yourself, but I don't let anyone on the walls until they're fifteen at least."

"My birthday's two months away."

"Then come back in two months."

Makara wasn't about to get the runaround. "I'm worth three of whatever guards you have, and you know it. I'm a good shot. Raine was grooming me for command."

"My brother wasn't as good at judgment as you seem to think he was," Ohlan said. "That's why he's dead, remember?"

He was testing her, to see she would go off. Almost every part of her wanted to.

"Please, Ohlan," she said. "I'm begging you to give me a chance."

He looked at her appraisingly, but as always, those glacier eyes were inscrutable. "Tell you what. We'll try you out. You can keep watch up there, and if you do a good job, well, we'll give you a gun like the rest of them." Ohlan smiled. "You'll have to wait for your birthday for that, though."

Makara's heart fell. If Makara didn't show up tomorrow

armed, packed, and ready to go, then Daryl would never give her another chance. Caravan leaders tended to talk, too, so there was a good chance that they'd find out about her malfeasance.

Maybe nobody would take her on after that.

But if she begged any more of Ohlan, he'd become suspicious of why she wanted a gun so bad that she wasn't willing to wait two months.

"All right," Makara said. "Let me start tonight. Watching, I mean."

"Well," Ohlan said. "We're a little short on the east side. Report to Terrance Shaw, and he'll see you set up."

It would have to be good enough. "Thanks, Ohlan. I won't let you down."

"We'll see. Now, get out of here. I've wasted enough of my time."

Makara walked quickly out of the hall and headed for the eastern wall.

Maybe she hadn't been given a gun, but she'd be around plenty of men who'd have them. She'd figure out a way to pilfer one of them.

Chapter 52

Makara reported to the eastern wall, as ordered, and talked to Terrance Shaw for the first time in a year. He looked much the same, though now he was sporting a full beard that covered his chiseled face. He wore sunglasses, even though it was night. Makara wondered how he could even see anything.

"Can't believe he's letting a little rug rat like you up here," he drawled. "Well, if you're lying about this appointment, I'll make sure you regret it."

"Nice to see you too, Terrance."

He gave a grunt. Makara wasn't sure if was supposed to be a laugh or not.

"Job's simple," he said. "Stand in that tower. Look out. If you see someone approaching, come find me. If you fall asleep on the job, then I don't want to see you back."

"Fair enough," Makara said.

Terrance turned and called out to the tower. "Varner! You're relieved."

A man started climbing down the ladder, and Shaw nodded toward it. "Hop to it."

Makara climbed the ladder and stood looking out at the

bleak desert. The entire land was covered with shadow. Barely any moonlight was getting through tonight. Makara had sharp eyes, though.

Not that it mattered, because she had no intention of keeping an eye out, anyway. She tracked the other guards' movements, along with Shaw's. All of them bore weapons, but it seemed that all the rumors she'd heard about guards falling asleep on the job were exaggerated. Everyone was alert, though it was still early in the night.

Makara herself was tired, too. She had to stay alert and find an opportunity.

At some point, Terrance left, leaving only the guards. There seemed to be three other guys covering the eastern wall, all of whom were standing and not looking tired in the least. Makara was starting to think this might be a bad idea.

She waited for the other guards to face away before going down the ladder. When she reached the rampart, she walked quietly, sticking to the shadows. No one seemed to be any the wiser.

This is stupid, she thought. *There's no way I can get a gun from someone who's fully awake.*

She ended up climbing down to the ground and standing by the wall. Could she try sneaking into the barracks? No, someone was bound to see her there.

She sat back with her back against the wall. Getting a gun before dawn was practically worthless.

There was one option, though. One she hadn't wanted to resort to. She didn't see another way, though.

She stood up and walked home. It looked like she'd have to take George's six-shooter.

When Makara quietly stepped in the cabin, both George and Emelia were still up.

"Where have you been?" Emelia asked, sharply. "We were just about to go looking for you."

George looked at her sternly, but didn't add anything to Emelia's question.

"Ohlan wanted some help with guard duty," she said, playing it off. "You can ask him yourself."

The two looked at each other, before Emelia turned back to Makara. "Well, a bit of forewarning would be nice. Why's Ohlan got you up there, anyway? You have school tomorrow."

"Well, mystery solved," George said. "I'm going to sleep."

Emelia watched him go quietly, not seeming very happy about it. When he'd retreated to the back room, she turned back to Makara.

"Is everything all right? You don't really want to join the wall guards, do you?"

Makara shrugged. "Maybe. I'm not much good at school, anyway."

"You just don't apply yourself," Emelia said. "You're a good student, but unless you work harder, few will want to apprentice you."

"Maybe I don't want that," Makara said.

Emelia blinked. "Well, what *do* you want?"

To be free. Makara kept that thought to herself, though. "Right now, I just want to go to bed."

Emelia shook her head. "Makara, we are just worried about you. We want you to fit into our community, but so far . . ."

"So far what?" Makara asked.

"Well," Emelia said. "If you can handle a bit of honesty . . ."

"I can handle anything," Makara said.

"I've been talking to some of the other townsfolk," Emelia said. "Many of them are looking for a bright, young apprentice to take on. There are so few young people these days. For all that, though, none want to take you on."

Makara laughed. "You thought my feelings would be hurt by that?"

"They hurt *my* feelings," Emelia said. "Me, who's been working so hard to get people to accept you. When you beat up the neighbor kids, or mouth off to the grocer, that gets around, Makara. You need to turn your attitude around if you're going to last here."

Don't worry about that, Makara thought. *I'll be out of your hair by tomorrow.*

"Well?" Emelia asked. "You don't have anything to say?"

"You're right," Makara said. "I'll try to do better."

Makara knew Emelia hadn't expected that answer. It seemed she had trouble accepting it, from the way Emelia just stared at her. None of it would matter by tomorrow, anyway.

"I hope you mean that, Makara. Will you try?"

"Yes," Makara said, pushing down her irritation. "Can I go to bed now?"

Emelia shook her head sadly. "I'm sure you're tired. As am I." She got up, poked the fire a bit, before retiring to the back room.

Makara went to her own pallet. The whole conversation had been irrelevant, but it still felt real. Her heart pounded at what she knew she had to do. Within minutes, she heard them both snoring back there. George kept the six-shooter in a drawer by his bed.

Could she really go through with this, after everything they had done for her?

I have to, Makara said. *It's the only way out of this place. It's the only way to be free.*

Besides, she was nothing but a drain, anyway. George was right about that. She'd bring nothing but disappointment to him, and eventually, Emelia too.

"I'll be gone, soon," she whispered. "Don't you worry."

She slowly eased out of her blanket and crawled on all fours to the bedroom, quiet as a mouse. She easily reached the side of the bed where George was laying. He was snoring loudly as Makara crawled forward. She reached for the handle of the drawer, pulling it open ever so slightly, timing it to move during the loudest parts of George's snores. It stood completely open, allowing Makara to scoop up the shooter, a carton of bullets, and a speed loader.

Makara gently closed the drawer, and eased back out of the room.

Packing was quick. Within minutes, she had plenty of food and a canteen full of water. She took everything she'd brought with her, including the matches, as well as some extra clothes to keep warm. It was all she could fit into the pack. The rest she'd have to leave behind.

Makara couldn't step out the door without making noise, so instead, she opened the shutters of the window, stepping out that way. She closed them behind her, finding herself on the dusty road outside.

She felt free, despite the fact she wasn't even out of Oasis yet.

There was no one out, but a guard could be passing by any minute, and it was obvious from her pack that she meant to leave. Makara went down some side streets, sticking to shadows where she could. Only one time did she have to allow a pair of guards to pass her, but thankfully, they didn't seem too vigilant. She made her way easily enough to the western wall, the designated area where caravans stayed.

She found Daryl's caravan, approaching the guard on duty. Before he could even ask her to state her business, Makara spoke.

"Daryl said I could join up if I brought a gun," she said. "I have that here."

She showed the old six-shooter, and the man gave the ghost of a smile. "Is that all it takes to join the Desert Foxes?" He chuckled. "Well, you can speak to Daryl in the morning."

"Where can I sleep?"

The man pointed with his head. "By the fire, with the rest."

Several men were laying around the fire, and there wasn't much room for Makara. She'd have to sleep on the outside, but she wasn't about to make a fuss about it. The only thing she was worried about was being in the open, where any of the townsfolk might see her. Hopefully neither George nor Emelia noticed her missing. The caravans were usually out of town before most people were awake.

It was only for one night and then she'd be out of Oasis for good and no longer under Ohlan's thumb. There were also a couple of tents set up, but Makara knew they weren't for grunts.

Makara set up her pad and lay down with her blanket thrown over her. She'd be out of here as soon as the sun was up.

Chapter 53

$\mathbb{S}$ he woke to the sounds of the camels being laden and the smell of biscuits over the cookfires. Several of the hardened men stared at her, but none asked her name or why she was there. She found Daryl and showed him her gun.

He gave a bark of a laugh. "I should have specified a rifle or a shotgun," he said. "But a promise is a promise."

"I can come with you, then?"

Daryl nodded, impatient. "Yes, yes. Bring me some food first, and I'll give you your assignment."

Makara rushed to obey, getting a couple of biscuits and butter for Daryl, which he ate quickly.

"We'll be out of here soon enough," he said. "What about your parents, girl?"

She shook her head. "Don't have any. The sooner we're out of here, the better."

"Wrap your head, then," he said. "I don't want any trouble with the authorities if they recognize you. Usually I wouldn't do this, but I need bodies. The road to San Fran is a long one."

Makara nodded quickly and wrapped her head until only her eyes showed.

Within minutes, the caravan and its train of twenty camels were soon trudging through town toward the north gate. Hardly anyone was awake this early, which Makara was happy about. When they passed by Emelia and George's cabin, there were no signs of them being awake yet.

When the gate came in sight, she felt a sliver of doubt. She was leaving behind safety. She was leaving behind a full belly every night, and at least one person who cared about her well-being, Emelia, without so much as a goodbye. She hadn't even thought to leave a note behind. It seemed a poor way to repay her kindness.

"I'm in control," she whispered. "I can be whoever I want to be."

That affirmation was enough for Makara. Ohlan would not get to decide who she'd become. Not even Raine could decide that. She'd done everything for him that could be expected, just as she had for Samuel.

It was her turn, now. Her life was her own, for better or for worse. It was a bit scary, but she was only here because of her own wits, so she deserved to call the shots for once.

She was surprised when she passed through the gate with the rest of them without incident. Daryl paid the gate captain a handful of batts, the town tax, and then they were on their way.

Makara let out a breath when the gates shut behind them. She looked to the east, where the sun was now rising, red as a drop of blood, over a high mesa.

"I'm free," she said.

Makara knew that it wasn't the beginning, but it was *a* beginning. Though she was almost fifteen years old, the responsibility she'd taken for herself made her feel a million times older. She was on her own now, with no one to watch over her for the first time in her life. It was a bit scary, but it also made her feel more alive. Every breath she drew tasted a thousand times sweeter.

Even if she didn't last long out here, at least she would be free. Sure, she was under Daryl's purview, now. But if she didn't like Daryl, she could always just leave the caravan at the first opportunity and join another.

It was all steppingstones to becoming a raider. Then, she would be truly free.

MAKARA FELL into life with the Desert Foxes. They followed the old highway north, making camp every night and picking up every morning. Sometimes they passed through small settlements, where Daryl would call a halt for a few hours to give the camels a rest and to refill water and food stores, if the town had any available. In exchange, they would trade some of the wares picked up in Oasis.

Shortly after, they were off again, heading northwest. A couple of days later saw them north of Bakersfield and the small community there, where they stayed a whole day to resupply and trade before making the next leg north, which would take them up to the ruins of Fresno.

Life seemed easier. There really wasn't much to do in the mornings and evenings other than making sure the camels were comfortable and fed, and during the day her job was to scan the passing landscape for signs of raiders. While Daryl's caravan had the right to pass through and trade in Raider Bluff and any outfits associated with their leader, Char, there were still many other groups not associated with Bluff, especially the further north they went. Things up north were wilder, according to Daryl.

That meant every group was for itself. But the best salvage was up north, since fewer dared take the risk to get it.

Makara survived her first ambush two days north of Bakersfield. Twelve raiders came upon them from the top of the hill and began to fire. Daryl and his men, about twice their number, fended them off, but not before losing four guards. Makara, luckily, was not included in that number. She had shot at them a few times but hadn't scored any kills.

The atmosphere became less jovial after that. She now saw what Daryl meant by needing a lot of bodies. If there were even one more attack like this, inflicting a similar level of casualties, they would be forced to turn back empty-handed, as the journey could no longer be made safely. Then again, that also meant more loot per individual for a successful trip.

Things were quiet after that. They reached Fresno and traded with several communities there. It was July, but still the temperature didn't get much warmer than the sixties. Daryl ordered the caravan on, not wanting to lose time. He expected to make San Fran by early August, and the camels' bags were full of food picked up from the south. Daryl hoped to trade that food for decent scrap he could sell for batts at Raider Bluff. Daryl's wish list included bullets, weapons, gadgets, copper, and gold, to name a few.

When they turned west from Fresno, Makara saw natural greenery for the first time in her life. They passed through some low mountains, and while the trees were mostly dead, a lot of the evergreens had survived. Here, Daryl paused for a few days to collect some timber, having the camels pull them on sleds. Makara hated the grating sound those sleds made on the tarmac of the broken highways, and didn't think she'd ever get used to it. Daryl told her that timber was a valuable resource, since trees didn't grow in many places these days.

Finally, after almost two full months of travel since they started, they made it to San Fran. Daryl and the Desert Foxes weren't going into San Fran itself. Instead, they set up camp outside the ruins, where several scrapper camps were located. These people were the ones who went into the city, and sold whatever they found to the caravans in exchange for food.

Here, the Desert Foxes stayed for a week, Daryl wheeling

and dealing while the guards mostly relaxed and fraternized with the other caravans. Makara learned a lot, then. She learned that San Fran's pickings were getting leaner, and that in a few years, the caravans would probably have to shift further north, toward Portland or even Seattle. Some caravans were already ranging that far, and it would be hard to do that in a single season, especially as the weather was becoming harsher. Others talked about Nova Roma, the new empire to the south, offering far better prices than even Raider Bluff. They would pay practically anything to get old tech or weapons, but the journey there was dangerous. There were talks of the Empire building a trading post at the mouth of the Colorado, so that the caravans of the Wasteland would not have to range as far.

Eventually, though, it was time to go. It was late August and already there was a nip in the air. Makara was glad to be heading south, this time by a different route closer to the coast. Daryl planned to unload some of his stuff on the way south, to make for faster travel, but to still save the best stuff for his end destination, Raider Bluff.

But the further south they went, the more worried Makara got. Their route might take them right into L.A. She wasn't quite sure what she'd do if that was the plan. It might be her one and only chance to find and kill Carin Black, but at the same time, she didn't think she could possibly get to him without being recognized. Maybe not everyone knew what she looked like, but a lot would know that Raine's adopted daughter was missing, and that her age and looks would match the description.

Once they'd reached Bakersfield, there was talk among Daryl and his top men about what to do. Some deemed the risk of selling to the Reapers worth it, as the spoils could be great. Others thought it too risky, that raiders would be taking advantage of the war trade to attack caravans trying to cross into L.A. from the north. In the end, Daryl decided heading east to Raider Bluff was the best call.

Things seemed to be going well at first. Until they were ambushed just east of New Barstow, with fifty miles left on their journey.

Chapter 54

S he heard the screams first, and then the gunshots.

She was up in a flash, jumping behind a rock for shelter and pointing her handgun into the darkness. Her heart pounded as the men around her fell, as the camels broke from their lines, a few of them even running off into the darkness. She hid behind the rock, and it didn't take long for her to realize that it would soon be over.

Within minutes, men were looting corpses of the fallen Desert Foxes' members, pulling aside dead bodies, and untying the camels on the hitch line. The beasts followed their new masters as surely as they would have their old ones.

Makara waited for them to notice her, and was surprised at how long it took for that to happen. Two men were arguing about a shiny trinket they had found, when one of them turned his head and noticed her sitting there, with her gun in hand.

"Well, well, well," he said, with a predatory smile. "It looks like it's my lucky day."

She could have shot him there, but doing so would almost certainly mean her own death. She decided to run, sprinting for the darkness outside the range of the campfires, but the man was faster. He grabbed her by the shoulders, though she still held her gun. She swung around the butt and knocked him good in the head. She pointed it at him, hesitating to pull the trigger.

"Shoot her, Dax," he shouted. "Shoot her!"

Makara saw she had no choice. She shot him, first, then ran, knowing the noise would draw every one of the assailants toward her. No shots rang out after her, and soon, she was cloaked by darkness. The brays of camels and the shouts of men faded. She ran as far as she could before the slope became too steep. She found a boulder to hide behind.

She was going to get caught. She'd already shot a man, so surrendering wasn't an option.

This was where she'd go down fighting.

Sure enough, she heard footsteps coming up the slope. They lingered a moment, as if not sure of where she had gone. But their footsteps grew louder, and Makara raised herself from behind her rock and aimed in the direction of the sounds.

She pressed the trigger, the gun kicking back into her hand. Just a moment later, a hand grabbed her from behind and applied pressure to her wrist, causing her to cry out in pain and drop her gun.

"None of that, now," he said. "Act nice and I might keep even you around."

"No!" Makara said, doing her best to wriggle free.

It was useless. He'd already picked up her gun, while his friend was coming to assist him.

"All right," he said. "Let's bring her to the boss."

Makara felt herself pulled away from the other man. "I found her. She's mine."

"You don't think he saw her run up this way? If you take her, the boss'll kill you for it."

The man was quiet, seeming to consider it. "Might be worth it."

She stomped the heel of her boot hard on the man's foot, where one of his toes was exposed through a hole. He yowled while the other man guffawed.

"She might be small, but she's no easy pickings," he said. "Come on, idiot. The boss is waiting."

Makara held back tears, of both fear and anger, as both men led her roughly down the slope. The cruelest part was that Oasis was not twenty minutes north of here, and if she hadn't been so stupid, she'd be there right now, warm and safe in bed.

Makara was led back into the camp, where thirty or so raiders milled about. Every eye was on her as catcalls and jeers followed her. Makara spat at anyone who tried to touch her, which was practically everyone.

Things got quieter when she was forced to her knees in front of a man sitting on a crate by the fire. She could feel his eyes watching her, but she would not let him see her cry. Men like this had no respect for tears or weakness.

"Look at me, girl," he said, his voice gruff.

Makara looked up, seeing a man in his late middle years, with cropped gray hair, sharp blue eyes, and a terrible marring on the right side of his face. He regarded her coldly as he held her gaze.

"Step back," he said to his men. "Don't lay a finger on her."

The men looked confused, but they did as ordered.

"What's your name?" the man asked.

Makara took a few steadying breaths while all of them waited for her answer. "My name's Jaz."

The man grunted. It might have been laughter. "Don't lie to me. Give me your name, now, or you'll be regretting it."

Makara did her best to keep eye contact with him. "Makara."

He nodded, as if satisfied with that answer. "Thought so."

The men around began to murmur. How did he know who she was?

"Carin Black's got a fat bounty on you," he said. "The only Angel to escape the grave."

Makara just looked at him, waiting for whatever came next.

"I say, any girl who could've gotten out of L.A. with the all the Reapers looking for her must be worth something."

"What do you mean?" Makara asked, forcing herself to talk.

"We taking her to Black, boss?" someone asked.

The man held up a hand. He took that same hand, and then extended it out to Makara. "My name's Char."

Char? From Raider Bluff? A thousand questions ran through Makara's mind.

"You're probably wondering what's going on, why I've slaughtered everyone here who's coming to my town, anyway. Well, that's a long story. Daryl broke a deal last he was with us. Probably thought I'd never figure out I was played. Thought himself clever, like I wouldn't ever figure out those batts were duds. Well, I figured it out. And he was stupid and greedy for thinking he could pull the same trick on me again." Char regarded her for a moment, seeming to gauge her reaction. "I don't know how you got yourself involved with a swindler like him, but I'm going to give you a chance, anyway."

Makara decided to remain silent on that point. "What are you going to do with me?"

"Well, you shot one of my men, but I can't fault you for that. You were just trying to defend yourself. Sometimes, you just get a feeling about someone." Char looked at her neutrally. "How'd you like to join us at Bluff?"

"Join you and do what?"

Char shrugged. "Become one of us. A raider."

The other men started talking at that. The two who had brought her to Char slunk behind the others.

"I'll do it," Makara said. There was really no other answer.

"Good," he said. "We're leaving tomorrow morning." He turned to the men watching him and addressed all of them at once. "Get some shuteye."

After that, Makara was treated with respect, even as if she were royalty. Men who thirty minutes before who would have raped and killed her were now treating her with deference. Somehow, unknown to her, she had become famous in the Wasteland. The angel who had gotten away. She realized that she had a knack for getting away, just as she had barely escaped Bunker One.

When Makara found her pack, which had been quickly returned to her, she unrolled it and was given a warm spot next to the fire. She still felt shaky as she laid down and closed her eyes, hardly able to process what was happening.

One thing she did know, however, was that freedom was only an illusion. Out here, she lived or died based on the whims of more powerful men.

Epilogue

Makara walked quietly with the rest of the raiders east, toward Raider Bluff. She saw the smoke of the city long before the city itself came into sight. They crossed the arched bridge spanning the Colorado and walked north, toward the high plateau upon which the city of the raiders had been built.

Along the river itself were the farms, manned by hundreds of people. Makara didn't have to ask. She knew they were slaves. The raiders walked up the road until they reached the city's front gates.

Makara entered with the rest of them, realizing that this was who she was, now. It was what she had wanted when she left Oasis, but all she could feel was empty inside.

With winter coming on, there wasn't much to do. Char took her under his wing and gave her a place to stay in his compound. There, she kept things clean and did basic chores. Makara thought that Char's reason for preserving her was less than wholesome. He was a raider, after all, and they weren't known for their moral scruples. She soon saw that he wasn't interested in her like that, and after that realization, she breathed easier. None of the other men bothered her, seeing how Char was looking after her.

Not that Makara needed much protection. She had her own gun, now, and knew how to use it.

Makara was safe for now, but life still wasn't worth living. Waiting out the winter was hard. It got terribly cold, to the point where no one went outside unless they had to.

But eventually, it warmed up enough when spring came along, and Makara started raiding with the rest of them. She was fifteen.

She did very well. Everything in life had been taken from her, so she had no qualms about taking it from others. Her days were spent scrapping, pillaging, and taking slaves back to Bluff to be sold like cattle.

She made a lot of batts doing it. With those batts, she rented out a nice room in the Bounty, which had plenty of good grub and beer, both of which were a welcome escape from the wider world that she wanted to shut out.

Her fellow raiders respected her. She was known for being brutally cold.

One day, she caught the eye of an especially gruesome raider, named Brux. When she saw the numbers of batts he got for his raids, she signed on with him immediately.

Times were even better after that.

MAKARA LIVED NEARLY four years at Raider Bluff. She was nineteen, now, and her old life was fast becoming a memory. Raine and Samuel barely crossed her thoughts, now, and that was to her liking. She was good a bottling all her feelings, so small that she hardly noticed them anymore.

Alcohol helped with that, too.

Makara agreed to another raid with Brux and his crew, even if he was starting to become too pushy for her liking. He brought in the batts, and that was all Makara cared about. They ranged further north than they ever had, making it nearly as far as Portland. For all that, though, they lost almost half their men in a sudden blizzard.

On the way south, Brux got intel about one of the government Bunkers out San Bernardino way. Makara was about desperate enough then to not veto the idea, agreeing to scout out the location and come back later with a larger crew.

Brux had a daring plan to get the Bunker to fall. The Red Sickness was coming back, and they'd nabbed a guy who seemed rife with it. They hauled him miles and lay him in the vicinity of the Bunker, hoping that if the government types found him, the people within would take the bait. Once the sickness ran them through, the Bunker would be ripe for the picking.

After they laid the sick man on the mountainside, timing it to happen just before the patrol was set to walk there, Makara had been the one to draw the short stick and keep watch on what happened.

She froze when she heard the voices, ducking behind a rock. When she poked her head above it, she was surprised to see two men. Well, one of them was a man, and the other just a boy. The older one wore desert army fatigues, well-built and looking every inch the action hero, while the other was a lanky boy, with wide, scared eyes and shaggy hair.

The boy was the one who had been staring at her with those fearful eyes.

She hid, but she knew she'd been found out.

Makara cursed herself and followed the ledge downward. When she reached the desert floor and was out of sight of the above patrol, she sprinted back to where Brux and the boys were.

"We've got to split," she said.

"Did they take the body?" Brux asked.

"Yes," she lied, though she didn't know if they had.

Brux nodded, satisfied. "Let's bounce, then. By the time we get back, we'll clear the whole thing out."

Makara nodded, but found herself thinking about the boy. She'd been like him, once. Living in a bunker and knowing nothing else.

Well, he was about to find out how rough things got on the outside.

About the Author

Kyle West is the author of *The Wasteland Chronicles* and *Xenoworld Saga* series, as well as a new science fiction series set for release in late 2020. From a young age, he's enjoyed just about anything science fiction or fantasy, with a particular fascination for end-of-the-world scenarios. His goal is to write as many entertaining books as possible, with interesting worlds and characters that hopefully give his readers a break from the mundane.

He truly appreciates his readers, and invites them to connect with him through his Facebook page, website, or mailing list.

kylewestwriter.com

 facebook.com/kylewestwriter

Printed in Great Britain
by Amazon